I0594268

BETWEEN DECISIONS

The City Between: Book Eight

W.R. GINGELL

Cover by Seedlings Design Studio

For everyone else still trying to figure out this love thing (and how it works)

CHAPTER ONE

HOUSEMATES CAN BE A HANDFUL. Mine more than most, but that's probably to be expected when two are fae and one's a vampire. It doesn't help when you live in a house that's halfway between the human world and what they call the world Behind, leaving you in a twilight sort of place that isn't one or the other. Between: that's what it's called. The sort of place where shadows move even when their owners don't, and visitors from Behind come through the linen closet door to look suspiciously at you as you tell them no, you have *absolutely no idea* who killed their commanding officer and there's no need to thank us. The sorta place where your fork could turn into a small, sharp-edged beetle more interested in slashing open your mouth than scuttling for cover.

What I'm saying is that it's an exciting life. Safe, no. Exhilarating, yes. There's always one more thing that can kill you, and there's always something unexpected around the corner to knock you on your rear. Not to mention that you get into this whole situation of being a pet to two fae and a vampire—then of being a sort of compatriot instead—thinking that fae don't have emotions and that vampires are just mildly obsessive-compulsive little gits, only to find out that the fae have grown inconvenient and potentially terrifying emotions in the dark like demented little mushrooms, and that the vampire can be an actually decent friend.

G'day. I'm Pet. Only on paper these days, and the vampire doesn't own me, so I suppose there's that. Things have gotten weirder, though, so it's not much of a comfort. It's not even that the Behind stuff is what's hard—it's the whole dealing-with-otherworldly-emotions-or-lack-thereof that's hard. It would have been nice if someone had made a primer for me to go by, but there isn't one.

No one teaches you this stuff—you know, what to do with a big white fae who has gotten far too cuddly lately, or how to deal with the gentle melancholy that seems to have settled over the fae butler, even when you brew him his favourite lavender earl grey and buy the really expensive shortbreads.

And there's no one you can call to find out what the heck is going on when the vampire declares love and outright challenges you to try not to fall in love with him in return.

I mean, he didn't even start with *I like you*. The flamin' little mosquito went right to *love*. Last night, right here in my room, the vampire had kissed me in a way that was definitely not all business, and then sauntered away smirking, daring me not to fall in love with him.

I still didn't know what the heck I was supposed to do about it. I'd already waited far too long to go downstairs this morning because I knew the entire place would be filled with JinYeong's presence as well as his cologne. Problem was, I couldn't even relax in my bean bag up here, because that was where—

I groaned and rolled back into bed, digging my face under the pillow. I'd managed to go downstairs right after JinYeong last night and complete my usual fighting practise as expected—and to do the little mosquito credit, he'd been completely business through our sparring sessions. I don't know what I'd expected, but it wasn't that. I mean, I'd been relieved, but I still didn't feel too comfortable this morning. Maybe that was because I'd dreamed about Jin Yeong's dark eyes glowing with laughter at me while he said, "You can't do anything about me being in love with you."

Or maybe it was because every now and then I'd catch a whiff of his scent in the room and have a distinct, if short-lived, memory of last night.

"I'm gunna kill him," I mumbled into the bedsheets, but I pushed the pillow away again. I had to do something about this. If I needed help finding something from a jumble of old papers and records, I could ask my leprechaun friend. If I needed help with something mixing magic and technology, I could ask my merman friend. When it came to anything from the world Behind, I had someone I could ask, even if they wouldn't always answer me.

Who on earth was I supposed to call about the vampire kissing me and declaring love, though?

I sat up straight, feeling bright all of a sudden. Morgana. I could call Morgana, right? She was a zombie, but at least she knew about crushes and makeup and could be depended on to tell me what the heck was going on and what I could do about it.

I grabbed my phone from beneath the pillow and pulled up her number.

Actually, now that I came to think of it, Morgana had been making weird suggestions for a while now—but she'd only said that it looked like *Zero* had a thing for me, hadn't she? And yeah, okay, Zero was acting suspiciously, but at least he hadn't actually *kissed* me.

My finger hovered over the call button, but before I could press it, someone knocked at the front door downstairs. I didn't have to look out the window to know who it was; the house told me it was my only human friend, Detective Tuatu. There's probably a lot to unpack there, but all you really need to know is that, yeah, most of my friends are behindkind, and no, the house doesn't actually talk. It's more that I can just kinda *feel* stuff. I'd thought at first that I could only tell if my three psychos were in the house or not, but either my senses or the house's ability to communicate had been growing stronger for the last year—and the last six months in particular. That was worrisome for a few different reasons, and I personally knew two of those Reasons.

Both of those Reasons had a house pretty similar to mine, and I wasn't too keen on what that might mean for me, even though my three psychos were all pretty sure I was human. They'd also been pretty sure I wasn't an Heirling, either, and—

Nah, let's go with one explanation at a time.

I shoved my phone into my pocket as I stood, then went downstairs to see what Detective Tuatu wanted. Hopefully it was something that would see me out of the house and helping him chase down something weird instead of making breakfast for my psychos and trying to figure out what to do about Jin Yeong.

They'd let Tuatu in by the time I got downstairs, which was a nice surprise; mostly they seemed pretty happy to let me answer the door and leave other humans on the doorstep if I wasn't there to answer it. That was fair, though: I usually preferred to let them answer the linen closet door to whatever came through there, so I couldn't complain too much about having to answer the front door most of the time.

I went right into the kitchen to boil the jug, grinning at Tuatu on my way through and skimming past Zero, who was just coming in from the backyard. He'd probably been exercising out there— stretches, or the particular form of practise that involves messing with Between and pulling stuff through the bit between Behind and the human world. He patted me on the head as I passed by, but I was so rattled by the waft of perfume that heralded Jin Yeong's imminent presence that I didn't even flinch away. That was good because I was pretty sure Athelas was watching and smiling from his usual chair. It's *really annoying* to have someone watching and smiling at you when you know they see a lot more than you're comfortable with.

Luckily, making morning tea and coffee was the usual, peaceful business it was when nothing unexpected had segued into the house through Between. That meant that by the time I came back out with the tray to find everyone except Athelas standing around kind of awkwardly in the living room, I was feeling pretty bright and not too worried. Tuatu's presence was a nice reprieve.

Still, I didn't look over at the bit of living room that was filled with Jin Yeong as I put the tray down on the coffee table. Of Zero, I asked pointedly, "You lot gunna stand around all day?"

I sat down in my own couch by way of an example, because apparently fae don't invite visitors to sit if they want to make them feel at home—they lay out poisoned food instead. Don't worry, you'll get used to that.

Jin Yeong sauntered across the room and pinched the front of his trousers to sit down elegantly beside me in his usual spot. Oh no. I wasn't having that.

I snapped, "Don't sit next to me!" reaching past him to grab Tuatu by the sleeve and drag him down into the seat instead.

Jin Yeong stumbled forward a step, his eyebrows flying up, and I saw the very tip of one canine through his lips. I thought he was snarling, but when he removed himself from the vicinity of Tuatu's legs and strolled around the coffee table, adjusting his cuffs, I saw that he was actually smiling, his eyes dark and dancing.

I should have known better, but it didn't occur to me that he'd just cross over to the other side of the coffee table, sit down next to Zero in the very slender space remaining, and lean back as he crossed one leg over the other. That seemed pretty harmless, and it wasn't until Detective Tuatu said, "There's something odd happening down by the waterfront these days," and started to explain what odd happenings were going on, that I noticed Jin Yeong was looking at me.

Not just looking at me: gazing at me, his head tilted very slightly to the side. He blinked once, precisely, every now and then, as if doing the required amount to keep up an appearance of normality, and when I scowled at him, he smiled innocently and tilted his head the other way.

"Flamin' heck, I'm gunna go mad," I muttered.

Detective Tuatu said, "What?" and Zero and Athelas both looked enquiringly at me.

"Nothing," I said grumpily. "Keep going."

The detective looked up and caught sight of Jin Yeong's bright gaze and unsettlingly regular-but-not-quite-regular-enough blinks.

"Good grief!" he said. "Has he been doing that long?"

"Nope," I said shortly. "You're just lucky."

"It's not me he's staring at."

"Yeah, I know," I retorted. "Forget about him. You said you're here about something weird happening down by the waterfront."

"Thank you so much for keeping us on track, Pet," said Athelas, swinging one leg gently. "It's delightfully unexpected of you. Correct me if I'm wrong, detective, but the strange happenings aren't confined to the waterfront, are they?"

Tuatu looked a bit fed up. "You know something about this, don't you?"

"You'll have to explain, first," Zero said, his cool blue eyes meeting Athelas' grey ones. "It's too early to know whether or not it's something we know."

"You're right," Tuatu said to Athelas. "It isn't just the waterfront: there are odd little things happening all over the place, and ever since you lot got rid of Upper Management from the station—"

"You're welcome," I interrupted.

"All right, I'm thankful, but it does mean that stuff like this isn't swept under the rug anymore—there's no need to tell me I'm welcome again, I'm willing to agree that it's a good thing, Pet! It's just that it gets talked about more, and there are...I don't know, *factions* forming in the station."

"I knew it!" I said, grinning a bit. "Some of your cops are behindkind or humans in the know."

He stared at me. "How could you possibly know that!"

"Well, maybe *know* is a bit strong. I guessed."

"The lower-ranking behindkind left behind by Upper Management must be feeling somewhat rudderless at the moment," Athelas said thoughtfully. "No doubt things will be very interesting for you, detective! Once you've discovered exactly who they are, it should be scintillating to observe their trajectory."

Zero flicked a cool look at him. "You think they'll be inclined to assimilate?"

"I think it very likely that they'll adapt to their surroundings if they've been abandoned," said Athelas. "We've seen it before, after all. Not all behindkind find humans as...troublesome as others—and living among them does seem to make a difference."

Was I mistaken, or did his eyes glance off Jin Yeong and straight to Zero? Zero's blue eyes chilled with a touch more ice, but he didn't say anything.

"Very scintillating," said Tuatu, his agreement disgruntled to the point that it sounded like disagreement. "At the moment, at least they seem to be trying to take care of the little things around town, but none of them seem to want to know what's going on down by the waterfront."

"They probably don't want to step on anyone's toes," Zero said. "Where specifically along the waterfront are you having trouble?"

"There's a nice little section between the Evans Street and Princes Wharf, where the *Aurora Australis* is docked."

"What, that big red ship that goes out to Antarctica?"

"I don't know where it goes, Pet; I just know that it's big and red, and people have been launching themselves over the side and into the water in what looks like some kind of bizarre suicide attempt each time. It's the latest internet sensation in Hobart: it even started trending worldwide last night."

Startled, I asked, "You got bodies already?" I hadn't heard anything about bodies down on the waterfront.

"No; we've got a couple of attempts, and one near miss—that one landed on the deck instead of in the water—but there are enough people around that area to make it a pretty safe place if you don't really want to commit suicide."

Zero sat back in his chair, frowning. "You don't think they're really serious about it?"

"I think it's a trend on the internet," the detective said dryly. "Or at least, that's what I thought at first. This morning I visited one of the kids still in hospital after nearly braining himself on the anchor chain on his way down, and—"

"Now you reckon it has something to do with us," I said, with some relish. It wasn't that I wanted kids to be trying to kill themselves—or being influenced or attacked by behindkind, if it came to that. It would just be nice to be able to get out of the house.

Or maybe just out of the perfume.

And speaking of perfume...

I risked a look across the coffee table at JinYeong and regretted it straight away. His eyes were still on me, and when he caught my gaze he smiled at me, slow and intimate.

"What makes you think it's got something to do with Behind, after all?" I asked Tuatu, looking away trying not to clear my throat.

"None of the kids were suicidal before they got to the waterfront, and only four of them had their phones on them. Out of those four, only two of them were actively streaming anything to a social media platform. People have been sharing video taken by bystanders, and I've seen kids talking about making it an online challenge. It's only a matter of time before they start showing up, selfie sticks and cameras in hand, streaming it for a dare."

"What about the kid you went to see?"

"That's the biggest thing," Tuatu said, chewing on his lower lip. "He's either a much better liar than some criminals I've met, or he doesn't remember a thing after getting on the boat until he hit the water."

"You said there are recordings?"

I glanced across at Zero in surprise. He wasn't usually the sort to ask about recordings—or anything that might be useful but came from the human side of things. He was usually more likely to send Athelas to try and do something sneaky with essence-seeking magic, or Jin Yeong to try and sniff something out of the scene. Or go there himself and try.

The detective looked surprised too, but he said, "Yeah, a few. I've got copies of all the ones that are trending, but there are a few more available. You want all of them?"

"Not copies, I believe," said Athelas. "We had a...mishap with our computer. Perhaps you would be good enough to show us what you have?"

Tuatu opened his mouth, shook his head, and closed it again. He took out his phone instead and said, "I won't even ask. Here. Have a look for yourself: the first one is just an example for the boss' sake, but you'll probably need it, too."

He put his phone down on the coffee table, then tapped the play button on the shiny screen with one dark, pink-padded finger and sat back beside me. Across from us, both Zero and Jin Yeong leaned forward. It was a relief to have Jin Yeong's attention on something other than me, but he still let his eyes flow over my face like a warm ray of sunshine, slow and thoughtful, as he sat forward.

Detective Tuatu shot me a sideways glance that I tried to ignore and Jin Yeong must have seen, judging by the brief sight of his right canine. From his side, Athelas inclined just slightly, enough to see over the top of his teacup, and allowed his eyes to dwell meditatively on the phone as the first fifteen-second video played in a bright burst of colour and sound.

Zero stared at it until it finished, leaving me hard put not to burst out laughing. From the look on Tuatu's face, he was having a pretty similar dilemma, though I was guessing the state of the kid he'd been to see this morning was what was keeping him from giving in to the urge.

"What," said Zero, his voice dropping nearly a full octave, "was *that?*"

"That's a kid dancing and lip-synching to a song," I said helpfully. "They upload it to that app, what's it called?"

"Click-Clock, or some such thing, I believe," said Athelas, surprising me more by the gleam of amusement in his eye that proclaimed his statement to be a subtle joke at his own grandad status than at the fact that he obviously knew exactly which site we were talking about. "No doubt a reference to the appalling noise in the videos."

"Close enough, Grandad," I said. "That's flamin' impressive; you got a computer hidden somewhere else?"

"Not at all," Athelas said. "I merely pay attention to what the children are doing these days. The application has impressed me with its susceptibility to manipulation for some time now. It appears that I was not the only one to think so."

"I don't think it's the site," Tuatu said. "That's just where the videos are being uploaded. I think it's the—well, I don't really know what it is, but I don't think the site has anything to do with it. If it did, we'd have videos from all around the world, but they're only here, in Hobart, at the waterfront."

On the coffee table, the video looped on itself and started again, which must have fascinated Zero with the same kind of fascination I feel toward spiders, because he stared at it with his lips pulled back very slightly from his teeth as if he couldn't look away until it finished again.

When it did, he shoved the phone back toward Tuatu. "What is this? Why would anyone do that? And why did you show me that video? No one fell or tried to commit suicide."

"Don't ask me why they do it," said Tuatu. "I'm old and grumpy, and no matter how many times North tries to make me—

never mind. I showed it to you because I wanted you to under-stand the format that these videos are appearing in. Once they're on the site, they're shared to other social media, but this is where they all start."

"Show me one of the real ones," Zero said. He could have been faintly exasperated, but it's always pretty hard to tell with him. I know him better than anyone except Athelas, and even I still have trouble telling his emotions apart occasionally. "Now that I understand the format—"

"Sure about that?" I asked, grinning. "Doesn't look like you understand it to me."

Ignoring me, he said to Detective Tuatu, "Now that I've famil-iarised myself with the format, there's no need to show me useless clips."

This time, the brief look that Tuatu shot me was bright with laughter. He was enough worried about his own health not to grin at Zero the way I had, though; he just flicked his finger sideways across the screen and tapped play on the next video.

"This is the first one," he said. "We managed to get the one of the girl hitting the deck off the site, but these ones are still allowed to be there for now. We're going to need a lot of international co-operation if we're going to get anything done about the others. There's a lack of blood, and I'm pretty sure the official stance is that it's just a joke."

"I'll have them taken down if it seems as though it's likely to jeopardise the investigation," Zero said.

Tuatu's brows went up. "I suppose you're useful for something after all," he said, but he said it pretty quietly, so I reckon he was saying it to me.

On the coffee table, a gangling fifteen-or-so-year-old boy in skinny jeans danced across the surface of Tuatu's phone to the upbeat strains of "Walkin' On Sunshine", in and out of a doorway and then back out onto deck. I could have thought he was actually listening to the song if I didn't know better: he wasn't lip-synching, but his face was bright and he didn't miss a beat.

"He's hitting all the right beats," I murmured, propping my chin in my hand.

Across the coffee table, Jin Yeong's eyes met mine; this time, instead of being provocative or challenging, they were thoughtful. "She is right, *Hyeong*," he said to Zero. "This boy dances as though he hears the music itself; this flourish—" he tapped the screen, where the boy shimmied his shoulders for the exact duration of the flourish of brass—"is in exactly the right spot. He behaves as though he is following it like a dancer."

"Heck," I said, staring at him. "Can you dance?"

"Of course I can dance!" he said, lifting his nose. "I am a *very good* dancer. I am known in all of the clubs in Seoul, and—"

"Yeah?" I interrupted. "What clubs? 'Cos you can't listen to this old-as-the-hills song and know where all the flourishes are and then try to tell me you go to regular clubs."

"I am the fastest swing dancer in Seoul," he said coldly. "You will see."

"Heck I will! I'm not following you to South Korea to watch you dancing in clubs!"

"Naturally you will not watch; I will *teach* you—"

"Jin Yeong," said Zero, his voice sharp and withering, "If you're going to be talking in the living room with everyone else, you can take the trouble to make sure everyone understands you."

I sat up a bit straighter. "Flamin' heck! He can do that? Exclude you two?"

"We do not speak Korean, Pet," said Athelas. "If Jin Yeong chooses not to translate for us—"

"I thought you blokes did that yourself?"

"We do," said Zero coldly. "But if he chooses to actively exclude us—"

"What are you doing?" I asked Jin Yeong.

Jin Yeong shrugged, and I saw his lips curve very faintly. "This is *our* business, not theirs."

I saw Zero's lips form the word *ours*, a deep line between his brows, and before he could say anything else, I said hurriedly to Jin Yeong, "There is no *ours*! Just talk to everyone! And before you start burbling about dancing again, all we need to know is that this kid might have been listening to the song live, right?"

Jin Yeong gave a small, precise nod. "*Kurae.*"

"Isn't that why we're hearing the song?" asked Zero, but his eyes were on Jin Yeong, not the phone. "He's dancing to it and recording it at the same time?"

"Nope," said Tuatu. "You'd hear background noise, and the sound as a whole would be different. What you're hearing is a track laid over the original recording, noises and all."

"Why can't I hear the original recording?"

"It doesn't exist," Tuatu said. "Not as far as we know. It's as though it was done live, already overlaid with the music. We don't know how, because it's not supposed to be possible."

Zero nodded. "All right. We'll have to start with the ship itself, then. You said it came from Antarctica? Do you have a travel log for it?"

"I'll send it to your phone once I get it," said the detective, nodding.

That made me smile a bit. We'd come a long way since he first met my three psychos; he'd originally been outraged to find that they'd pretty much been given the key to the station.

"Let me know if anything turns up," he added. "I've got to try and figure out what's going on along Collins Street for now—in the whole of the shopping and business district, actually."

"Yeah, you said there was something going on around the place," I said. I was pretty sure I knew what it was; the psychos had to be thinking the same thing I was thinking, too. The human world, linked to the world behind, was experiencing the magical equivalent of sympathetic labour.

While the world Behind spiralled into a freefall of chaos in the lead-up to a change of management—well, of kings, but the whole thing was terrifying enough to make me want to push it away with a healthy dose of flippancy—the human world couldn't help but experience the fallout from that change. We'd known it was coming, but I think we'd all been hoping for a bit more time before it actually began.

"What exactly is it that bothers you so much about Collins Street?" asked Athelas.

"I told you earlier," said Tuatu, shrugging his shoulders in discomfort.

Athelas nodded. "Yes, but I'm more specifically interested in your observations of those newly occurring phenomena."

"It's...uncomfortable," he said. "The world doesn't feel balanced right now, and I don't know how else to explain it. It probably sounds stupid."

"It doesn't sound stupid," said Zero. I would have said he was trying to comfort the detective if it wasn't for the grim edge to his voice that suggested he regretted a state of affairs wherein a human could notice any such thing.

"It is, in fact, distressingly perceptive of you," Athelas said, confirming my suspicion. "For a human."

"And that's not to mention—" The detective hesitated, as if he wasn't sure how to go on. There was a bit of a quirk to his lips, and I wondered if this was another thing he thought we might already know about.

"What else?" I prompted, elbowing him. It was no use holding back stuff; and besides, he might not trust the other three fully, but I was pretty sure he trusted me enough to tell if I asked. "Don't tell me North has been learning to drive?"

Tuatu went very white. "No, thank goodness! She says she prefers to walk, but I'm fairly certain she doesn't walk anywhere."

"That would be a fair assumption," said Athelas, smiling into his tea. "I'm surprised she hasn't offered to take you along with her."

"She has," said Tuatu. "I said no. I get airsick."

"A very wise decision, then."

"That's what I thought. No, it's nothing like that: someone tried to kidnap me the other night. I was hoping you knew them."

I stared at him, forgetting JinYeong for a blissful moment. "Hang on, you hope we know the people who are trying to kidnap you?"

"Are those people still alive?" Zero asked.

I mean, it was a fair question. North is pretty protective when it comes to people she likes, and the incarnation of the North Wind can do a heck of a lot of damage when her back is up.

"I just thought that on balance I'd rather it was someone you knew than someone you didn't; I didn't actually think you were trying to have me kidnapped. And yes, they're still alive. North wasn't there."

"Bet she was a bit stroppy about that," I said, grinning.

I wondered if he knew how softly the smile came and went on his lips. Tuatu is Islander born; with lips as full and wide as his, all the smiles are pretty soft, but this one was different.

"I'm surprised she's letting you walk around by yourself today, then," I said.

"I'm a fully grown man and I'll walk where I want," Tuatu said, with some indignation. He added, after a moment, "Anyway, I'm pretty sure she followed me. You might as well let her in if she's out there."

"She can get in by herself," I said. There was a stir around the house that I'd just thought was my own disturbed state of mind, but now made more sense. I called out, "Come in, North! There's tea!"

It started as a bit of a tickle around our ankles, sweeping from the back of the house toward the front door, then became a gust, sweeping dust bunnies along the hall and past the kitchen. When a banshee tumbled past, wailing, it heralded the small, soft sound of North's footsteps along the hallway, then the frothing, windswept edges of her frock. The North Wind herself whirled into the living room a moment later, her black hair fluttering and coiling around her on the breeze.

"My lady, the tea!" said Athelas reproachfully.

"I knew there was something," North said, stepping lightly down into the living room with a flutter of skirts and breeze, her eyes on Tuatu. "I knew you weren't telling me everything when you came home with a black eye."

I raised my brows at Tuatu, and Athelas did much the same in North's direction. North only shrugged her elegant shoulders and perched herself on the arm of the couch by Tuatu, leaning on his shoulder while he darkened in his version of a blush.

"It wasn't your lot," he said up at her. "They weren't super-human or anything—they were tough to fight, but they didn't have extra arms or spit poison. I don't think they were trying to hurt me, either; they grabbed me behind the bottle shop and tried to drag me off somewhere. That's why I said *kidnap* instead of *kill*."

"Flaming heck!" I said, realising what must have happened. I sent a look in Zero's direction and asked, "Reckon this was Abigail and her mob?"

JinYeong made a soft *tch* of laughter. "*Ah, jaemisseo*! They were not trying to kidnap you."

He spoke in Korean, as he always did, but the curling edges of Between translated it for Tuatu.

Tuatu said grimly, "It felt a lot like an attempted kidnapping to me."

"Yeah, they're a bit...funny about being seen in public," I explained. "Reckon they were just trying to get you somewhere quiet for a bit of a talk."

"I think I can do without that kind of a talk," the detective said. He still sounded pretty unconvinced.

"I recommended you to them."

North shot me a rather cool look beneath her dusky lashes.

Tuatu said, "Thanks. Do you think you could not do that?"

"I didn't think they'd try to mug you behind the local bottle-o!" I protested. "Figured they'd approach you like professionals and introduce themselves. You hurt any of them?"

"I don't think I could have if I wanted to," Tuatu said, a bit grimly. "I don't know what they were using as armour, but every punch I landed felt like hitting memory foam, and they didn't even grunt."

"Looks like those two know something about it," I said, tilting my head at Zero and then Athelas. They might be good at communicating only through looks, but once you know how to interpret them, there's a pretty good chance of being able to eavesdrop whenever you need to.

Zero looked faintly exasperated, but he said, "Your human friends—"

"Never going to get used to people qualifying nouns with *human*," muttered Tuatu.

"—already mentioned that they had something to share. I imagine they're using the same things that they would have shared with you."

"Ohh!" I said. "You mean they used the *artifacts* they were talking about to help 'em fight against behindkind *magically*?"

"I think it very likely that they're using fae elements," Athelas said.

North said delightedly to Tuatu, "Let's take them! They're fun!"

Tuatu eyed her askance. "What are fae elements, and why do they want me to take them?"

"They wanted to talk someone into taking care of 'em," I explained. "They said they weren't getting much good out of 'em anyway, but I s'pose they figured that out. They reckon life is gunna get more dangerous for them from now on, and they want somewhere to store the stuff so that humans can keep looking after themselves when their little cell is...gone."

I nearly said *dead*, and even though I'd already talked about it with Abigail before, I felt a chill for the first time. It wasn't just the little cell that was in danger: from now on, things would continue to get more and more dangerous for me, too. I had Zero in front of me and Jin Yeong behind me, and Athelas somewhere in the shadows, but Abigail and the group had no one else. If Hobart was going to start getting dangerous again like it apparently had a few times over the last century, there must be another way to protect them.

"A sensible way to look at life," said Athelas. His eyes dwelt on Tuatu and North in turn, and he asked, "Will you accept the humans' appeal?"

"We haven't made up our minds yet," North said, with a particularly bland smile at him.

That smile said *don't interfere* and *don't try to trick us into accepting* all at once.

Tuatu jerked a thumb up at her and said, "What she said. Right, we'll be off; I have a lot of ground to cover."

"Are you a part of the police force too, now, my lady?"

This time, North's eyes danced when she answered Athelas. "I could ask you the same thing, old man."

"Yes, it's appallingly quick-witted of you. Oh, are you really going now?"

"I have about four reports to follow up on, starting from Collins Street and flowing up toward the Brewery," said Tuatu. "And I've got the feeling it'll be best to go on foot, so it'll take some time. I'll call you if I find out anything else; please do the same."

They didn't promise him, but Zero did nod, which was enough to get Tuatu and North out the door with at least one of them thinking there would be a phone call if we discovered anything. I mean, never say never and everything, but my

BETWEEN DECISIONS • 19

three psychos aren't the most communicative people out there.

When the door closed behind Tuatu and North, there was a brief flurry of action as Zero retreated to his alcove to start strapping on weaponry and JinYeong went to change his shirt. Even Athelas stood and, removing his houndstooth jacket, laid it neatly across the arm of his chair.

I watched him do it, then gazed at him as he stood there in his vest and shirt-sleeves, tidying his cuffs, and said, "That's flamin' scary."

A couple of lines creased beside his eyes. "Is it? Why?"

"Never seen you take off your jacket to fight before," I said. "You expecting trouble?"

"One never exactly *expects* trouble at the correct moment," he said. "The human world is presently in flux, and I think it wise to be ready."

"Okay, but don't come back half dead again," I told him, as Zero and JinYeong returned from different directions.

"You stay here, Pet," said Zero, with a brief glance toward JinYeong. "Try to contact Abigail—at least tell her not to try to kidnap the detective again. We'll check out the waterfront and see if we can find anything obvious there. Athelas, see what you can find in the main business district: start with the older buildings and whatever infrastructure you can find out about that might be problematic."

"I should come with you," I said, shifting uncomfortably. I don't like being left out of the action. "What if someone tries to come through the linen cupboard?"

"Don't open it," Zero answered briefly.

"What if it's Palomena? You want your dad to be wondering what you're up to?"

"Don't open it," he repeated, this time pinioning me with his eyes. "My father already has far too much access to you; I'd prefer that he not get any more."

"Might not be a bad idea to let him at me again," I said thoughtfully. "It's thanks to him that I got some memories back, after all."

"We shouldn't neglect the fact that my lord's father might also have those memories as a result of your encounter," Athelas said mildly. "And if you are saying that you wish me to be more adversarial, Pet—"

"It's not that I *want* it," I said. "But I know there are other memories—there's that whole night I can't remember. I can't just keep avoiding it."

"You certainly can," he said. "Judging from your young friend Morgana, it is entirely possible to attempt to live your life without stirring up uncomfortable feelings and memories. But since I have no doubt that you'll prefer to do things otherwise, we had best come to some consensus on how the thing ought to be attempted."

"It ought to be attempted when I'm in the house," Zero interrupted. "And when we can be sure that no one inconvenient is likely to be helped by the memories that spring back up again. In the meantime, we have work to do. We can talk about this later. Athelas, JinYeong: it's time."

Maybe I shouldn't have done it. It wasn't like it was against the rules, and Zero hadn't told me I couldn't do it: it was more that I knew he wouldn't approve. The problem was, I didn't think I was wrong, and while I was in that mindset, it wouldn't be right not to do it.

It being contacting a not-so-old adversary of ours.

I pulled my phone out of my pocket, and when I unlocked it, Morgana's number was the first thing that flashed up on the screen. I hadn't exited out of the phonebook when I locked it again this morning, and my morning's interrupted decision was still there to be seen.

A bit sadly, I flicked away that screen and went into my texts instead. One of the last ones I'd received was still there, clear and direct. It said, *Thanks for helping me out. I'll be seeing you. Blackpoint.* None of us had actually meant to help him: we'd been chivvied into doing it without knowing we were doing it. But now that he'd escaped, he was probably the only person who could help Abigail and her crew. He was probably the only one they'd accept real help from, if it came to that.

Well, so long as they didn't discover that he was actually fae.

My thumbs hovered over the screen for a few seconds of hesitation, then I started typing. I didn't type much, but I made sure it was to the point. When I pressed the *send* button, only a single sentence was there.

If you don't want your lot to end up dead, you'd better do something about it.

CHAPTER TWO

ZERO AND JINYEONG didn't come back that night, though Athelas did. I gave up on the other two after midnight and cleared away the dinner I'd made—plated it up into two portions for easy reheating later with the rest in a bigger container. I even found a lid for the container. The banshees had started getting into the cupboards lately, using knives for caber toss and lids for projectiles whenever they were too annoyed about things, so it was no mean feat.

When the kitchen was tidy, I mizzled away into the lounge room where Athelas sat, reading, and tried to settle on the couch. I'd already had a brief, partially coded message exchange with Abigail via text—during which she'd apologised, as much as she ever did apologise, for making Detective Tuatu think he was being kidnapped—and checked to make sure that Blackpoint hadn't messaged back. I could have gone upstairs and tried to settle in bed, but that seemed even harder: if I settled in bed, I would fall asleep, and I didn't want to fall asleep.

I'm not afraid of falling asleep. I'm afraid of the nightmares. And technically, the Nightmare-with-a-capital-n doesn't hang around when my psychos are in the house, but ever since I'd gotten a big clump of memory back a little while ago, I'd started getting normal nightmares, too.

You know, the kind a person gets when they've been kidnapped as a kid and then seen a slightly fractured montage of their kidnappers being torn apart by a murderer who is very good at reducing flesh creatures to strips of flesh. Not to be confused with the night that person's parents were killed by the same murderer—the night I could never properly remember despite my attempts to do so. The night that gave me the Nightmare as well as nightmares.

I'm special. I get a personal Nightmare, too.

"Pet," said Athelas, looking up from his book after ten minutes of me wriggling around on the couch and vainly trying to get comfortable. "Do you suppose you could refrain from flopping around like a landed fish?"

"I'm trying to get comfortable."

"I should have imagined that the last ten minutes would have been sufficient to convince you it's a vain endeavour."

I sat up again, moodily. "The couch is flamin' uncomfortable tonight, that's all."

"Indeed?" said Athelas, with a slight lift of his chestnut brows. "There is usually a vampire at the other end and significantly less space. One presumes that you are now acclimated to the lack of space and find it difficult to adapt once more."

"One shouldn't be presuming," I told him grumpily. "Anyway, even when he's not sitting there, his flamin' perfume is, and that takes up enough space."

It was true: Jin Yeong may not have sat on the couch with me since two days ago, but his cologne was still very much ingrained, and could be said to be occupying the space I hadn't allowed him to occupy.

"Perhaps you would be so good as to make tea, in that case?" he suggested.

I got up straight away. Athelas hadn't actually asked me to

make tea much lately, which was unusual. He was still probably recovering from the latest fight he'd been in, despite the fact that he looked fine on the outside. He'd also been a bit quieter the last couple days, and that was worrying me in more than one way.

When I came back with the tea tray he was still reading, but I had the feeling that he wasn't fully absorbed in his book. Was he trying to avoid conversation with me, or let me know that I could talk and he'd answer?

"How's your gut?" I asked, by way of opening up the conversation, as I set the tray on the coffee table and pushed the biscuits closer to him.

"The same as ever, I believe," he said, bookmarking and laying his book on the coffee table.

That put a bit of a damper on the conversation, but he had put his book down—and he'd done it before I poured his tea, too.

"Well, it was looking a bit ventilated the other day after the fight. Figured you might still be tender for a while."

Athelas took his teacup and gazed at me for a few moments before he asked, "Is that your way of telling me not to eat too many of the biscuits?"

It surprised a chuckle out of me. "Nah. I wouldn't dare. You know I ask stuff because I'm concerned, right? I don't have to have an ulterior motive to be concerned."

"A most unwise way of proceeding through life," he said.

"Better than getting my stomach ventilated every few months," I pointed out. "Wouldn't have said that's exactly healthy, either."

I saw the rim of his teacup reflected in the sudden, amused glow of his grey eyes. "Perhaps not."

I sipped coffee and he sipped tea, but although there was silence, he didn't pick up his book again—which meant either that he wanted to talk to me about something that he wanted, or that he wanted to know something.

At last, into the silence, he said, "You appear to have something on your mind, Pet."

I stared at him. "I've got lots on my mind: I'm an Heirling without enough behindkind blood to be anything special, and my owner's dad is always trying to kill me or form weird alliances with me. That's not to mention that my best friend is a zombie with an identity crisis and the vampire is—"

I stopped, and Athelas' grey eyes grew luminous with amusement or fondness, I wasn't sure which. Maybe it was both.

"Yes?" he said encouragingly. "The vampire is...?"

"A flamin' pain in the neck," I said. "That's not the important thing. The important thing is that I'd have a lot more information —we'd have a lot more information—if I could just shake out a few more memories. I'd be able to find out who killed my parents, and you lot would be able to catch your murderer."

"Is this your way of asking me to try again? I was not entirely successful last time."

"Maybe," I said, propping my chin on my palms. "I've gotta do something, and apart from Zero's dad, you're the one who's had the most success jolting stuff free."

"I've already told Zero that if we proceed, I will have to be significantly more adversarial."

"Yeah," I said. "I know."

Athelas' voice was light and questioning. "Are you asking me to try now? I believe my lord said you would be best served to wait until he was back in the house."

Both of us knew that Zero hadn't said anything of the sort— or at least that whatever he had said, he had said as a command. We were not to do anything while he wasn't in the house, and that had been an order.

"No," I said, hardening my heart against that promise of safety. "If you wait until Zero's back in the house, it won't matter how adversarial you are."

He gazed at me. "Did I not tell you that becoming fond of people was a weakness that few of us can afford?"

"It's not because I'm fond of Zero," I said, rather grumpily. I didn't want to say exactly what it was, because he wouldn't approve of that, either. The fact was that when I had Jin Yeong at my back or Zero in front of me, I didn't feel afraid—or at least, not afraid enough to lose my head—and I was pretty sure that in order to get more of those sneaky memories, I needed to lose my head a bit.

That way, I might be able to avoid losing it around Zero's dad, too.

"It's more that I trust Zero not to let me get hurt," I told Athelas.

"Even more dangerous, I would have said," he murmured. "I'm glad to know that trust doesn't extend to myself; I like to think I've taught you better."

I narrowed my eyes at him. "It's not that I don't trust you," I said, very bluntly. It was hard to tell if he was genuinely glad I didn't seem to trust him, or hurt in his own twisted little way. "I just trust you to a different extent. I don't trust you not to hurt me, but I reckon I trust you to hurt me only as much as necessary."

"A foolish trust," he said sharply. "How many times must I—"

"All right, all right, I'm an idiot," I said soothingly. "Feel better? You want more tea before we start, or what? Reckon that lot's gone cold."

"My tea is sufficiently—as a matter of fact, I would like more tea, yes. Thank you, Pet."

I may have grinned a bit. Zero often loses patience with me, and Jin Yeong is as likely to melt down about something inexplicable as he is to confess love from what seem like equally incomprehensible motives, but Athelas very rarely loses his patience, even for a moment.

Looks like tea really is his Achilles heel.

"Not enough sleep last night?" I asked him, pouring the cold remnant of tea into the little pot for the old tea leaves and refreshing his teacup. That was nonsense: fae need far less sleep than humans. But even if I wanted to prod at the memories in my head and get out the things that had, apparently, been buried there far too long, I also very much didn't want to—a state of things that led to me being facetious, inclined to joke about stuff I shouldn't joke about, and in general an annoying person to be around.

"Nothing of the kind, Pet. I merely had a brief moment of fellow feeling with my lord. Are you perhaps stalling for time?"

I gazed at him as I crossed my legs beneath me. "It's really rude how you tell the truth so politely."

"I might return the favour and inform you that it's highly impolite how often you tell the truth in a rude manner, but since I'm inclined to think that you're again stalling for time, perhaps we should begin. I shall not go easy on you this time."

"Yeah," I said, with a dry throat. I took a sip of coffee, but it didn't help much. "That's what we're going for, isn't it?"

"Indeed," said Athelas, setting his teacup down despite the steam rolling up into the ceiling. I followed that steam with my eyes and saw it curling around the greenery growing there.

Heck. How long had there been ferns growing from the ceiling of the house? Just this morning, if the rate they were growing was any indication; otherwise we'd have been choking on them during breakfast.

"Where should we begin?" asked Athelas, his voice as light and multifaceted as the steam from his teacup. "Your memory of being—what did your young human friends refer to it as? Being *out of state?*—we already regained. Should we attempt a discovery of the surrounding events, or should we attempt to pull up something else?"

"Reckon there's a few specific things I don't remember," I said. *Like the night my parents died.* "But the surrounding events are really clear each time I remember a specific thing. Like all the little things that didn't make sense—all that stuff I just forced to be normal instead of weird—was easier to shove underneath other thoughts because the big stuff it related to was gone."

"Are you saying that you don't know what you don't know? That is...not particularly helpful, but I suppose we can attempt much the same kind of interrogation as Zero's father did—by ignoring your own questions, we might perhaps gain some insight."

"What, you reckon it'll help if you ask me about stuff you want to know about?" I pulled my gaze away from the ferns on the ceiling and looked suspiciously at him. There had been a brief few hours not so long ago where I had suspected him of something so dark and ugly that I didn't like to think about it again—collusion with Zero's dad, and a part in the murders that Zero had been trying to solve for so long now—and while I didn't suspect that now, I knew it was still very wise to suspect him of ulterior motives to...well, *everything.*

"I do," he said tranquilly.

I looked at him for a while longer before I asked, "What have you been wanting to ask me, then? There must be something you really want to know if you're gunna be picking the questions."

"If I had not just warned you about trusting behindkind too much, I might have plaintively asked why you should imagine me to have an ulterior motive," sighed Athelas. "Alas! I must remember to be less forthcoming with my warnings."

"Rubbish," I said. "You like giving warnings for the sheer delight of watching people take 'em the wrong way and do exactly what you wanted 'em to do in the first place."

"Dear heavens!" Athelas said, sipping his tea. "You appear to have been listening, after all. How inconvenient of you."

"I always listen," I said, one of my legs bouncing a bit in

nervousness. It seemed as though the chair behind him was moving very slightly, a movement that churned up the kind of motion-sick feeling you'd get from looking at a wheels-within-wheels setup where the wheels turn in opposite directions. "I just don't always do what I'm told; it's different. We gunna start, or what?"

"We have already started."

"'Zat why the house is halfway Between?" I asked him.

"Oh, I should imagine we're more than halfway Between! We're likely to be able to walk anywhere Behind that we wish before long."

I flicked a look around the room and then back at him. "Maybe we should try that one day."

"If you have a death wish, Pet, I do not. There are far too many people Behind who at this moment would be greatly pleased to find me alone."

"I'd be with you," I pointed out, but I didn't need the creasing around his grey eyes, or the subtle amusement that glowed within them, to realise how ridiculous that was.

Hang on, though. If he wasn't too keen to be Behind, why was the house sinking closer every moment? I jerked my chin at the most nebulous of the areas around the living room and asked him, "You do this?"

"I did not. I wonder if you realise how much you affect the house?"

"You saying *I* did it?"

"Shall we split the difference and conclude that the house itself has done a great deal of the work, under direct impetus from you?"

"If you want," I said, shrugging. It wasn't like I knew better; I didn't even realise I'd been doing anything.

"Even so," Athelas said, as though he perfectly understood my thought. As he spoke, the living room sank a little and began to feel spongy beneath the couches. "Perhaps it would be useful if you attempted to explore just exactly how you're doing it."

"Just blame the pet," I grumbled, but we were here to puzzle out exactly how I knew the things I did and how I did the things I did, so I tried anyway. I sat quietly on the couch with a feeling of not-quite-reality around me—as if the chair wasn't exactly in the right spot, or I wasn't exactly in the right spot of reality to be able to interact with it properly—and explored the feeling of skewed reality, and how it connected to me.

Something fluttered away in the back of my mind: Athelas, and something very like a worm, burrowing deep into my mind. I ignored them both and focused on the house instead, trying to feel with the part of me that could usually feel Between—trying to use that sense to see exactly how I was connected to the house.

"Something isn't right," I said, gazing around me. The room should have been closed-in, like a normal room, but there were thin patches in reality all around me instead: a moving shadow of deep grey beneath the stairs; a glimmering, beckoning thatch of moonlight cobwebbed in the kitchen entry; the sense that if I climbed up into the rafters, I could keep climbing through the greenery and into some sort of dense, claustrophobic forest. "Things aren't like they usually are."

"I very much doubt you'd know," Athelas said. "You don't even know why you're connected to the house."

"'S'pose it's the same thing that keeps Morgana and Ralph connected to their houses," I retorted, averting my eyes from the leaves above with a bit of a shiver. Athelas' worm chewed that up and dug for more, nibbling away at the roots of my mind. "The murderer killed their parents too, so there's no reason to think it'll be different for me."

"You," said Athelas, "are very different from the other two."

"Yeah," I said, my voice fading into the soft shadows of the room and the whispering advance of the greenery above. "My parents died for me."

Athelas' voice was amused. "You're very trusting of the words of a nightmare."

"It never talked before," I told him. "And I'd already half-guessed, anyway. Oi. What would happen if we just...went through one of these thin patches?"

"We'd be deep Between and very nearly Behind," he said. "Why? Do you wish to choose one?"

"Dunno. Reckon Zero'd be annoyed, but he's probably going to be annoyed anyway."

"That's an interesting direction," said Athelas. "Why not go that way?"

The suggestion was directly at odds with his earlier warning, but despite that, I followed the potential path of the thin patch with my eyes. It trailed off into the darkness of a corner that shouldn't have been as dark or deep as it currently appeared to be. It definitely shouldn't have smelled of old, grey, wet rock.

"Yeah, I don't think that's a good way to go," I said, but I rose anyway. I felt the uncomfortable muddle of movement in my pocket as I did so, and absently patted that pocket. Three tubes of something that felt plasticky lurked beneath the denim, and when I pulled one out, it was a needle. "Flamin' heck," I said. "This is the lot I got from that goblin way back when!"

What were they doing in my pocket? I kept them upstairs with the necklace-that-had-been-a-snake, hiding behind my marbles. That's probably a metaphor, but the important thing was that they were now in my pocket, and I didn't remember putting them there.

The worm nibbled furiously now, chasing something slippery and dark.

"Isn't it odd," said Athelas' voice, "how things seem to move around the house? Always in just the right place to be useful."

I tore my eyes away from the dark, grey space in the corner and said, "Yeah. Handy, I s'pose. Was that bit of...stuff...always in the house?"

"I believe we mentioned being surprised the house hadn't sunk into Between or been the site of more strange occurrences."

"That's a nice, creepy yes," I muttered. The worm wriggled and chewed, and that was uncomfortable, but I wanted to know what it was chasing so furiously. The closer I got to the shadows, the more furiously it moved. To Athelas, I said, "C'mmon. Looks like this is it, after all."

I didn't have to see his face to know that he had a brow raised as he followed me; the amusement in his voice as he said, "Oh, after you, of course, Pet!" was enough. He followed me, though, and that was the important thing.

We passed through the plaster and into cool, damp rock, far too tight around us for comfort. Athelas had to move slowly, and I wasn't much more comfortable: him behind and the rock pressing in from the sides made me feel as though I couldn't quite breathe. Maybe it would have been easier without the worm constricting my mind as well, but by then it was something of a relief to have that to focus on. I caught a brief flutter of memory, and let the worm eat it as I stood still to capture it too: it was a memory of myself, shambling sleepily through the house to get to the kitchen and wandering instead through a mossy glade. Soft beneath my feet, the grass made me giggle drowsily to myself. I could still see the kitchen light ahead of me, and I wasn't afraid until something big and shadowy cobwebbed itself into the divide between wherever this was and the safety of the kitchen.

It reached for me, and I screamed, high and sharp. Something big and fast that smelt like dad swept past me, and an urgent hand tore me away, spinning me to face the other way too quickly for me to be truly frightened at what I saw.

Mum's face; Mum's eyes, so bright and grey. She knelt before me, cupping my face in her hands, and although my younger self didn't think anything of it the me that remembered it now realised for the first time that she had also covered my ears against the muffle of sound behind me. We stayed like that for a few minutes, and I remembered how my heartbeat had slowed down with my face in her hands and my toes scrunched into the moss.

When she let me go, my toes were scrunched into the carpet instead. She looked down at it, then shot a quick glance behind me before she got up.

"You're sleepwalking again," she said, and I knew that it had to be true. I felt the brief warmth of her hand around mine, as if she actually had reached through the memory and grasped my hand here and now. More insistently, she added, "You just had a bit of a nightmare. Forget about it. Come back to bed, Pet."

She didn't say *Pet*, of course.

She said my name, but the sound of it was blurred within my mind. I heard, or felt Athelas' amusement somewhere behind me.

"I am somewhat comforted," he said. "It seems that you don't trust me as much as I'd thought you did. Your mother was a surprisingly gifted magic-user, it would seem."

"For a human," I said, adding the qualification he hadn't.

"I'll thank you not to put words in my mouth. It seems as though you were inclined to wander where you shouldn't wander as a child, too."

"That's pets for ya. Always getting into stuff." I wondered, suddenly and coldly, exactly how many of my memories of the old mad bloke had been altered. I had used to wander around after him a lot after we moved here, and something fun and exciting always happened when I went out to chase after him.

I found that my memory of those episodes wasn't quite whole: it was there, but I had carefully forgotten the way the world changed around me as I followed him, and the strange people we met on the way through that changing landscape.

How often had I followed the old mad bloke into Between without knowing about it? And did he remember it all, or had he been made to forget it too?

"You should stay away from that one," said Athelas, and the

worm grew sharp and insistent as it ferreted out memories of those adventurous days to chew on.

I let it do its work, shaken by the familiar yet not *quite* familiar memories that wriggled to the surface of my own mind: memories that I remembered, and now viewed through a slightly different lens—or perhaps simply a different point of view. I felt as though I had become something not myself.

I tried to move forward in the tunnel to give my body something to do while my mind churned in discomfort, but it ended abruptly, closing me into the dark, stuffy recess of my own mind.

"Now this is interesting," murmured Athelas, his voice cold and amused and speculative. "Do stop trying to run away, Pet."

For the first time in a very long time, I felt actually frightened to be alone with him. As much as the stone pressed in around me, did Athelas and the worm press in on my mind.

I said unsteadily, "Maybe we should go back."

"There is no going back," said Athelas. "I am very much afraid that you are at my mercy. I did warn you before we began that I would not be kind to you."

I tried very hard to steady my breathing, but it felt as though the very rocks themselves were pressing against me, suffocating me. "You brought me down here on purpose?"

"As you yourself mentioned, my lord is somewhat of a deterrent to this sort of endeavour," he said, soft and thoughtful. "He is unlikely to find it easy to reach you, even if you call for him; I shouldn't rely upon that tracker spell working, if I were you."

"Yeah? How annoyed d'you reckon he's gunna be if I yell out for him and he has to come rescue me from you?"

"Try it," he said, the last vestiges of light glancing off the curve of his lips and catching in the depths of his moonlit eyes. "I won't wait for you to do so, but I won't stop you."

I reared back against the stone behind, then surged forward to try to push through Athelas, but both alike were immoveable.

"There's no way forward and no way back," he said. "Now. Let us see exactly what memories can be squeezed out of you."

I very much didn't like the way he said *squeezed*, or the way that the rocks seemed to constrict as he said it. I couldn't help the small, panting breath that escaped me as I pushed fruitlessly against the rock in burgeoning panic.

The worm bit me this time, deep and hard and searingly painful, and I choked on a cry of pain, battering at the stone around me until I seemed to feel the blood run down my arms. No matter how hard I pushed, against the stone or Athelas, nothing moved. It grew tighter instead, and the worm tore strips off my mind, careless of importance and pain alike.

For a brief instant, I was caught in a floating, clear whiteness, teetering on the edge of descending into the madness of panic and pain; and in that moment, I had time to think just one thought.

Hang on.

Hang on.

Zero was able to find me when even *I* didn't know where I was —when he didn't have a tracker on me, too. There seemed to be a connection that brought him to me when I called for him. Where on earth had Athelas tricked me into going that Zero wouldn't be able to get in? There was nowhere Between or Behind that Zero couldn't find me, especially if I called for him.

And as I thought that, I understood.

I stood up straight, and this time I could do it: stone and pressure alike vanished.

"You flamin' *liar*!" I said in shock. "We're not in the house! We're not even Between or Behind—we're in my head!"

The scene changed in a moment from claustrophobic tunnel squeezing the breath out of me, back to our living room once again: Athelas in his armchair with one leg crossed over the other and me on my couch where I always sat.

Only this time, I knew it wasn't the real thing, so the feeling of not quite being in synch with my surroundings didn't put me off like it had before. The relief of not having the worm tearing strips off my mind left me awake and sharp and highly focused, too.

And now, I was stroppy.

"I do wonder why you expect me to tell the truth all the time," Athelas said pleasantly. "It really is no use glaring at me."

"Because you always do," I said. "You tell it in a way that makes people not believe it, but you tell the truth."

"How exactly is that different from lying?" he enquired.

"You never lied before," I said. I couldn't help still feeling shocked at that. Athelas had always told the truth before—albeit in such a way that made it a weapon of deception instead of uprightness. "Not really."

"Perhaps you have not been paying enough attention, after all," said Athelas. "Don't attempt to struggle, Pet; you're here in my power, and I don't think I'll let you out so easily, after all."

I narrowed my eyes at him. "Zero's gunna be pretty cranky at you," I said again. We were still inside my mind, and now that I knew it, I also knew that Athelas didn't really need the worm. Here, he was the worm.

"Perhaps so, but Zero isn't here to help you," he said pleasantly. As he said it, a wealth of vines grew up and around the couch, coiling around me with shocking strength. "And I don't recall setting any kind of limits. I believe you have already mentioned that you have no trust in me not hurting you, after all. We will begin."

I pulled with all my strength against the vines, straining my neck and arms, and felt something make a distinct *pop* between neck and shoulder. I didn't miss the slight lift of one of Athelas' brows; he might as well have called me an idiot, and that was very useful.

Insulting, yeah. But flamin' useful.

I laughed to myself as I realised the ridiculousness of straining physically against bonds that were real only in my mind, and this time I focused all the anger and pain that I had felt in the last fifteen minutes into finding the source of my power here in my mind.

There was no visible power, but I saw the world around me shift until it was a morass of particles of thought instead of a coherent whole, and that was a terrifyingly unsettling thought. I tried to grip the particles of that world, and as I did, another memory wriggled to the surface. I sat upstairs in the second living room, playing with dust motes that swam in the morning sunshine, and there was a warm contentedness to me that curled like a blanket around me. The walls moved and sighed with greenery, sending a fresh, sweeping breeze of heavily oxygenated air through the room, and something shuffled through the leaves nearer the floor as I smiled my content around the room. I breathed in wonder as I remembered how it had felt, and felt a tickle of delight in my chest. I had once been so familiar with the world Between that it had seemed friendly to me. I wondered if I would have felt so safe if I remembered all the things my mother had obviously made me forget.

The shuffling across the room grew and resolved itself into a canine sort of form that slinked out of the leaves and surveyed the room. It caught sight of me, and I heard it sniff the air, deep and snuffly.

It looked like a dog, and it was pretending to be a dog, but I could already smell something very wrong about it. I felt my brow furrow.

I said to it, "Good dog?"

It snarled and leaped for my throat, its jaw elongating and splitting to display a double row of teeth, top and bottom. I didn't scream this time: I used the free-floating edges of Between to sweep it up mid-leap, then tumbled it over and out the window. It shattered the window, howling, and disappeared from sight, and I heard it hit the ground outside.

Footsteps pounded against the stairs and my parents tumbled into the room, panting.

"It wasn't a dog!" I said, my breath coming too fast. "I didn't ask it to come in!"

My father crossed to the window, picking through the glass, and I heard his breath hiss inward. "There's another one out there."

"This is...not working," my mother said heavily. She knelt beside me, methodically checking all my limbs for wounds, then settled back in relief. "We're going to have to teach you to forget, Pet."

The name was still blurred around the edges, but there was a purposeful sort of rounding of the sound that gave me a thrill of fear that Athelas might just be able to make it out if he listened hard enough or thought well enough.

There was a very heavy silence before my father said, "Isn't it safer if we teach her how to fight them?"

"She already knows how to fight them," said my mother, her voice tight with worry. "That's the problem. Every time she interacts with *that land*, she's in danger; they can sense her. Once she gets stronger, they'll come for her. They always come for them. Unless she learns to forget, she'll keep drawing danger to herself."

Dad's lips pinched in, but he nodded. "You look after it," he said. "I'll go find those...*things*...and put them down."

"I didn't do it on purpose, Mum," I said, as he left. "It just came through."

"I know," she said. "That's why you're going to have to learn how to forget."

I let the memory go, and the worm appeared again to eat it up. Eating, it grew, and turned back for more. There were more memories there for it to eat, and now that they had begun to surface, they pushed from beneath, wanting to be free. I could access these memories without the worm, and I wanted it *gone*. I wanted it gone, but it wouldn't stop eating, and I knew Athelas wouldn't stop it.

I pulled in a breath that probably wasn't real, though it stuttered as though it was. There was no Between in here—at least, not in the way that there was outside my mind. But it was *my* mind, and that was enough. Just like my mother had bound me to forget things—just like she had obviously bound me to make myself forget things—Athelas had a binding around my mind. Only instead of keeping memories in, it was keeping *me* in. It was magic, but I already knew about magic. More importantly, now I knew that I had once known how to use it.

Despite the lingering sadness at Athelas' duplicity, that thought, and all the implications of it, warmed me. It was time to take away the bindings. I had once been a child, and now I was grown: it was time for me to break free and fight instead of hiding and forgetting.

I drew up the corners of my mind as if they had been the corners of a sheet, gathered all the knowledge and strength from every thread of it, and shoved it all at Athelas, or the worm, or maybe both of them, because they were one and the same.

The vines curled away and vanished as if they had been seared and burned to ash in a moment, but we were still in my mind. Heck. I'd figured that would work. How on earth was I supposed to get him out when I didn't even know how to get myself out?

"No, I think not," murmured Athelas, wincing only slightly. "You will not throw me out so easily as you did last time, Pet; nor, I think, will you be able to do so to Zero's father a second time. As...special as you are, it would be foolish to think that you're equal to either of us when we're aware of your methods."

"Yeah," I said, climbing unsteadily to my feet as the world turned lazily around me. The memory of my mother had been useful in more than one way, because it had reminded me of something that I had learned only recently. "But I've got the element of surprise, remember?"

He looked faintly amused at that, but it didn't weaken him in any way: the binding he still had around my mind was tight and sticky, digging roots into places I didn't want brought to light and pulling upward.

I crossed the room that was my mind, and sat on the arm of his chair, pulling my legs up until my feet rested on the seat of it, snuggled between the arm and his legs. I slipped my arm behind his neck and curled it there, then leaned my head into his shoulder and linked my other arm with the one around his neck. I'd sat like this with Dad more times than I could remember—and those memories remained, whole and unbroken, in my mind.

Silence, heavy and complete, remained unbroken until Athelas said, "What do you think to accomplish by this episode, Pet?"

"Dunno," I said, pushing my face more firmly into the scratchy, warm brown shoulder of his jacket. I could hear his heart beating, steady and quiet. "Don't think I was thinking, actually. It was more of an instinct."

Athelas seemed to sigh; a faint thing in and out, and the world flickered around us. I hugged him a bit tighter, and this time when he breathed in, I heard his breath shudder, too. I had heard that kind of breath only once before, and that was when my father cried, so I held on a bit tighter and didn't look.

Instead, I concentrated on the scratchiness of Athelas' jacket and, in the very tangible strength of that feeling, drew us both out of my mind and back into the human world. There, I had somehow made it to Athelas' chair as well, and if I had before laid my head on his shoulder with the visceral instinct that it was the thing to do, now I couldn't quite raise it again because of how heavy and tired it was.

I mumbled into his neck.

"A moment, Pet," he sighed, and soon I felt his hand, heavy and energising at the same time, on my shoulder.

I didn't remember him using his healing talents on me before, though I'd seen him use them on Zero. It didn't feel anything like what I would have expected it to feel like. It didn't really *feel* at all. It was more as though I had eaten after fainting from lack of food, and my energy was finally being allowed to store itself again.

Before I could gather that energy to get up, I felt a flutter of Between around the front door, and a roar fairly shook the house.

"Pet! *Pet!*"

"Ah heck," I said, as something big and white snatched me away from the brown scratchiness that was Athelas. "Reckon Zero's back."

CHAPTER THREE

BLUE EYES DAZZLED ME, much like the sunlight at present pouring through the windows.

Flamin' heck. It was already morning?

I said accusingly to those blue eyes, "You interrupted an experiment."

Zero's gaze flickered past me to Athelas, and the coldness I saw in it chilled me right to the bone. He said to Athelas, "If you think I won't carve out your stomach, you're very much mistaken."

"I'm under no such misapprehension, I believe," said Athelas.

His voice sounded light and amused, so why did the words make a sob catch in my throat?

"What are you doing?" I asked Zero, wriggling against the arms that held me. He'd picked me up as though I was a baby, and even if I didn't think I could walk right now, that was insulting and unnecessary. "I can stand on my own two feet."

"No, you can't," he said briefly. "Not for another few moments, I think. Are you all right?"

"'Course," I said, and where I hadn't really been able to feel

Athelas using his healing talents on me, I definitely felt Zero pushing magic into me, bright and wild.

I yawned and pulled my head away from his shoulder where it had drooped again. I suddenly felt as though I could walk again, but it didn't seem as though Zero was going to put me down any time soon. Since the whole world was too bright to bear at the moment, maybe that wasn't a bad thing. Maybe it would also stop him from hurting Athelas; his arms were already in use, after all.

That thought both cheered me up and left me free to gaze at the room around me. I hadn't seen it when my head was tucked down on Athelas' shoulder, but the entire world was awash with particles of light and auras in glittering essence of Between. Even compared with the brightness of morning sunlight, it was dazzling.

"Heck," I said, trying to blink away the brilliance of it all. "Reckon I busted an optical nerve or something."

"Athelas," Zero said, his voice sharp with command. "Explain."

Ah heck, I thought, chilled from my ears to the pit of my stomach. He wasn't going to stop, and as soon as he put me down...

Something hard and uncomfortable pressed against me, forced by the unyielding bulk of Zero's stomach muscles into the softer flesh of my leg, and I had a crystal-clear recollection of what it must be.

Flaming heck. I'd actually brought them down to me in the real world as well as my mind. I wriggled a bit more, and with a stifled sigh of exasperation Zero shifted me just far enough to allow me to slip a hand into my pocket and pull out one of the syringes that I'd stolen from a goblin a long time ago.

I flicked the cover from the needle with the nail of my thumb and manipulated the whole contraption until the plunger was beneath my thumb, narrowly avoiding sticking myself with the needle. I would have stuck it in his neck, but I couldn't quite reach, and I didn't dare do it while I couldn't see where I was putting it.

Instead, I had to wrap my arm around his neck, pulling myself closer. From there, I could just reach far enough to snatch the needle from one hand to the other, so I did it, breathless with panic because Athelas still hadn't said a word to exculpate himself, and I was half afraid he was actually trying to antagonise Zero.

I s'pose it could have seemed like I was scared and looking for comfort, because Zero's arms tightened straight away.

"You had better not have hurt her," his voice said in my ear, fairly radiating fury, "or—"

Got it! I plunged the needle into the soft bit between shoulder and neck and depressed the plunger as quickly as I could.

"Pet," said Zero in shock, swaying slightly. "What did you do?"

"Mickey-finned you," I said. "You better put me down before you drop me."

He did so, staggering slightly, and tried to focus on me. "Why?"

"Because you said you were gunna gut Athelas," I explained, swaying a bit. We were a fine pair, hardly able to stand up to face each other. "And that's not fair, because I'm the one who made him do it."

"I very much doubt," Zero said, blinking heavily, "that you made Athelas do anything."

Yeah, that was fair enough. Still, I'd been the one to ask him to do it, whatever his motives or expectations had been—and he *had* warned me.

"Doesn't matter," I said, trying to make my way around the coffee table, which seemed determined to follow me no matter where I went. Zero dropped down onto the couch and put his head in his hands. "I still asked him to do it, and I'm not gunna let you hurt him because of it."

"What did you think you were doing?" demanded Zero. He

looked as though he was trying to get up but couldn't quite manage it. His shadow, threaded with light, looked like it was trying to pull away from him.

"It is not your business, *Hyeong*," said JinYeong's voice. I felt his hand plucking at the back of my collar to stop me falling over, and he steered me around to my side of the couch. This time, the coffee table didn't follow. "She wishes to get her memories back, and she is not hurt. Just drunk."

"I'm not drunk!" I said. "It's just hard to stand up and stuff is... weird. Where did you pop up from?"

"You are drunk," he said. "Sit down."

I sat down because I couldn't do much else by then. I wished the room wasn't quite so separated into tiny pieces of light.

My attention caught on an interesting group of light particulates across the coffee table: a buzz of brightness around Zero's pocket that resolved itself into a form I recognised. Zero had a USB in his pocket. I said to Zero: "You went to the library."

JinYeong gave a crow of laughter and dropped down beside me on the couch. After yesterday morning's performance, I couldn't tell him to move, and he knew it, the smug little git. He'd just stare at me from across the table, and the room was already dizzying enough as it was.

"*Jal haesseo*," he said to me, his eyes still bright with malicious laughter.

Zero said rather thickly, "How did you know we went to the library?"

"I can see the USB in your pocket," I said. My voice came out a bit gloomy, but that was probably only because I didn't know why I knew it was the USB. And maybe a bit because I really was something very close to drunk. "The one I exchanged the house for. You never told me what was on it."

"No," said Zero, sinking against the back of the couch, his eyelids dropped low over his eyes. As though he couldn't quite stop himself from saying it, he added, "I didn't stop the merman from letting you look at it. You can't blame me if you walked away before you saw what was on it."

Jin Yeong, his voice amused, said, "Ah, *jaemisseo*! *Hyeong*, you are drunk too!"

"Perhaps you should retire abovestairs for a few hours, my lord," suggested Athelas.

"No," said Zero, his voice obstinate and very slightly slurred. "I want to have a word with you."

I snorted a bit and overbalanced against Jin Yeong, then pushed myself away. "Good luck doing anything but sleeping after that lot."

Zero tilted his head to the side and fixed a hazy look on me. His shadow, while technically doing the same, looked a good deal more alert, and that made me giggle. Jin Yeong gave a sniff of laughter beside me.

Zero, suspicious and sleepy, said, "How did you see the USB when it's in my pocket?"

It wasn't so much that I could see it as sense it. It seemed as though the room was inside one of Blackpoint's computers, and all the lines of code that went to make up the room around me were still buzzing with the connection, lighting up all the interesting points around the room in a soft but pervasive kind of purple halo that fit within the sparkling matrix of the rest.

My three psychos weren't immune to that effect, either; they weren't purple, but they were each lit up to a greater or lesser extent. Zero was a steady glow of Between particles, Jin Yeong another beside me where it was hard to see, and Athelas lit up his side of the room.

"Dunno," I said. "Reckon that's something to do with getting back a few of my memories. I'm seeing the world in a different light."

It made me giggle again, and although Athelas shut his eyes briefly, the corners of his mouth turned up in an instinctive smile.

"Stop dripping on the carpet," Zero said to Jin Yeong in irritation. I was pretty sure he was trying to stop himself from smiling, too.

JinYeong gave another sniff of laughter. "I do not need your concern, *Hyeong*. I will heal."

"You're dripping on the carpet."

"You do not care about the carpet. You are picking a fault."

I sputtered a laugh into my sparkly elbow but said to JinYeong, "Don't drip blood on the carpet; I gotta clean that up afterwards."

"I shall shower," said JinYeong loftily, and disrupted the world around me by removing himself from the couch.

I tipped over again, straightened myself, and said to Athelas as the buzz that was JinYeong disappeared into the shower, "This is your fault."

"Should I apologise, or inform you that you're welcome?" he enquired.

"Pft," I said, and fell asleep for a while.

Luckily for Athelas, Zero seemed to do the same, because when I woke up again, his eyes were closed and his breathing had deepened. The balance of the couch had been reset, by which I knew JinYeong had returned from his shower, and the world was still bright and formed from particles and lines of light. At least Athelas and Zero weren't quite so bright anymore.

"How come everything still looks like we're in the Matrix?" I asked Athelas, rubbing my eyes. He had been in my mind with me for the memory recovery, so hopefully he'd have a good idea what was going on.

"It would appear that you've always been able to see and manipulate magic—and Between," said Athelas. "As an Heirling, that is to be expected. From a full human, however, it is less common; but then, a fully human Heirling is...unprecedented. The way you see the world would naturally be different to that of a fae Heirling."

"Yeah, yeah, same as usual: I'm not supposed to be able to do this and no one knows exactly why," I said soothingly. "A bit late saying that now, isn't it?"

To my surprise, Zero's eyes cracked open. With an air of very great concentration, he managed to say, without slurring, "It could be a way of dealing with Between that is peculiar to humans who have so little other behindkind blood that they have no other facet by which to view Behind and Between. The fact that the revenant and the zombie can also do something of the sort with their houses leads me to believe that our conclusion that they're Heirlings is correct."

"Look at me, being right and stuff," I said, narrowing my eyes at the very bright glow of particles beside me that was JinYeong. I was less tired than before, but it would be nice if things stopped being quite so bright; I might feel a bit less dizzy, then.

Through the glow, JinYeong grinned at me, and the glow pulsed a little stronger.

"Good grief!" I said, annoyed anew at him. "I know you think you light up the room, but do you *have* to be so flamin' literal about it?"

A softly glimmering Athelas murmured, "You have such a unique method of communication, Pet."

"You telling me not to provoke fights in the lounge room?" I enquired, rubbing at my eyes to try and help dissipate the glow further.

"I will not fight," said JinYeong, as I remembered that doing something physical wouldn't fix something that hadn't been affected by a physical thing. "I have just showered."

I sighed and closed my eyes, reaching out to put a hand on top of the head of hair nearby that wouldn't stop glittering. I shouldn't have needed to touch him, but touching Athelas had made the effects of what I'd done so much stronger that it seemed like a reasonable crutch to use.

JinYeong, sounding significantly more startled than I'd expected, said, "*Mwoh hae?*"

"Belt up for a bit," I said, curling my fingers into his hair so that he couldn't get away. It was a good thing he had just showered: his hair was soft and faintly wet rather than thick with gel or wax. "I'm turning your wattage down."

"*Bulkaneunghae*," he said, with conviction. His voice was a bit closer, which was sensible if he didn't want to lose hair.

"Garbage," I told him. "All light bulbs can be turned down. You just need the right mechanism."

From across the coffee table, Zero's voice said coldly, "What are you doing, Pet?"

"You can have a pat on the head later," I told him. Neither Zero nor Athelas glowed as brightly as Jin Yeong; typical, that. Even today, Jin Yeong was being a headache. "Go back to sleep."

"I don't know why I bother," muttered Zero. There was an element of hopelessness to his voice, and maybe of wonder, too.

"Me either," I said cheerfully, trying to relax the hyped-up part of my brain that was straining to see and understand. I needed to relax, not stop seeing stuff altogether.

There was a brief silence. Then Zero said, *sotto voce*, "I'll expect a pat on the head. I won't forget."

Jin Yeong huffed a short, derisive breath out at him, but I couldn't help smiling. The first time Zero had been the recipient of a goblin syringe, he had gotten soft and warm and approachable. It looked like that was a fairly consistent reaction for him. It was nice to know that he wasn't always an iceberg—or maybe just that on the inside, he never had been.

I took another moment to relax my mind, breathing in and out deeply. Then I opened my eyes to find a far less brilliant Jin Yeong gazing at me with a curious expression on his face—a face that was a lot closer than I'd expected it to be. That confused me until I realised that I still had a good handful of his hair and hurriedly let it go. Jin Yeong straightened, re-establishing the space between us, and turned his face away from me.

"A pleasant interlude," said Athelas, his eyes faintly mocking.

He was no longer glowing at all; neither was the room around me. There was a *more*ness to everything that suggested I could open that sight again at will, but for now everything was tucked away in the fashion it should be tucked away.

Across the table, Zero stirred and seemed to wake again. Still slightly slurring, he said, "Pet, go out with Jin Yeong. I need to have a discussion with Athelas."

"I don't want to go out with Jin Yeong," I argued. "And if you're going to ventilate Athelas' stomach again, I'm not going anywhere. I told you: he only did what I asked him to do. And he did it flamin' well, too—you do want me to get these memories, right? You haven't been chasing this murderer for so long that your life won't have purpose without it?"

"I've been chasing the murderer for an insignificant length of time, considering my lifespan," he said, stubbornly precise with his words despite the obvious difficulty. "I'm hardly likely to suffer from a lack of purpose in my lifetime."

"I believe there is rather a surplus of purpose than a lack of one," Athelas murmured.

It probably would have been better if he hadn't said anything; Zero's eyes flickered back to him and hardened.

"Out," he said to me, swaying in his seat. "I won't tell you again."

I threw a look in Jin Yeong's direction, and he tipped his head toward the front door, his eyes bright with malicious laughter.

"*Wae? Shilleoh?*"

"Exactly," I told him. I had absolutely no desire to be walking the streets with Jin Yeong, who was still full of laughter and sultry looks. To Zero, I said, "And it's not much good trying to intimidate me when you can't even stand up straight."

There was a huge, gusty sigh from Zero. "Pet—"

"I'm not gunna leave the house while you're half-drunk and likely to hurt Athelas," I told him. "Me and Jin Yeong'll go upstairs. That's enough. If you start trying to kill Athelas down here, I'll know. Otherwise, we'll leave you alone."

I got up and headed for the stairs before anyone could argue further. Jin Yeong followed with a spring to his step that suggested he was delighted with the way things had turned out, and that was worrisome. At least I'd be able to leave him in the upper lounge room and ignore him from the comfort of my own room if it got to be too much.

The first thing I saw when I got upstairs was the open window. It was only open a crack—just the amount I used to leave it open so that I could wriggle my fingers beneath the sash and lift it to climb in. Still, it wasn't usually open these days.

"Who left you open?" I muttered, crossing to close it. As I did, I caught sight of a shiver of movement along the fence at the side—on the neighbour's side, I was pretty sure. I'd just missed seeing whatever it was that had made the movement; a moment too slow at looking down. I frowned, and Jin Yeong exhaled a small *aish* of sound by my ear, startling me by his sudden proximity.

He said, "That crazy *halabeoji* is out there again."

"I know," I said, my eyes flicking across the house next door.

"How do you know? You can't smell him."

"I can see him," I said, tipping my chin just slightly toward the lower windows of the house opposite. Reflected in one window was a scruffy figure that crouched below the level of the fence, creeping stealthily toward the front of the house and, presumably, freedom via the front yard.

Jin Yeong's brown eyes grew thoughtful. "Who taught you to do that?"

"Dad," I said. "And before you say it's strange, I know."

He grinned, then asked unexpectedly, "How long have you known it is strange?"

I stopped and stared at him. "You're not as dumb as you look."

"I am charming," he said, with certainty.

I almost expected him to do what he'd done more than once before: lean forward and encroach on my space, warm and worrisome.

Instead, he leaned back into the window frame, still gazing down at me through his lashes.

"Stop looking at me," I complained, looking away and back out the window. "You reckon he was up here? The window was open."

"*Hyeong* would not allow that," Jin Yeong said.

I stared out the window again, hoping to avoid his eyes, and caught sight of something even more interesting than the old mad bloke creeping around in next door's yard.

"Flamin' heck!" I said, staring in disbelief at the moving truck. "Got a new neighbour! That isn't supposed to happen, is it?"

There hadn't been a steady neighbour here for a good while; that's the way it turns out when you live in a street where weird stuff happens and there's a double homicide to crown it all.

Jin Yeong's expression grew curious. "I wonder if *Hyeong* knows?" he said softly. "This should not happen. I wonder..."

"You wonder what?"

"I shall not tell you," he said, lifting his nose. "You don't tell me anything."

That surprised a laugh out of me, but I said, "You reckon Zero's dad has found us, don't you? It could be a spy moving in."

"Perhaps," he said darkly. "We will tell *Hyeong* and the old man."

"Good idea," I said in relief, starting back across the room. That would give me an excuse to get out of the distracting and disturbing solo presence of Jin Yeong, and at the same time an excuse to make sure that Zero and Athelas weren't fighting. I hadn't heard the sounds of death, but neither Athelas nor Zero tended to make a lot of noise when they were at their most deadly.

Jin Yeong caught at my sleeve and tugged me to a stop. "It is too early."

"What do you mean, too early?" I asked him, hunching my shoulders. "You saw how he was looking at Athelas, and I haven't heard a peep out of either of them."

"*Hyeong* will be very quiet and very threatening," he said, releasing me. "The old man is not like me; *Hyeong* cares for him in a different way. It would be rude to...ventilate him like *Hyeong* did to me."

"You're pretty blasé about that for someone who nearly died," I remarked, but I sat down on the closest armchair to stop myself from going back down the stairs.

He shrugged and threw himself into an armchair at right angles with mine, curling up with his arms folded on the fat arm of the chair and his eyes resting on me.

He looked soft and defenceless: hair freshly washed and down in a heavy fringe across his forehead instead of swept away, high and sophisticated; wearing a soft jumper and the most elegant pair of trakkie daks I'd ever seen. But Jin Yeong looking soft and defenceless was the most dangerous Jin Yeong, in my experience, so I narrowed my eyes at him.

"What?" I demanded. Athelas' safety aside, this was exactly the reason I hadn't wanted to leave the safety of the other two. The room felt far too warm and closed-in with Jin Yeong's eyes on me. "What do you want now?"

"I wish to know something," he said. "I wish to have a name for you."

"Yeah, but do you have to keep staring at me?" I complained.

Jin Yeong only rested his chin on his folded arms and continued to observe me, catlike. "I cannot keep calling you *friend*," he said.

"Rude."

He lifted his chin from his arms and narrowed his eyes at me. "Don't throw wrong meanings at me."

"You learn flamin' quick," I said. I meant to glare at him again, but there was a laugh burring in the back of my throat, and it was hard not to give into it. I didn't quite give way, but I didn't glare, either. "I'm not giving you my name just yet."

"Very well," he said, but he didn't look as though he was disappointed. "Then I want something else."

I must have looked pretty suspicious of him, because he grinned, sharp and mischievous. "Not that," he said, on what was almost a purr of laughter. "I wish to look at those papers again; I had a thought."

"Yeah? All right, but you'd better not go showing them to Zero or Athelas." I still felt a bit warm in the face, but at least it was something reasonably harmless he wanted. For just a fraction of a second, I'd actually thought he would tell me he wanted a kiss.

JinYeong made a small, dismissive sound. "There are no secrets from *Hyeong*. He knows everything."

That was surprisingly touching, and more than a little bit naïve. "Maybe from your perspective," I told him. "From mine, he's not as all-knowing as that. Athelas is the one I'm more worried about."

A small frown twitched into place between his brows. "Why do you worry about the old man?"

"Because he made Tuatu get all that stuff," I said. "The papers you saw last time, I mean. And I can't figure out why. I don't know what he was looking for—don't even know if he found it—but I'd rather he didn't know I have it all now."

"Mmm," said JinYeong. "Then nothing makes sense."

"Tell me about it," I said, and started for my room.

"I already told you," he said, following me.

"Nope," I said, when he tried to follow right into my room. I grabbed him by the arms and physically turned him around, then pushed him back into the living room. He didn't try to resist, but he looked so ridiculously pleased with himself that it made me want to kick him.

"I will wait," he said instead, and padded back over to the armchair to sit down again.

I ducked into my room and looked around at the mess in there. You gather a lot of detritus when you live with two fae and a vampire, somewhere between worlds. Stuff like a necklace that used to be a snake—or maybe was just pretending to be a necklace for a while to lull humans into a false sense of security—and a frog that used to be a tie. Stuff that couldn't be counted on not to be something else at an inopportune time.

But there was also the detritus I'd gathered that was a bit more...human-related. That kind was even harder to sort out, even if you didn't have to worry about it turning into something weird and strangling you while you were asleep.

It was just paperwork, and it shouldn't have been such a big pain in the neck, but it was. Most of it was stuff that Athelas had had Detective Tuatu searching the internet for, but some of it was information I'd gotten from Abigail and her group of humans. Most of it was gathered in one area, so I picked up an armful and poked the rest of the bits and pieces into another pile with my toe and sighed a bit. One of those pieces of paper was missing, too, I was certain. I hadn't seen it since last week—a photocopy of my great-grandma's license that I'd originally thought was my mother's—and worse, unless a certain tie-turned-frog had taken off with it, I didn't know who *had* taken it. Jin Yeong was the only one who came into my room with any regularity—a mistake that was going to be rectified from now on—but if I'd had to pick from one of the three psychos, I would have guessed Athelas. Only he never came into my room, and Jin Yeong and Zero both had.

I huffed out a sigh and combined my pile of papers, then went back out to Jin Yeong.

"I wish to know," he said, when I put the heaping pile down

on the floor between the chairs, "I wish to know why the old man was so careless."

"What do you mean, careless?"

"So careless that he used the detective to do this."

"Tuatu didn't know not to say stuff like *I owe you*," I told him. "Reckon that's how Athelas got him."

JinYeong made a small hum that was hard to decipher as either agreement or disagreement. "I agree. But that is not *why*; that is *how*."

"Dunno what to tell you," I said. "Maybe he thought Tuatu was the one who had the best access to what he wanted?"

"Perhaps," said JinYeong, but he didn't sound convinced. He pushed a few bits of paper aside, picked up another, then sorted rapidly through the rest, picking up and discarding at will. "This one, this one, no, ah here it is! This one, no, this one."

I stared at him. "What are you looking for?"

"I am not looking, I have *found*," he said, wafting the little sheaf of papers he'd found at me. "It is as I thought."

"What did you think?" I took the papers from him mostly to stop him brandishing them in my face, but none of them made a lot of sense in conjunction with each other. "They're all bills? I can see that; what about it?"

"These numbers are the same," he said.

"What numbers?"

"What is this? P.O.? The number is the same, but the name is different."

I blinked a bit. "Flamin' heck. They are, too. Five didn't mention it to me last time I talked to him."

"The leprechaun knows about this?" JinYeong looked faintly offended. "Before me? Also, if he did not see this, he is blind. What is P.O.?"

"Post office box," I said, amused. "And I didn't say Five didn't see it; I said he hadn't mentioned it to me. He seems to work on collections of data points that make a map instead of picking out this or that. Hang on. If this is a post box number, how come all these bills from different addresses are being sent to the same box? And why are the names all different?"

"This person does not wish to be known," said Jin Yeong, as if it were perfectly natural. "So they give a false name."

"Yeah, but why is someone paying bills for several other people?"

"Bills?"

"They're bills," I said. "You know, electricity and water and stuff?"

"One is for this house?"

"Yeah," I said, and as I looked down at the water bill for my own house, it dawned on me exactly what it was that was important about this bill. It was a bill from two years ago—which meant that someone had been paying for my water, knowing perfectly well that I was here. More slowly, I added, "This is the water bill for this place. The others...well, that's the power bill for —flaming heck!" I looked up at Jin Yeong with wide eyes. "This one's the power bill for Morgana's place. Want to bet there's something here for Ralph's place too?"

"That sneaky old man," murmured Jin Yeong. "What does he want with this information?"

I wanted to know that, too. I didn't like the idea of beginning to suspect Athelas again when Zero had given such a good reason for trusting him, but I also didn't want to be as blind as Athelas regularly accused me of being.

Still, it wasn't as though trying to find out who knew about the three of us human Heirlings—and was actively hiding us— was the same as being involved in the murders. Athelas could even be under Zero's orders by doing so, and they just hadn't told me—as usual. We already knew that someone like Upper Management was involved in keeping Heirlings hidden from the murderer, and it was likely that whoever had paid for our power and water while hiding the fact that they were doing so, was someone from that group. It made sense for Athelas to be looking for that person.

I took a photo of the P.O. Box number on a couple of the bills, careful to get the names in the shot. Nemo Keiner. Vivien Nunc. Two would do for now, but when we found the bloke, I was going to ask him exactly what joke he was playing with his names.

"Might have to go to the post office later," I said, sliding my phone back into my pocket. "Bring along your mojo and see what we can find out."

Jin Yeong elevated his nose very slightly, looking pleased with himself, but said as if it was a very great consideration, "Perhaps I shall do that."

I managed to stop myself from snorting rudely, and asked him, "How'd you see this, anyway?"

The addresses were all in different places on the bills, and the names were all different: the only common denominator was the box number and the suburb: P.O. Box 681, Hobart, 7050.

He shrugged. "I like numbers. They are peaceful. I will look at other things now—that one. I want to see what that one is about."

"It's a police report," I told him, but I passed it anyway. Jin Yeong might not have much human sense, but it was obvious that he had a useful point of view despite that. "Good luck finding useful numbers on that one. I read it last night: it's an overall report of crime going up in the area up toward the old brewery from about ten years ago. I reckon that's probably when Abigail moved into the area."

Jin Yeong gave a small sniff of laughter. "Ah. Then the crime did not grow; it was stopped."

"Yeah, but I bet they left a bit of a mess when they were first starting," I said. "Might need to suggest to them that they move out of that area soon. If someone knows how to find them by picking up police reports..."

"This is all interesting," said Jin Yeong. "The things the old man has gathered—they are things that someone would gather if they wished to keep you close and safe. He is looking for that person?"

"Yeah," I said soberly. "That's the bit that doesn't make sense to me: who would be looking for us, apart from Zero's dad or the king? And if they've already found out this much about us, why are we all still alive? If it's Upper Management that's looking after us, why wouldn't they have made a move already?"

JinYeong, his eyes fixed on the page, made a soft sort of *mmm* sound.

"*And*," I began to add, when there was a snap and tug at the bit of Between that edged the house. "Hang on, reckon someone's here."

There was a dull thud from below, followed by Athelas' voice, sharp and negative, and a wall-shaking *crunch* that was ridiculously familiar to me. My head jerked up: someone or something had just gone through one of the downstairs walls.

"Flamin' heck!" I said in exasperation. "What now?"

JinYeong's eyes met mine: we scrabbled to get all the papers together, then he thrust them into my hands and I dashed off to throw them in my room while he darted downstairs.

When I got down there, the first thing I saw was JinYeong, hands in pockets and his eyes alight with laughter, observing Zero from just beyond the stairs. Zero—who was currently sprawled on the floor with his head partway through the living room wall and Palomena's knee on his chest, her knife at his throat.

"Is that you, Pet?" she asked, without looking away from Zero. He looked a bit dazed, but I didn't really blame her for not taking the chance: even a dazed Zero is a dangerous Zero.

"Right here!" I said cheerfully. "I don't know why you two don't just go out for coffee or something."

Zero's eyes focused on me for a moment, then went back to Palomena. "I am drunk," he said to her, very clearly. "Enjoy the moment: it won't happen again."

"I'm not sure that I would have said it was enjoyable," said Palomena, withdrawing her knife. She replaced it in its sheath and used that hand to gently massage the wrist of the other hand, which was purple and bruising fast. "Are you usually drunk before noon, by the way?"

"Why?" Zero asked, curling away from the wall and lurching to his feet. He shook his head, staggered a bit, and seemed to gain his balance again. "Looking for more information for my father?"

"I report on exactly what I'm asked about," she said. "Nothing more, and nothing less. For example, after this meeting, I'll make a report to my commanding officer that details everything I happened to notice about the Pet and her apparently changed position within the house, despite the fact that I previously had no information to suggest there was such a change. I'll pay especial attention to how that change has affected her interpersonal relationships among the three of you. My commanding officer will then pass that report on to Lord Sero's father."

There was a very long silence while Zero gazed quizzically at her, then at Athelas; and Jin Yeong, out of sight of the rest of them, dabbed his fingers toward me in a *come here* gesture. Oh yeah. Zero's dad thought we were a couple.

It looked as though Jin Yeong thought it would be a good idea if he continued to think that, too. I considered him silently for a moment, then stepped away from the staircase and joined him by the entrance to the kitchen. Zero's dad would definitely want to know what was up if that particular "relationship" had changed.

"Don't reckon you're supposed to tell us what your orders are," I said, leaning into Jin Yeong's inviting side and allowing his arm to circle me naturally.

"Indeed I'm not," she said, turning a little toward us. I noticed, not without a bit of amusement, that she didn't seem to be able to bring herself to put her back to Zero entirely. "I think you'll agree that I haven't told you what I was ordered to do, however."

Zero, looking more alert by the minute, exchanged a worried look with Athelas—who, to my relief, looked unhurt, if rather tired. "Why is my father so interested in the Pet's position?" he asked Palomena.

"That is something I can't tell you," she said. "Even if I wasn't directly forbidden to do so, I don't know. I'll make a report on the appearance of changes due to her apparent change in position, and that's as much as I can do."

Did she put emphasis on *change in position*? I was pretty sure she had.

"Ostensibly," Palomena added, "I'm here to see if you need any assistance in dealing with the occurrences that are reported to be happening along the waterfront. I get the impression that my help is supposed to lean more toward covering up the incidents than finding the source of them, but I wasn't given clear enough directives to be...*completely sure* of that."

Zero's eyes grew lighter blue, and I'd have sworn they danced a bit. "You're offering us help."

"I believe that's my job," she said.

I poked Jin Yeong in the ribs, and he bared his teeth at me but glanced toward Zero and then grinned for real, shrugging one shoulder at me. So Jin Yeong agreed: Zero was amused.

More importantly, it looked as though Zero was prepared to accept real help from Palomena, and that Palomena without her nearest commanding officer was inclined to help as much as she could.

"We would appreciate the assistance," Zero said to Palomena.

Nothing much changed in her expression, but there was the briefest little upward pull on one corner of her mouth that made me think she was pleasantly surprised. That was fun and rather nice: she'd come prepared to offer help—had even given us information for free—without expecting that it would be accepted in the spirit it had been offered.

"I'm being very useful to Zero these days," I said helpfully, smiling brightly at both Zero and Athelas. "Very hard working and supportive and all that sort of thing. Anyone who wants to know how things are going should know how useful I'm making myself."

"I'm quite certain my commanding officer will be interested to hear that," said Palomena, with a very slight glow of amusement to her eyes. "No doubt if it gets...further than him, anyone else hearing it will be glad to know. There seems to be a great deal of interest in whether one human pet is as loyal to her master as everyone would like to think."

"Consider it confirmed," said Zero, the amusement fading from his face completely.

"Then I'll be on my way now that I've had it confirmed and offered my assistance. When shall I make myself available to you?"

"Tomorrow, dawn," Zero said.

"I look forward to it," she said. She bowed to us—even to me, which was nice—and headed back toward the linen closet door.

I don't know when it started to be normal for people to pop in and out of the linen closet, but even if it hadn't been exactly normal by now, it still beat Zero's dad knocking down the front door to get in. So long as the linen closet was the only way his minions had of getting into the house, we were all a lot safer.

Well, mostly me. I was a lot safer.

"It seems as though I'll have to make it clear to my father that you're not to be touched," said Zero to me, after the door closed behind Palomena.

"You believe he wants to hurt the Pet?" Athelas' voice was light with surprise. "I had thought quite the opposite."

"I don't believe he wants to hurt her, but I think it's a common side effect of my father's interest," Zero said shortly. "I don't want him interested in her and I don't want him following her. Jin Yeong, get your arm *away* from Pet."

"Heck!" I said, startled. I hadn't realised it was still there, warm behind me and snug against my waist. I was supposed to be making myself very distant from Jin Yeong—I'd obviously got far too used to him being close.

Jin Yeong surprised me by removing his arm without a challenge to Zero, but he did glance down at me with a curious, tentative little smile that was almost terrifying in its honesty.

"It's all right, I'm not gunna try to hit you," I said, looking away. "I knew what you were playing at."

"I'd like to know what you were playing at," said Zero, but he was looking at Jin Yeong.

"Your dad thinks we're a couple," I said hastily. It wasn't great, but it was better than the whole explanation, and right now I didn't trust Jin Yeong not to come out with it in an excess of either honesty or mischief. "You going to see him right now?"

"Yes," he said, after a moment of thought. "I want to know that you're not going to disappear one day while you're out on the street."

"You just don't wanna cook your own dinner," I said, grinning; and when he grinned back reluctantly and put his hand briefly on the top of my head as he passed me for the linen closet door, it didn't make me instinctively shy away.

I didn't know why it had weirded me out so much when it first started happening, apart from Morgana's insistence that Zero liked me—didn't know why it suddenly didn't now—but for now it was just nice not to feel uncomfortable around him again.

I called after him, "I'll go get some groceries, then. We're out of steak and nearly out of onions. Make sure you come home hungry, 'cos we're having barbeque tonight."

CHAPTER FOUR

ZERO WAS SUPPOSED to be out seeing his father, so when I nearly collided with that father along Elizabeth Street just before I got to the mall, it was a bit of a shock. Luckily for me, I saw the flower first, growing where it shouldn't have been growing. It had sprouted up in the pinch between the boards of an A-frame sign, nodding its little head while the very tall, very beautiful fae behind it scanned the footpath opposite.

I ducked behind the sign before he could look around and see me, staring sickly up at the flower with memories and nightmares stirring at the edges of my thoughts and threatening to come out before I had the chance to ease them out, nice and gentle, to examine each one carefully and emotionlessly before going onto the next.

I stayed behind the sign for nearly too long, heart pounding; then I whisked myself into the alleyway closest to the sign without looking to see which one it was. That was probably pretty stupid, because more greenery grew around me as I hurried into the bricked, covered alleyway that should have held tables for the charming little restaurant that was usually part of this bit of Hobart. As I scurried through, the hanging lights coiled and moved as though trying to follow me—or maybe just trying to keep an eye on me. The sound from Elizabeth Street muffled and then silenced completely as ferns closed in around me, but I couldn't turn around and go back. Zero's dad would be out there, waiting. My only hope was to push on ahead and hope that I would be able to access the other entrance to this alley that in the human world was at right angles with the one I had used.

There were two problems with that particular hope.

Firstly, I was no longer in the human world—or even quite sure that I was still Between. There was an awfully solid feeling to the flagstones beneath my feet, and a dreadfully ancient chill to the air that was far too akin to the air of Behind than I really wanted to acknowledge right now.

Secondly, I was not the only person in this not-quite-Between-and-not-quite-Behind patch of existence. Ahead of me, a man sat at one of the three black tables, reading a library book. He looked up as I approached, one dirty-blond eyebrow lifting very slightly; but I was pretty sure he was surprised, not contemptuous.

He looked as though he didn't know he was tall, dressed in soft, comfortable trousers that were a bit too short and a loose cotton shirt with sleeves not quite long enough, his vest unbuttoned and hanging in folds from his shoulders. Square, useful gold-rimmed glasses perched on his nose, and his shaggy, dirty-blond hair was just slightly too long: the whole of him looked like a wolfhound crossed with a golden retriever who had been turned into a doubtful sort of human.

Unlike a wolfhound or a golden retriever, however, this bloke had a book in one hand and an enquiring look on his face.

"Sorry," I said. "Didn't mean to interrupt you."

I wasn't supposed to be here, that much was obvious. I also didn't particularly want to be here, because this was definitely Between-shading-to-Behind, and there was a really good chance that this bloke was fae, deadly, or wanted to kill me. There was also a good chance that he was all three.

"You didn't," he said. "I was about to go upstairs, anyway; I've finished my book and need another."

I would have told him that I was just passing through and tried to make a break for it down the other side of the alley, but by then I was far enough in to see exactly what lay down the left-hand turn I would have normally made to exit onto Bathurst Street. What I could see now, instead of an open view into the street, was a long, vast lane of greenery that followed the gentle swell of a hill and reached a crest that showed only blue, glassy sky beyond it.

"Flamin' heck," I said slowly.

"You seem to have closed the doors behind you," said the fae, drawing my attention back to him.

I looked at him doubtfully, taking in the stubbly chin perched on his palm and the curious eyes behind those glasses. I couldn't tell if he was joking, but any fae should know that humans couldn't do things like that.

"Don't reckon I did that," I said.

"I don't think it was me," he said. He made it sound really polite, like he didn't want to call me a liar but knew it hadn't been *him* so...

That made me want to laugh, but an inconvenient thought chilled the impulse. Heck, if he hadn't done it, who had? Had Zero's dad...?

Ah heck.

"Come up and see the books, if you'd like," the fae offered, pushing away from his table. "The alley will probably open up by itself later, anyway. I'm going to get another book."

"Aren't you going to tell me that I shouldn't be here?" I asked him. I was reasonably sure that he was fae, and he should be pretty well aware that I was human. Still, he didn't seem to be about to try and kick me out, or to tell me that humans shouldn't be able to poke their noses into his quiet little courtyard.

He shrugged and pushed his glasses up on his nose. "Who's to say you're not supposed to be here? That's the *thing* about Behind, isn't it? The intersection of the worlds: reality meeting up with another reality at odd points and things happening because of those connections. The entirety of the succession rests on that intersection. Perhaps you're here exactly where you're meant to be, at exactly the right time."

"Right," I said, blinking a bit. I hadn't expected him to talk so much—or to *say* so much, more to the point. He must know I was a human, but he was telling me things humans weren't supposed to know.

Was he planning on killing me? He must be.

Still, I wasn't dead yet, and there were definitely flowers creeping up around the edges of the alley from which I had entered.

So when he said, "Come on if you're coming," and moved across the courtyard at a long-legged lope that was nearly as hard to keep up with as Zero's, I jogged after him and followed him all the way up the metalwork stairs there. I didn't particularly want to go upstairs with a strange behindkind, but I didn't particularly want to stay down here and see how long it would take Zero's dad to get in if he hadn't been the one who closed the place up, either.

The stairs felt nice and human as we climbed, shaking and echoing the way they would have in the human world, but a layer of moss crept down to meet us, and by the time we were at the corrugated landing, it was soft beneath our feet as well. There was also a lot more greenery in the alley than there had been when we were down there, and I didn't think that was due to Zero's dad.

"Is that the green man?" I asked, tilting my chin at the court-yard below, where waving fronds curled up and along the curving roof of the alley in both directions. It would be nice if it was the green man; I'd feel a lot safer, too.

"I would like to think so," said my companion. "But I haven't seen a leaf or twig of him in many years. Did you come here in search of him?"

"Nah," I said, pulling back from the railing at the end of the landing and moving toward the door. There were definitely a few too many flowers for comfort near the entrance of the alley. "Just would've said g'day if it was him, that's all."

"Would you? I heard he's quite picky about who he talks to. You'll have to introduce me."

"I can't tell if you're joking," I said bluntly, following him through the door and into an antechamber that had more stairs. Much to my relief, there was no instant tug of magic or Behind, and the interior, although dark, still felt very human.

"I wasn't joking," he said over his shoulder. "I've been trying to get an audience with him for a while now. You'd think he was the King Behind with how hard it is to meet him."

"Oh," I said. "Well, I wasn't trying to meet him; I had something he was interested in. He sorta pulled me in."

"Some people would call that a compliment."

I didn't have much to say to that, actually; I was still too ignorant of the world I kept accidently impinging on to know how much of a compliment it was. So I kept quiet, and we climbed the stairs that were still a fusion of metal and moss, echoing and silencing our footsteps in a syncopated kind of rhythm that led us toward a small window straight ahead at the top and an entrance to the left that allowed soft light to fall on the mossy stairs.

Turning into that open doorway, the fae stepped onto a wood-boarded floor that stretched out in long, peaceful lines, and I came out a little after him, looking around me curiously. There still wasn't too much of a feel of Behind about the place, and I felt more at home than I had in the courtyard below.

That is, until I got a bit too close to one of the windows.

I felt the pull of them trying to interest me, so I was already feeling cautious about wandering over toward the nearest. I went over anyway because I was still able to pull back pretty comfortably from the tug. When I rested my hands on the windowsill, gazing out at the totally unexpected view there, I could see exactly why they had tugged at me.

This window should have looked out on plain, red-bricked wall. There shouldn't even have been a window here, considering that this building was supposedly co-joined with the buildings on either side of it. Instead, I saw deep, dark ripples of a blue that was immediately familiar and touched a bittersweet chord of mingled fondness and hurt in me. It could have been a giant pool I was looking into, like the pool that existed in the upper-story apartment of my friend and local merman, Marazul. Was this fae keeping merpeople in his house, or did he have a mer-housemate?

Then I saw that the light from the next window was decidedly different from this one, and quickly stepped a few paces over to look out that window instead. I saw a garden, bright and green and peaceful, and when I craned my head to gaze along the wall, without quite daring to touch the glass, there was more wall there.

All right. So it wasn't a pool actually attached to the house— might not even be a pool. It was a view of somewhere else— whether pool or ocean, I wasn't sure. I'd seen windows like this before: windows on a house that was so steeped in the malleable influence of Between that you could see out into Behind through the glass. Ralph the revenant's house, to be precise. Just quietly, Ralph was one of the aforementioned Reasons I Personally Knew for being worried about a house that was a bit too inclined to follow you when you tried to leave.

Still, despite my unease, the windows were magical—literally as well as figuratively—and it was hard to pull my eyes away from them to see what the fae was up to. He didn't seem to be too interested in the windows; he passed across the room to the nearest bookcase instead, without even glancing toward the enticing windows, and put his book back. Then he bent his knees a bit and ducked his head to look on the bookshelf below the one he'd just replaced his book in, as if he was trying to figure out his next read. Maybe he was. I just hadn't picked fae for being peaceful readers of books.

Zero reads books, yeah, but he doesn't do it exactly *peacefully*. When Zero reads a book, you know he's trying to find a monster or figure out a spell, or maybe just work out what laws he's going to be very careful not to break this week.

I went back to the first window, and was in the process of watching the light from the ripples play across my skin when I heard the fae sit down. I turned my head and saw him at the long table that drew the centre of the room toward itself, sitting on a bar stool with a wide base and a wide back. It looked comfortable and welcoming: if I had time to read and sip coffee in dancing beams of sunlight, this was the sort of place I'd choose to do it.

"The other windows have better views," he said, opening his book. "I'm not sure what you'll see today, but it won't be a dirty human street, at any rate. Hobart is on the pretty side, but there are views that are nicer than the bare city street."

"Fair enough," I said, backing away and moving across the room to look at the other set of windows. At least this bloke wasn't starting by running down the human world like Zero and Athelas still too often did. "You own this place?"

"Yes," he said.

That made me smile a bit. Athelas would have said something like *You could say that* or *Well, something like that, Pet*, because he understood that even if he had taken over an area in the human world by owning the piece that connected with it either Behind or Between, it didn't mean he owned the human bit of it. Looked like this fae didn't have that knowledge.

"What do you use it for?"

"Thinking," he said, then gestured vaguely with his book. "Reading."

"Do you need the glasses?"

He took them off and looked at them as though seeing them for the first time. "I don't know anymore. Perhaps. They're comforting when I'm in the human world. Perhaps I'll need to reconsider that."

"You're fae, though," I pointed out. He looked a bit fuzzy without his glasses, but not in an obscuring-spell-on-the-specs kind of way: it was more like he was the kind of bloke that always looked a bit less real or clear around the edges without glasses.

"And you," he said, putting his glasses back on and then leaning over the table on his folded arms, "are human."

"Got it in one."

"Be careful about the windows, then," he said. "Don't open them, I mean: it could be hard to stop yourself climbing out."

"I'll watch out for that," I murmured. I'd already felt that tug, urging me to open the window and climb out, but it wasn't difficult to resist. I didn't want to tell him that, of course. It's not a good idea to surprise fae with what you can and can't do.

Even if I hadn't been able to feel the pull of the windows, I would have been fascinated with them. The one right over at the stairs, at the head of the stairwell, was small and double-paned, and it should have looked right onto the brick wall of the place next door, too. When I stepped briefly back into the stairwell and tiptoed to get a look over the sill, I saw the brittle blue sky of Behind instead. As glittering and blue as breathable glass, it was a thing of beauty that looked as though it could kill you just by breathing in its air. Whatever place this window looked out into, it was unfathomably high and perilous: I saw birds flying through the air far away, swooping and darting around each other like eagles, but as they drew closer I saw how soul-crushingly *huge* they were.

"Beautiful," I said, beneath my breath. I had read Sinbad the Sailor: these were rocs, and I was enchanted. The fae laughed from his seat at the table, but he might have been reading his book.

The birds, sharp and fast and terrifyingly large, spread wings that spanned longer than my house and the two houses next door combined, and spiralled down in a playful dance around each other. I couldn't help pressing closer to the window as they disappeared from sight, hoping for a last view of them, a sigh of disappointment on my lips.

A beak larger than me shot upward, making an arrowhead that curved downward into two terrifyingly large wings that were pointed almost straight at wherever the ground was in preparation for a massive upsweep. Feathers whistled through the air, rattling the window panes, and I caught a brief glimpse of the longhorn beef cow gripped carelessly in one dangling claw as the roc shot up past the window.

"Wonder whose farm they pinched that off?" I muttered to myself, my heart pounding in panicked little beats that timpanied around my ears. It wasn't likely to have been a human farm, at any rate—or at least, not one from around Tassie. There weren't too many longhorn beef cattle around the state.

I let out a shaky breath and moved away from that window, too. It wasn't that it felt safer away from it, but for the first time in my life, I actually understood what behindkind could see in a world that seemed more inclined to deal in death than in life.

It was savage, but it was beautiful.

Just so long as you weren't the beef cow, of course.

"These all the same place?" I asked, walking along the back wall to catch a glimpse through the other windows. I knew they weren't all the same place, exactly. I was pretty sure they were all gunna show parts of Behind, though.

"That depends," the fae said, turning a page. "They tend to show different places to different people. They're very obliging: they like to show you things they think you'll like to see. If you've always wanted to visit a particular country, I'd advise thinking about it; you might persuade the windows to show you something from that country."

I wasn't sure if that was cool or creepy.

"Is that safe?"

"Not at all," he said. "But it's possible. There's coffee in the kitchen, if you want it."

"No thanks," I said. "I don't know the rules for regular coffee drinking with fae. Mistakes are pretty permanent around here."

He abandoned his book again for a moment to say, "You know the rules for irregular coffee drinking?"

"I know some of the business rules," I explained. "Had to go to a contract-signing once."

"Contract-signings are very boring," said the fae. "I don't attend them if I can avoid it."

"Don't blame you," I said, moving onto the next window. I wanted to look at the bookcases, too, but the windows were too enticing right now.

I'd only caught a dark, moonlit glimpse of whatever was in the next one when a cold, amused voice from behind me said, "There you are! I lost sight of you on the street for quite some time; I didn't expect to find you here!"

I whipped around, shock making my heart stutter at the back of my throat, and over at the table, the spectacled fae stood up, his book still gracefully open with the leaves wafting up to meet each other in a half-circle.

He said, "What an unexpected surprise."

Zero's dad visibly moved backward, the rictus of a grimace passing swiftly across his face. Had he not seen the fae, or was he just surprised at actually being confronted about wandering into someone else's house?

With a very slight pull at his lips that could have been contempt or anger, he asked, "What are you doing here?"

"I could ask you the same thing," said the spectacled fae. He didn't come across as antagonistic, but I was pretty sure he was enjoying himself by startling—or maybe annoying—Zero's dad.

I was enjoying it, too.

He added, "You are the one trespassing, after all."

"I came in to fetch that little human," said Zero's father, once again cold and collected. "It ran away from me out on the street, and I have a few things I wish to discuss with it. We have an agreement of sorts."

I slid my hand into my pocket, because I didn't expect the fae to do anything but hand me over, and I wanted to at least text Zero before his dad nabbed me. That way, I'd have a good chance of living until Zero got there to take me back again.

Then I heard the fae say, "I don't see why that's my business. You came in here without an invitation to take away a human I'm talking with? I think not."

Zero's dad didn't quite gape, but he did catch his breath on what seemed like an unexpected gasp and said with difficulty, "The human has nothing to do with you! It is completely below your notice, and if I wish to take it back, why should you stop me?"

"Are we going to have an argument about it?" asked the spectacled one. "Really?"

"It would be foolish to argue about a valueless human," Zero's father said disdainfully, but there was an undercurrent of quivering anger that I didn't miss. I was pretty sure the other fae hadn't missed it either. Fae-like, he seemed to be enjoying it, too.

"Humans are never valueless," he said. "But that's something you've yet to learn, I suspect. Good day."

Zero's dad didn't like it, but he left. That didn't make me feel too much better: he'd probably hang around like a bad smell until I came back out of the alley, too. Luckily for me, I had other options.

Options that definitely didn't include climbing out of one of the windows up here.

I waited until the last of the flowers wilted away before I said to the other fae, "Thanks for that. I'm Pet, by the way."

"You can call me the Librarian," he said. "It's not my name—"

"Yeah, figured that."

"—but it's close enough. I wouldn't leave just yet, if I were you."

"Yeah, figured that, too," I said. "He'll probably be waiting for me. Reckon I'll call my um, owner—see if he's got time to come and pick me up."

The Librarian's brows lifted a little. "Oh, you're a companion?"

I couldn't help chuckling. "Nah. I'm a pet. Couldn't picture my owner having a companion; he'd have to smile more than once a month, for starters."

"I see: not your name, but your function. You seem to be quite self-governing, for a pet."

"Yeah, my owner likes me to be useful," I said glibly. That was true. It was also true that not a lot of the behindkind coercive methods worked on me, but that wasn't something I was going to tell him.

"Sero was pretty concerned about you," he said, while I texted Zero.

My brows rose. So they were both called Sero? Zero and his dad? That was nice and confusing.

"I don't usually see him that worried; he's usually very careful about what he gives away. I'm surprised at him coming this far for a human, too; he has agreements with them, but as far as I know, they're usually the lowest, chattel kind."

"Yeah," I said, and I didn't try to hide the disgruntlement in my voice.

The Librarian laughed again and sat down. "Yes, it's always been like that. The problem with behindkind like Sero is that they see the value of humans only up to a point. It makes them blind to a lot of things that would otherwise be helpful to them."

"No need to be opening their eyes, then," I said, as I pressed the send button.

It was a simple text. *SOS. Courtyard corner of Elizabeth and Bathurst.*

"Will your owner come for you?"

"Reckon so," I said, putting my phone away again. "He doesn't like people playing with his toys, and I told you: I'm pretty useful every now and then."

"I got that impression," said the Librarian. "You might as well go downstairs, then. I've got the feeling it's opened up again. Sero won't try to get back in right now; he likes to show that he respects the right people every now and then, even if it doesn't extend to respecting them behind their backs."

"Yeah, I got that impression," I said, copying him. I trailed back across the floor, not quite eager to leave the comparative safety of the building for the more perilous courtyard below. I didn't want to antagonise someone who had sent Zero's dad off in a huff, either, and I remembered to say, "Thanks for the help," before I left.

I also remembered not to say anything like *I owe you one* because despite how low-key this fae seemed to be, I wouldn't trust him not to hold me to it. Athelas would have been proud.

I didn't come out of the courtyard until I had a text from Zero that said, *Come out. I'm waiting.*

My brows lifted in surprise, but I came out regardless. Zero was leaning against a streetlamp when I did, arms folded and attracting the eyes of pretty much every woman within cooee of him. He didn't look even remotely drunk now, so whatever he'd been doing instead of talking to his dad, it had sobered him up pretty well.

"What, didn't you want to come in?" I asked him, looking around furtively to make sure his dad wasn't still nearby as I crossed to his side of the footpath.

Zero looked down at me unreadably for a few seconds before he said, "I couldn't get in."

I stared at him with my mouth open for quite a bit longer than he'd looked at me, and maybe that irritated him, because he pushed himself away from the streetlamp and brushed past me to start up the road in the wrong direction.

"Hang on, what?" I said, darting after him. "You couldn't get in? How come? Why are we going the wrong way?"

"I don't know why I couldn't get in," he said shortly. "Why did you go in there? What happened?"

"Your dad found me," I said. "Reckon you can make him stop waltzing around the city streets and growing flowers all over stuff? I've already had enough heart attacks for my age. I thought you were talking to him."

Zero's jaw tightened just slightly. "I tried to do so and was prevented. Pet, how did you get in there?"

"Just walked in," I told him. "Same as always. Reckon someone was bending the rules for me again?"

"It wouldn't surprise me. You said you met my father?"

"Well, more like I was running away from your father. We're still going the wrong way, by the way."

"I'm taking a shortcut."

"If you say so. Anyway, your dad came after me, but there was another fae in the courtyard who was pretty rude to him in a very polite way, and after they'd both made a few remarks at each other, your dad went away. That's when I texted you."

Zero looked down at me briefly, his brows winging up. "Then you must have met one of the fae lords. Seelie, it would seem, since you're still alive and still right-ways in."

"Okay, that was a mind-picture I didn't need," I complained.

Zero gave vent to a quick, hard sigh of irritation, then grabbed my hand and pulled me down into the nearest graffiti-decorated alley and right into a dark, twisty part of Between where the graffiti grew wild instead of sitting politely on walls. Once there, he stopped and turned me to face him.

"Pet," he said. "*Please* stop wandering into the demesnes of fae lords and consorting with people like the green man."

"I would *love* to do that," I said earnestly. "And maybe if your dad would stop chasing after me every time I step out onto the streets, I could be a bit more careful about where I go."

"I will make it clear to my father that you are assisting me," Zero said flatly. "And that if he interferes with you again, I'll take it as a direct attack against myself."

"Reckon you'll want to keep an eye on Athelas as well, then. Your dad wasn't too pleased with Athelas when I spoke with him last, either."

Zero huffed another one of those quick, gusty sighs. "Let me look after Athelas. You just stay home for the next day or two—or go out with Jin Yeong if need be—while I try to encourage my father not to make mistakes."

I made a face, but it wasn't as if I could really get away from Jin Yeong after all. I'd already told him that he wasn't allowed to fall in love with me, and the sooner he got that idea into his head, the better. In the meantime, I just had to live with it.

"Fine," I said. There were a couple things I could do for the case from home: contact Abigail, for instance, and see what chatter Marazul could pick up online. I was also overdue a call to Morgana.

"Home, then," he said.

"Steak first," I said. "Then home. You can carry the bags."

The house wasn't exactly fraught that night, but it wasn't exactly comfortable, either. Zero might have recovered both his temper and his sobriety completely, but there was a kind of watchfulness to Athelas that made me feel vaguely off-kilter, and the fact that Jin Yeong came in to watch me cook dinner instead of sitting with the others in the living room left me more unbalanced.

"What did you blokes find down at the waterfront, anyway?" I called into the living room, to escape the quiet, closed feeling of being alone with Jin Yeong. How did he manage to take up so much *space* when he was so flamin' skinny! "And don't think I've forgotten about the USB, Zero! You can't go doing stuff secretly and then expect me not to ask about it!"

There was a moment of silence from the living room before Zero said unemotionally, "It must be very hard for you to bear."

Which meant, of course, that he was not the only one who was doing things secretly, and that I was being called out. I grinned a bit.

"Want me to guess what's on it?"

"Absolutely not."

"I do believe that sooner is better than later," murmured Athelas' voice, and I looked up to find that Jin Yeong's dark eyes were on me, his head tilted.

His eyebrows went up: an expression that said *Really? He's going to tell you?*

I shrugged at him.

"If you hadn't left the merman's house in such a hurry, you'd already have seen what was on it," said Zero, appearing in the doorway to lean against the frame.

Jin Yeong and I turned our heads to look at him.

"Yeah, well, someone went and corrupted my source," I said pointedly.

"Someone stole my USB."

"You can't say I stole it when someone gave it to me," I protested. "I bargained with you, and it was mine before that."

"You were in the process of stealing the contents."

"Okay," I said, going back to cutting onions. There was a lot more to that story than Zero knew, too: the USB I'd given him hadn't been the only one I'd had, and I was pretty sure he still thought the glass USB I'd taken to Marazul belonged to the merman instead of being mine all along. "That's fair. I did that."

"Never acknowledge an offense, Pet," said Athelas, in a pained voice. "In some circles, it's tantamount to acknowledging debt."

"Fine," I said, and pointed my knife at Zero. "How about this, then? Prove it, mate."

Jin Yeong hissed with laughter and snaked out a hand to steal a round of pineapple. I let him; if you haven't seen a vampire gleefully chowing down on a round of pineapple with both canines like an oversized fruit bat, don't judge me.

Zero pointed at the sight and asked coldly, "What's that?"

"That's a vampire eating pineapple," I told him. "Don't change the subject. You were going to tell me what's on the USB."

"I wasn't, and I meant, why is there pineapple when we're having a barbeque?"

I stared at him. "You gotta barbeque the pineapple, too! What are you, a savage?"

Zero closed his eyes briefly in a pained sort of a way and said, "I think I preferred talking about the USB. I'm *not* going to eat that."

"Suit yourself; more for us," I said, tilting my chin at Jin Yeong.

That was a mistake: he smiled at me over the top of his pineapple, warm and glad and a little bit questioning. I looked away at once and snapped at Zero, "You might as well tell us what's on the USB; it's not like Athelas doesn't already know."

"You," he said, "are not Athelas."

But he came into the kitchen anyway, which was a relief, and Athelas followed behind, languid and silent. I left the onions to make us all a cup of tea and get away from Jin Yeong's pineappley face.

"All right," I said, conceding for now. I filled the jug and tapped the on button. "What did you blokes find along the waterfront, then?"

"At first, a rather large mess; at length, an adoring crowd," said Athelas, sitting down at the table in his usual place to cross his legs. "Zero was especially active; in fact, you might find him on the internet, along with the latest intended victim."

Both Jin Yeong and I stared at Zero, who settled on the bar stool closest to the living room with an expression of irritation.

"I'll see about getting the videos taken down," he said. "The merman can take care of it."

"That seems a shame, my lord."

Athelas was making a lot of subtle, amused digs for a bloke who had come within an inch of his life the other day, I thought. The thought didn't stop me from taking full, gleeful advantage of the opportunity, though.

I filled the teapot and coffee plunger and demanded of Zero, "What did you *do*? Were you making yourself obvious to humans? Isn't that against the rules? Was she very pretty?"

Zero stared at me. At last, he asked in bewilderment, "Was *who* very pretty?"

"The girl you rescued," I prompted him. I glanced at Athelas, and just a look was enough to tell me that I was right. "She was pretty, right?"

"Almost inhumanly so," he said, his eyes bright with amusement. "And my lord was sufficiently dashing as to capture the hearts and minds—"

"—and cameras," interrupted Zero grimly.

"—of every onlooker. It was quite the rescue. The girl already has a good following online; I've no doubt she'll have an even bigger one after this escapade."

Zero sighed: a big, gusty thing heavy with exasperation. "She was dancing on the top of a building—"

"Could you hear the music?"

"No. She was dancing with her phone set up behind her, and she danced right off the edge of the building and down four stories."

I shivered a bit, and poured a cup of tea for Athelas, breathing in the warm, calming scent of lavender earl grey.

"I s'pose you were there to snatch her out of the air, since you're not talking about her in the past tense."

"Almost inhumanly so," Athelas said once more, with a rather pointed look at Zero.

"What song was she dancing to?" I asked them, carrying the teacup across the kitchen.

Athelas accepted his cup of tea with a wondering look. "Must you know, Pet?"

"Got a feeling about it," I explained.

Zero looked a bit suspicious, but JinYeong only leaned his chin on the palm of his hand, grinning and waiting. I don't know if he was thinking the same thing I was or if he was just happy that I seemed to know something Athelas and Zero didn't. He likes things that cause trouble.

"The detective was on the phone with me at the time," Athelas said. "Apparently he receives notifications whenever something of this kind goes up on the website. We were communicating in real time as the event occurred, and I believe the song I heard was 'Believe it or Not'. I confirmed it with the detective."

"You think it's important?" Zero asked me. That was nice: I still wasn't really used to him asking for my opinion on stuff, even stuff I had been the one to ask about.

"Dunno," I said. "But the first video we saw had someone singing 'Walking on Sunshine' while they walked into thin air on a sunny day. If this one was 'Believe it or Not'—yanno, where they sing *believe it or not, I'm walkin' on air*—and the one with the boy who got hung and strangled in the hook and pully setup was choking to the sounds of 'Hooked on a Feeling', I've got the feeling that someone thinks they're funny."

"How very interesting," said Athelas. "And we've been told that no one uploads the videos; they merely appear there, music already attached."

JinYeong laughed and said a word in Korean that I didn't understand.

"Yes," said Zero grimly. "It does sound like a siren."

CHAPTER FIVE

"FLAMIN' heck!" I said, impressed. "There are modern day sirens who know how to use the internet?"

"Apparently so," said Athelas. He didn't seem surprised, but I didn't know if that was because he'd already begun to suspect or if he was just trying to seem like he knew what had been going on. "A rather deplorable state of affairs, I would say."

"That merman," JinYeong said darkly. "He has been *talking* too much."

"You can't just blame everything on Marazul," I objected. "I mean, yeah, he might sell stuff to dodgy people and do dodgy stuff in general, but he doesn't like it when people are hurt. He tries to stay away from stuff like that."

JinYeong sniffed, and Zero said unemotionally, "You don't know the merman anything like well enough to say that."

"Fought with him for half a day," I pointed out. I went back to my onions so I'd have something to do with my hands. Talking about Marazul with my three psychos was still awkward-verging-on-uncomfortable. "And even when he dealt with you instead of me, it was because he was scared of you. Besides, we would have known about it before now if sirens had had this kind of ability, wouldn't we?"

"I've not consorted with many sirens," Athelas said. "But I believe this sort of thing is generally in their purview."

"Okay: a modern day siren who knows how to use the internet. Fine. But why did it just suddenly start trying to kill people in Hobart now? And why like this? Don't they usually just sing at people?"

"Sirens don't usually come to places that are well-inhabited," said Zero. "They prefer the open seas and a ship or two to tempt sailors away from, one by one. They tend to work alone, which is good for us."

"Most interesting," Athelas said thoughtfully. "The result is similar to the historical norm—the method, however! I would have assumed it to be truly new."

"I have never heard of this before," Jin Yeong said, with certainty. He tried to pinch another slice of pineapple but retreated with a small snarl when I threatened him with my knife.

"So we reckon someone gave tech to the siren," I said. "I mean, apart from Marazul. Why would a siren go to him for this sorta thing? How would it know?"

Zero folded his massive arms across fully half of the kitchen island, crowding my onion chopping. "We said that the cycle is beginning again; if we can tell, other people can, too. Upper Management, for example—they might be approaching useful people."

"Other people who have an interest in the cycle beginning again," agreed Athelas.

"Not the king, then," I said, scraping all of my chopped onions into a bowl. "Reckon he'll be wanting to poke his nose in and find out what's happening, though? If people are stirring up sirens and making trouble around town?"

Zero looked distinctly tired. "Almost certainly."

"Then I s'pose it's most likely to be Upper Management giving stuff to the siren, if the siren isn't just doing its thing."

"Almost certainly," he said again. "But I'll check with Marazul first; no doubt he'll know who is capable of doing something like this. He might have even worked with the person who did it."

I set up a skillet almost as big as myself on the kitchen island, impinging on Jin Yeong's space in the hopes that he would abandon his place at the island and sit at the table. He didn't, but he did sit back a bit with watchful eyes and fold his arms across his chest.

The skillet wasn't a proper barbeque, of course, but it was the closest thing I had to it.

"We gotta buy an outdoor barbeque one day," I said to Zero. "Y'know, after your dad is dead and the king is dead and everyone stops trying to kill everyone else."

His eyes went bluer. "Is my father's death a pre-requisite to that?"

"Well, that's up to you," I said. "You're the one who thinks he killed your mum."

"I didn't say that," he said.

"You didn't have to," I said. "You can't be going around trying to find out dirt on your dad and mum, threaten to kill me because I got the info before you did, and then try to pretend it's not because you suspect he killed your mum. You're trying to find proof so you can kill him legally."

"I'm not permitted to kill high-level fae," Zero said shortly. "They have to face the behindkind justice system—unless they're killed in capture."

"Don't worry, I'll kill him for you," I said, flippant in my discomfort. "Trade you for info on what was on the USB."

I said it as a joke—a way to lighten the mood again—and turned away to get out the tongs and egg-flipper so he could take the opportunity to smooth away the frown from between his brows.

"The USB," said Zero, to my surprise, "has remarkably little on it. What it does have concerns my mother...and connected elements."

"Knew it," I said quietly to the cracked little tile over the sink. "Knew that's what it was."

"If you knew that, you might have given it to me as soon as you got it from North," Zero said, with some exasperation. "Instead of running away and making life hard for everyone."

"Yeah, but that's no way to make trades," I told him, fighting off a twinge of guilt when I remembered that JinYeong had been the one to pay dearly for that. "Athelas would think badly of me, and I can't have Athelas thinking badly of me."

Athelas said rather plaintively, "You might remember that I'm already *persona non grata*, Pet. Kindly don't give my lord any further reason to dislike me."

"What about your mum?" I enquired of Zero, ignoring Athelas. "And what connected elements?"

Zero's gaze came to rest on me, as inquiring as JinYeong's had been earlier, but for what I suspected were entirely different reasons. Did he think I'd actually looked at the files Marazul had pulled from the USB? I was pretty sure he was trying to figure out if I was being sincere in my question. I had confused him, at the least, and that was fun. Confusing Zero is always nice: he's so lofty and so rarely confused that it makes a nice change.

"If you're gunna call me a liar, you should do it out loud," I told him.

Athelas smiled into his teacup. That was pretty usual: he likes tea *and* smiling mysteriously, so why not do both at once? Still, there was that pull, or maybe tiredness, of sorrow around his eyes that had been there a lot over the last week, and it worried me.

Was it just that he was sad about Zero, or was there something else?

"The USB," said Zero at last, levelling a very blue look on me, "only had things that concerned my mother's life before she came to live Behind."

"Before she was kidnapped," I corrected. Zero already knew that, but euphemisms for being kidnapped and married by force didn't strike me as a good thing to get used to using. "Figured it had to have some info on it about your mum or the murderer, so it's no big surprise. Looks like you found it surprising, though."

"Not surprising," he said. "Merely limited in its usefulness. As you already said, it was from North, so I couldn't be completely sure the information on it would be correct, but from what I've lately been able to confirm from other sources, it seems to be."

"Yeah? What were you able to confirm elsewhere?"

Again, there was that thoughtful look that made me think he suspected I already knew what I was asking about. "A number of things: the most important of which was that my mother was not alone when she first arrived Behind. How North discovered that from the human side of the world, I've yet to discover; she had even come up with a birth record."

That made my ears prick up a bit, and I had to work very hard not to look at Jin Yeong—who, I was very well aware, had his eyes on me. Abigail's group had records and information very similar to what Zero mentioned being on the USB; they also had some information about me, I was pretty sure. They'd known more about me than they should have, and with what I now knew about fae and names, I had begun to be very curious about whether or not they also knew my name.

"How's that help you, though?" I asked. "You're trying to prove your dad killed your mum, right?"

"Not precisely," said Athelas. "My lord's mother was not fae, and therefore doesn't fall under protected persons by Behind law. However, if we can show proof that he kidnapped her without a contract in place, we'll be able to show Exploitation and Endangerment of the world Behind, not to mention that the King Behind frowns upon fae/human relations formed with the idea of producing an heir—as one might imagine. There is, of course, always the argument that the fae at fault simply fell in love, but that is rather hard to prove."

"And in my case," said Zero, without a shred of emotion to his voice, "impossible. Especially if it's proved that he killed her. The King Behind has been looking for a reason to take care of my father for years; he would jump at this opportunity if he thought it would prevent me challenging him and taking the throne."

"You don't want the throne, though," I said.

"It is remarkably hard to convince a power-grasping person that someone else isn't out to steal that power," said Athelas, shrugging.

"You want to try and trace where your mum came from in the human world," I hazarded, turning back to Zero. "So that you can prove she didn't leave willingly?"

"It won't be easy," Zero said. "I have no idea of where to look here in the human world, and very little to go on. What I do have, I'll give to the merman."

He looked at me again as he said it, and I felt a tug of unease. He definitely knew I was hiding something from him, but why did he think it was about him or his mum? Did he know that Abigail had records of people who had disappeared Behind? It wasn't like that was a secret, though; we just hadn't really discussed it.

"We might as well ask Abigail to look through her records," I said, hoping to shift some of the discomfort away from me. "She even had a bit of info on me there."

Zero frowned. "They have your name?"

"Dunno," I said. "They didn't tell me that. Thought you said that names weren't important when it comes to humans."

"Normal humans, perhaps," he said. "Besides the inconvenient fact that you're an Heirling, we have to consider that you can do things you shouldn't be able to do."

I narrowed my eyes at him through the heat shimmer of steak cooking. "You calling me weird?"

"You are very weird," said Jin Yeong, with certainty. "You should not let people have your name."

"No one asked your opinion," I said sourly, tipping the onions onto the skillet. "Oi, Zero: what are we going to do about the siren?"

"At any rate, we'll need to try and find it before more people die," said Zero. The smell of onions cooking rose on the air, and both he and Jin Yeong instinctively leaned forward. "See if you can convince your human friends to go out with us. We'll need to spread ourselves as wide as possible without leaving anyone at risk."

"Don't tell me that even big, bad fae can be lured in by a siren!" I said in disbelief.

"Not me," said Jin Yeong demurely.

"I didn't say anything about vampires," I told him. "And what do you mean, not you? If fae are susceptible, why not vampires?"

"Because I am too beautiful," he said. "I will not be tempted. If I wish to look at something beautiful, I shall look in the mirror."

Zero's eyes narrowed very slightly with amusement that he refused to show. "Beauty has nothing to do with it. Sirens lure humans—and behindkind—via sound. No matter how beautiful you think you are, it won't prevent you from being lured. I suggest that you invest in a pair of earplugs."

"What if you're really good at not being persuaded by sneaky people in general?" I asked.

"Then you might last long enough to stuff your ears if they're not already blocked," Zero said crushingly. "Even Athelas will take precautions now that we suspect a siren."

"Flamin' heck!" I said, impressed. It was one thing for Zero to wear earplugs: despite his cold demeanour, he was susceptible to persuasion in ways that the apparently more gentle Athelas wasn't. I would never have said that aloud, but I was certain it was true. "All right; want me to give Abigail a call?"

"Tomorrow," said Zero. That made me a little bit happy, because there was no reason to wait until tomorrow except to make it easier to co-operate with our human friends, who slept at normal times and worked best during daylight hours. "Make sure the humans know to have something to stuff in their ears if need be—or better yet, something already in their ears."

"Boy are you gunna be happy to know about foam earplugs," I told him. "You can use 'em to block out ambient noise and still communicate by text if you need to. Two bucks a pop at any corner store."

"You arrange for the earplugs," he said. "And get us a meeting with the humans."

Athelas went out after dinner, but Zero must have known about it, because he just went out into the backyard to start stretching. Luckily for me, it didn't seem to be one of those nights where I was the recipient of his training; he went right on to his own training after stretching, and with no Athelas in the house, I gleefully tidied the kitchen as quickly as possible and legged it upstairs, from where I would—hopefully—be able to sneak out in a way that was less obvious than using the front door. He'd never said as much, but I was pretty sure that Zero had some sort of monitor on the front door that pinged him whenever someone came in or out—and that included people who went out without actually opening the door.

Luckily for me, Zero tended to push himself for longer than he pushed me and was likely to be outside for at least an hour and a half, maybe two. That should give me just enough time to take a bus down to the post office, figure out how to break in, and help myself to their computers to check out a certain P.O. Box's owner. I still wasn't ready to tell either Zero or Athelas what I was up to, and I definitely wasn't going to be inviting Jin Yeong out at night when he was still looking at me all the time in a way for which I would have loved to kick him. Mostly because, having done so, I wouldn't be able to explain why I had done it to the others. Since I couldn't do that, I'd just have to make sure that I didn't go off on my own with him too often.

Unfortunately for me, I didn't realise that Jin Yeong had followed me up the stairs on his narrow, silent feet, apparently curious to know where I was sneaking away to. There was enough of his cologne already upstairs that I didn't notice him enter the living room, either, until I was halfway out the window and something gently pulled at my right wrist.

"*Noh*," he said, pinching the cuff of my hoodie so I couldn't get away. "What are you planning?"

"None of your business," I said, as indignantly as I could manage in a whisper.

"You should not be on the street alone at this time," he said. "It is not safe. Come back in."

"Or what?" I said resentfully. "You'll tell Zero?"

He scowled at me. "I will not tell *Hyeong*."

That made me stop and blink a bit. "Wait, you're not threatening to tell Zero? How you gunna stop me, then?"

"*Nado molla*," he said, clearly disgruntled.

So he didn't know either. I nearly grinned at him but stopped myself just in time because he probably would have taken it as encouragement.

Jin Yeong's expression became reproachful. "I cannot stop you, but I do not wish you to go," he said. "This is not pleasant."

I stared at him. "Are you—are you *sulking*?"

"I am not sulking," he said stiffly. "I am annoyed because it is dangerous, but you will go, and I cannot stop you."

"'Course you can," I said, propping my foot against the opposite side of the window. "All you have to do is yell out to Zero through your bedroom window and that'll be the end of it."

"I am not *Hyeong*," he said, looking away.

There was no reason why that should have made me want to

cry, but I had to swallow a definite lump in my throat. This was exactly how someone like me ended up thinking the vampire was a friend, and then apparently finding myself wrong in two very different ways.

"I wasn't going to be stupid," I said, turning in the window frame to dangle both my legs back in the room. "I was just gunna try and get a look in the post office's computer system for that bloke's contact details. You know: the one who's been paying the bills on my place and Morgana's and Ralph's."

"Of course," he muttered. "Then I will come with you."

"Good grief, no!" I said. "Zero might not notice me leaving if he's in the back yard, but he'll definitely notice if we both go!"

"*Hyeong* and the old man would worry if you go alone," he said. "It is not *safe* anymore."

"It never was safe out there for me," I told him. "I'm starting to get an idea of that now that I'm getting a few memories back."

JinYeong didn't answer, but although he shoved one hand in his pocket and looked away moodily once again, he didn't let go of my hoodie.

"Fine," I said, dropping back down to the floor. "I'll go during the day when there's people on the streets and people waiting in line. Happy?"

JinYeong made a sound that was close to *eung* in the back of his throat, and put his other hand in his pocket. I hadn't heard him use that word before, but the bit of Between that translated it for me said that it meant *yes*. It was the softest and least defensive yes that I'd ever heard from him.

I must have stood looking up at him for just a fraction of a second too long, because he turned back toward me, hands slipping out of his pockets, and stepped toward me. For one frozen second, I thought he might actually be going to try and kiss me again. I would have moved if I could have, but I just stood there as he leaned in—and then around me to close the window.

I stared at his chest, barely two centimetres away from my

nose, for a rather breathless moment before I said sharply, "Stop it!"

JinYeong looked down at me with an inquiring lift of the brow, and I saw amusement flit briefly across his face. He put the palm of his hand against my shoulder and gently scooted me out of the way, then finished closing the window.

"*Myan*," he said; another softer, less defensive form of the word he might usually have used to apologise with—if JinYeong ever did apologise for things. "You feel a distance from me, but I do not feel a distance from you. I forgot. I will make a boundary."

"You flaming better," I said crossly. I didn't like dealing with this disarming version of JinYeong: it felt rather like dealing with shoeless JinYeong—dangerous when you least expected it. "I'm going to bed. Don't sit up here; I don't want to smell your cologne."

Tuatu was already waiting for us down by the chocolate shop when we got to the waterfront the next day. So was Ezri, who must have been sent by Abigail to scout out the area to make sure it was safe before we all met up. That was probably a good thing, because Ezri was keeping a pretty good eye on the detective, and he was keeping just as good of an eye on her. Palomena was there too, watching everyone with a wondering eye.

"Recognising some old friends?" I asked Tuatu, grinning.

He jumped a bit, then said, "The kid looked familiar. I was just thinking that I'd have to keep an eye on her for shoplifting or damaging property, but now that I come to think of it, she's about the height of the kid that tried to smack me in the back of the head with a cricket bat."

"Okay, but we weren't told whether she wanted you alive or dead," Ezri said, strolling over to us. "So technically it's not my fault."

Tuatu shot her a look that was more dislike than fear and said,

"Hitting a person on the head with a cricket bat is something you have to take personal responsibility for."

"This is our police officer," I told Ezri, and there must have been a bit of a chill in my voice, because she froze for just a second before her usual *hit-me-and-see-if-I-care* attitude took over again.

"All right, no need to get territorial," she said.

"Actually, I said *no needless injuries*," said a familiar voice from behind us.

Abigail emerged from the chocolate shop, and this time Tuatu tensed up.

"You!" he said. "You're one of them, too?"

"What?" she said, grinning at him. "Wasn't I useful when I was helping you pick chocolates for your girlfriend?"

"Dear me!" murmured Athelas, as Tuatu's cheeks darkened with embarrassment. "It would seem that you've had a second meeting despite yourself, detective."

Tuatu snapped, "North is not my girlfriend!"

"You keep telling yourself that," I said. "Oi, Abigail; this is Detective Tuatu. Tuatu, this is Abigail: she's the one that tried to have you kidnapped."

"I didn't actually tell the kids to kidnap you," she said to Tuatu. "Sorry about that. We just wanted a quiet chat with you; we have to be really careful, these days."

"Yeah, me too," he said, with more than a bit of sarcasm in his voice. "If it's not Upper Management trying to frame me for murder or cave trolls taking a pot-shot at me, it's a group of humans trying to hit me on the head with cricket bats."

"That was your friend's murder they tried to frame him with, by the way," I said to Abigail. "I told you about that; you blokes ought to have a bit of a chat about it later. In the meantime, everyone better figure out how we're gunna communicate and think about putting in some earplugs."

Detective Tuatu's eyebrows went up. "We're supposed to be

working together today? What's to stop them trying to hit me again later?"

"What's to stop me hitting you right now?" demanded Ezri, scowling.

"Be quiet, Ezri," said Abigail. "He's got a right to be concerned. Things didn't...go well the other night. We were a bit hasty. There won't be any friendly fire from our side, all right?"

She said that directly to Tuatu, and he must have thought she was sincere, because his shoulders lost a bit of tension, and he nodded.

Zero said expressionlessly, "Are you all finished?"

"Sorted," said Abigail.

Tuatu said, "Yeah."

"We'll split into groups of two," Zero said. "It'll be safer that way. If you find the siren, try to keep hold of it, even if it seems dead. If it retreats to its nest injured, it won't come out again until it feels safe. Abigail, you'll need to liaise with your people to make sure they have something to block their ears: if we're in groups of two it'll be safer, but we'll still need to be careful. Athelas—"

"I'll go with the delightful young lady who wields a cricket bat," said Athelas. "I'm sure we'll manage well together."

"All right, old man," said Ezri. "But you'd better be able to keep up."

I grinned; Ezri might think she was tough, but she was no match for Athelas. I said to Zero, "How about I go along the Salamanca side where the *Aurora Australis* is docked? Might be able to ask a few questions or sneak on board. A few of the videos came from there."

"I will go with you," said Jin Yeong at once.

"Make sure your earplugs are in and your phones are on," Zero said briefly. He asked Abigail, "Do you know what you're looking for?"

"Water fairy," said Abigail, nodding.

"It's not fae," Zero said shortly, surprising me. "It's a different kind of thing altogether. Sirens share no bloodline with fae."

"Hm," Abigail said, but she didn't sound too surprised. "In our records, they're called water fairies, but I suppose you know what you're talking about. They come from your side of the world, don't they?"

"Yes."

"A siren, you reckon?"

"Yep," I agreed. "It sings at you and convinces you to throw yourself overboard—or in this case, convinces you that you're dancing on something when there's only thin air beneath you."

"Right," said Abigail, a line digging itself between her brows. "So we go in groups of two, keep in our earplugs, and make sure that our partner is okay at all times. You said it'll have a nest? Our records don't have anything else other than a basic description."

"In its true form, it will have made a cave for itself: something underwater or above the water, but not far from the water. It could be big or small. Look for little collections of rocks and shells and anything bright that could still be pretty beneath water."

"Like I said, we have a description of the true form," said Abigail. "What about when it's out and about among humans?"

"In its glamoured form, it will look just like a human."

"How will we know when we've found it, then?" asked Ezri. "We usually try to get a look at stuff through our cameras—"

"Lots of 'em look different in cameras than they do in real life," Abigail explained quietly to Tuatu. "It's a pretty decent constant—enough to make life safer for us when we have our camera apps open most of the time."

"Use whatever human devices make it easier," said Zero. "We have nothing to give you, so you'll have to be careful."

"We brought a few things along," said Abigail, and there was a gleam to her eye. "You know, a few of the things we thought the detective might like to hold onto for us. Give him a bit of an idea how useful they might be."

"Sort it out between you," Zero said shortly. "Palomena, you're with me. Athelas, Ezri; JinYeong, Pet—spread out. We'll meet again in the park by the government building in an hour. Communicate via text if you find anything—do not take your earplugs out until you know the siren is dead or gone to nest."

He turned and left before any of us had a chance to reply, but I reckon Palomena must have been used to dealing with uncommunicative male bosses, because she was right there beside him when he went. Unlike me, she didn't have to adjust her step to keep up with Zero: she walked effortlessly and steadily at the same pace. They were well matched—might even have looked like a normal couple out for a walk along the waterfront if there wasn't something so suspiciously warlike about the shadows they cast. I could almost see the impression of all the weapons I knew each of them had hidden on them, but maybe that was just because I knew them so well.

Ezri and Athelas melted away together without a word, and JinYeong and I left while Tuatu was saying suspiciously to Abigail, "Is it anything that's likely to change me into anything not human? Because my grandmother said—"

There wasn't too much to see on our side of the boardwalk apart from a lot of seabirds, though. Not a lot of conversation, either, after JinYeong finally let me put the earplugs in his ears, complaining the entire time. I squished the bright orange foam between my fingers to put plugs in my own ears, then caught JinYeong's eyes and jerked my head in the direction of the bright red hull of the Aurora Australis. Usually, if you try to get aboard without a government pass on a day that isn't set aside for tours, it isn't possible; today, I had a vampire with me.

The vampire proved to be as useful as I'd thought he would be. More than usually annoying, but useful. It wasn't that he was intrinsically more annoying than usual, either; it was just that he was so flaming *present* all the time, and I didn't seem to be able to ignore him walking along beside me like I usually could. I couldn't really blame that on him, either, unless I was blaming him for telling me that he loved me, which had precipitated the whole uncomfortable state of affairs.

Nah, I was gunna blame him for it anyway.

"You're still a pain in the neck," I told him, even though he couldn't hear me. Maybe particularly because he couldn't hear me.

I must have startled the bloke who had been hanging around and watching us slowly make our way onboard, because he seemed to stammer something at me even though I couldn't hear him. From the bit that I could tell by lip-reading, he'd said, "You can't be here. Are you deaf? I've been yelling at you."

I waved Jin Yeong in front of me to take care of the bloke, and he did so silently. Dunno what he said to the bloke, but he stepped aside and seemed to have forgotten that he could look anywhere else but the gangplank. We kept going along the lower deck and around aft, because that was where it was easiest to get in, passing a huge buoy that had been slung up on deck for whatever tourist group had passed through most recently. Just under cover, we came across some sort of a station that looked like it might be used for collecting water or specimens of some kind: great big pipes with doors in them, and capsules that looked tiny inside of them until you saw one on the deck and realised they were nearly waist-height, glittering with salt water and bubbles along the glass sides that sparked rainbows.

"That's right," I mumbled to myself. "It's a research vessel."

Jin Yeong kept walking, one hand in his pocket. He didn't seem to be too interested in the site, so I followed him through a round-edged doorway that led into a small, narrow room with computers on both sides of it.

There was a window facing out—did they still call them portholes when they were flaming huge?—and on the ledge that surrounded it, I saw a collection of plastic toys, ornaments, and even a plant or two.

I raised my brows at that and shot an inquiring look at Jin Yeong. I could feel a scattering of Between to the room—cabin?—and there had been a trace of it out and about on the deck outside, but not enough to make the walls move or anything.

Was it enough to be considered a nest? Or was it just the sort of thing that a crew member, stuck on board a ship with the same crewmates for months on end, would put up around the place to feel a bit more cheerful? And was the bit of Between just a natural residue from a siren who had already lured a couple of kids into danger, or a sign that it was still around?

Jin Yeong was more interested here, prowling up and down the room with narrow eyes and both hands in his pockets until someone came into the room from the opposite end and approached us both with an enquiring look on his face.

I grinned at the bloke—if he was a siren, he was a portly, not-too-good-looking one—and said, "G'day. We're with the college group."

I saw his lips move, but I couldn't hear what he said. I almost reached to take out my earplugs, but even if he was just a human that didn't seem like the brightest idea. There was too much Between about this ship to make me feel safe being able to hear when a siren could start singing at me any moment.

Jin Yeong took care of him anyway, though he didn't bite the man, to my relief. He just told him to do something, and the man, looking confused, continued on through the room and went out onto the deck. Maybe Jin Yeong had sent him to join the other bloke, who knows.

I felt the buzz of my phone in my pocket as I was taking a closer look at some of the computer screens, and took it out to see what was up.

It was a text, short and grim. It said, *camera app NO. text only, and not much. Siren sorted; didn't find nest. cu @ park.*

I showed it to JinYeong, and his brows went up as if to say *What's this?*

I shrugged and mouthed *Athelas* at him. The text had come from Athelas' phone, though I was certain that Ezri had been the one to send it. Texts from Athelas were few and far between—even more so than texts from Zero—and it certainly wasn't his style.

So something had gone wrong with using the camera app, had it? I put my phone away, wondering what it could have been, but not too worried: Ezri or Athelas had still been alive to send the text, which was the important thing, and it seemed as though they'd taken care of the siren in one way or another. Still, it might be a good idea to find the nest if we could.

I went back to the computers, getting a quick look at each one as I passed onto the next. It was mostly hard-to-read lines of text and meaningless numbers, but there were a few diagrams, too, and they were familiar.

"Looks like they're taking samples," I said, frowning at a diagram of the same sample containers I'd seen in the tubes out on deck. I couldn't tell what most of the readings were, but I was pretty sure some of them were co-ordinates for where the samples had been taken.

I don't know why I bothered saying it aloud; I couldn't even hear myself properly, just heavy, stifling silence with the *almost* wordy vibration of my voice. JinYeong wasn't paying attention either. He'd wandered to the further end of the room while I was looking at the screens, and now he vanished into the next area. I followed him a bit more slowly. If there was nothing here that suggested siren to him, who was I to argue? I'd never met one.

We continued up and through the ship, and I had the distinctly grumpy feeling that we would have been better off waiting for a tour day or vamping someone into giving us a tour, because there were so many decks and so many rooms on each of those decks that our time vanished away before we were ready to come down to the dock again.

In the end, we were moving through the space so quickly that it didn't seem possible that it was doing much good; we also ended up with a couple of silent hangers-on, though they didn't approach closely enough for it to be worthwhile trying to talk them out of following us.

"They'll probably just put us in their report," I said to JinYeong, who, shoulders stiff, very obviously didn't care to be followed and had taken out his earplugs in his annoyance. At least we didn't have to worry about being sung to now that Athelas and Ezri had taken care of the siren. "C'mmon, let's get through this last lot and shoot through. We're gunna be late, and you know how Zero gets when we're late."

"This is a useless job," he said, a sliver of teeth showing. "I do not like doing useless jobs."

"Me either," I said, removing my own earplugs. "It's about as good as we're gunna get and still get back to the park in time. You want to explain to Zero why we're half an hour late?"

JinYeong sniffed. "*Ani.* I do not fight when there is no use."

"The heck you don't. You've been trying to pick fights with Zero since I've known you."

"That," he said, stopping in the gangway to face me, "is different. There is a reason."

"Yeah, your sister," I said, nodding. "I know."

He considered that, then nodded. "JiAh is one reason. You are another."

"Oi!" I protested, as he started down the gangway again. "What do you mean, I'm another? What did I do?"

"You did nothing. *Hyeong* is overprotective."

"Tell me something I don't know—hang on. Do you mean—"

"I mean," said JinYeong, sending a bright look at me over his shoulder, "that *Hyeong* does not approve of me and you."

"Zero can mind his own business!" I said indignantly. "I already *had* a dad, and—hang on. There is no *me and you*!"

"And if *Hyeong* has his way, there will be no me and you," he said. "He threw me through a wall to remind me. You remember."

I stared at his back. "You said it was because he was reminding you to call me *Pet*."

One shoulder shrugged. "It is the same. *Hyeong* knows why I do not call you Pet. What else would we argue about?"

"What else? Pretty much anything, as far as I can tell," I said crankily. "You fight over *everything*. And you'd better stop discussing me with Zero; I'm not going to have the two of you deciding who I can and can't date. I don't need his permission!"

"That is what I told him," Jin Yeong said blithely. "Ah. We have run out of ship. This is the outside."

I followed him out onto the deck, blowing out my cheeks and feeling in need of the slight, cool breeze that tickled around my ears and cooled the neckline of my hoodie.

"Right," I said. "We'd better get back down there pretty flamin' quick, then, otherwise we're gunna be late."

More importantly than that, I had the feeling that I was going to end up talking about things with Jin Yeong that were definitely dangerous to be talking about—things I hadn't even let myself think about.

I was very good at not thinking about things that I didn't want to think about, and it was no time to break the habit of a lifetime.

CHAPTER SIX

WE WERE ONLY fifteen minutes late to the meeting spot, but Abigail was pacing by the time we got there. All of the humans except for Ezri were back, along with Tuatu, who stood with his back against a tree as though he didn't trust anyone not to hit him on the back of the head. Maybe he didn't; I'd expected him and Abigail to be getting on better after working together, but maybe it would take a bit more time.

Zero was still gone, too, which might have worried me if I'd had time to think about it. I didn't, because as soon as Jin Yeong and I got into the park, Abigail was striding toward us.

She hadn't quite reached us when she demanded, "What took you so long? We had an agreed-upon time."

"The only way to get down in time would have been to take a dive," I told her. "We were at the top of the ship by then; I've heard how that turns out, and I didn't fancy it much. Anyway, Jin Yeong's wearing his good suit."

Jin Yeong nodded once, faintly approving, and appeared not to notice Abigail's withering look.

"What's up?" I asked her. "Zero's not back, either; you gunna have a go at him?"

"I'm not used to working with fae," she said, frowning. "And I'm used to people answering to me, not the other way around. Where's the old man? He's got Ezri with him."

"She's with Athelas—she's safe. I figured they'd be back first, actually, if they sorted the siren out."

"I'll go look for them," she said abruptly.

"Hang on!" I protested. The siren might be taken care of, but who knew what else was out there these days, with everything stirred up. "Wait for me! We gotta go in lots of two, remember?"

The look she threw over her shoulder at me was slightly amused, but she called out to the others: "Stay here. Pet and I are going to have a look to see what Ezri's up to."

"We'll be back," I said to Tuatu, with a cheeky grin. "Don't kill each other while we're gone, all right?"

I didn't notice until we'd cleared the park again that Jin Yeong was still beside me, a shadow in scent and blue silk.

"You don't need to come along," I told him. "And it's no use pretending not to hear me; I can see the bump where you've got the earplugs in your breast pocket."

He grinned but refused to answer.

"Fine," I said. "But it's still not a date."

Abigail threw me a bit of a weird look, but didn't stop moving, and it took me a few minutes to remember that she still probably thought Jin Yeong and I were dating. I could tell her differently, but that would open a whole different can of worms that I didn't particularly want to open right now.

I said, "We're on a break right now."

She gave me another sideways look, but all she said was, "Which way do you think they'll have gone?"

I threw a look around and pointed toward a café that was inside one of the older buildings. "There. Reckon Athelas would hunker down there if he needed time to heal after a fight. Plus I'm pretty sure that's the building one of the girls took a dive from the other day, so they could have found the siren there."

She raised a brow at me. "We didn't hear about that one."

"Yeah, Zero saved her before she hit the ground. Reckon that's not as much fun for the siren; Tuatu says that the live broadcast was stopped as soon as it was obvious that the kid was going to be okay."

"Typical," she muttered.

I couldn't help grinning, because it was something I might have said myself.

We nipped across the road before the city tour bus could pull in, avoiding the line-up of cars behind it, and I thought I saw the frosted white of Zero's spiky hair somewhere out near the Pier Restaurant, alongside dark, oiled braids that belonged to Palomena.

That reminded me of a few questions I had for Abigail before anyone more dangerous than Jin Yeong was there to hear them.

"Oi," I said to her as we threaded through tables outside one of the waterfront restaurants. "You said you had records of me in all of your...records. Was it just the police records, or did you have other stuff?"

"Just the police records," she said. She must have heard the worry in my voice, even if she didn't see the frown on my face, because she added, without looking at me, "Don't worry: your name isn't there. It took us a while to figure out that it was you, actually. We were only sure when you turned up. You don't have to worry about names and stuff like that, you know. The fae can't do anything to us with names."

"It's harder," I said gloomily, "but I reckon it's not impossible. And my parents went to a lot of trouble to make sure that my name wasn't out and about, so I think there must be something to it for...people like me. Plus Zero said—"

"People like us have more things to worry about than our names getting out there," she said.

"*Hotsori*," said Jin Yeong, and added for my ears alone, "Do not listen to this woman. She is wrong."

"You're the one always trying to get me to tell you my name," I pointed out.

"I am different."

I opened my mouth to say, Flamin' *different*, but I found that he was looking at me already, just waiting for me to say it—almost *daring* me to say it, with the glitter of play-hunting in his eyes—and shut my mouth again. That must have pleased him, because he did the smallest little click of his teeth in delight, eyes dancing. I looked away, feeling a bit too hot around the cheeks again.

"It's redacted in the police files, too," Abigail said, dodging a couple of tourists in puffer jackets and leading the way up the stairs. "There's almost nothing in the regular ones, actually. The ones we've got are the um...extra ones. One of the groups before us had someone in the police station for about ten years, and we've got a fair bit of extra info that the regular cops don't have: they made their own files."

"Hopefully Upper Management don't have it, either,' I muttered. "What do they call me in the extra files?"

"No name: just *female juvenile*," she said. "Even that's missing from the official files, though. Like I said, we were only sure it was you when we got to know you a bit better: we just knew you were The Pet—heard about you on the grapevine. We'd been looking for you for a while; figured you might like to join up with us if you were still alive."

"Cheerful," I said, blinking my eyes in the darker interior of the café after bright sunshine. "Oi, reckon you could have a look a bit later for the name of someone I know?"

"Got a full name? You'll need at least first and last names for me to be able to say I've found the person you're after for sure. Even then, we've had misidentifications. You trying to track a bloodline?"

"Yeah, you could say that," I said. "I've got a photo, too—if I can find it again. Haven't been able to find it for the last week or so, but if I can lay my hand on it again, I'll come see you."

"All right," she said, only half listening. Her eyes scanned the room, and I saw her frown clear away. "They've been here, but they're gone."

It took me a moment longer to see what she must be talking about, and when I did, it made me frown. There was a skirl of Between pulling the fronds of two small potted palms toward each other and slightly *inward*—though exactly where that inward was, was difficult to see.

"Someone's been here, anyway," I said. For all I knew, it might not have been Ezri and Athelas. Frowning, I asked, "How did you see that?"

I knew that behindkind weren't the only ones who could see Between, because I could see it too—as could Sarah and the old mad bloke—but it wasn't something that humans could typically do, in my experience.

"Told you," she said, grinning. "We've got a few useful things."

"Tuatu agree to anything?" I asked, shooting another quick look around the room before heading out again.

"Not much," said Abigail, faintly disgruntled but reluctantly admiring. "Someone seems to have taught him not to be too hasty about saying yes to things."

Jin Yeong gave a small sniff of laughter.

I said, "Yeah, experience'll do that to you."

"It was not the old man that came through here," said Jin Yeong to me in untranslated Korean. "We should keep looking. This human is too energetic."

"Nah, you're just old," I told him, grinning.

That didn't seem to worry him, because he only grinned back, and it occurred to me that it had been a while since I had just joked with him, without a sting and without it being anything other than friendly. It was nice to know that things weren't going to become quite as awkward with Jin Yeong as they'd become with Zero when Morgana first told me he liked me.

Maybe it was just because I'd heard about the liking from the actual source, and that made it less of an unknown danger than the possibility of Zero liking me. Heck. There was a thought. What was Zero going to say when he found out that Jin Yeong had actually spoken to me? I didn't think it was going to be good. For that matter, what would Athelas say? He had once or twice warned me about loving any of my three psychos, and at the time I'd thought he was warning me against loving them as family, but now I wondered if that was what he'd meant.

I was still wondering about that when I saw Athelas himself, just ahead of us and across the road.

"There," I said, pointing.

He strolled in a leisurely way along the boardwalk beneath the trees, the glimmer of an insubstantial sword sweeping from his left hand and another just vanishing from his right hand as he walked. Ezri almost skipped beside him, her boots untied and in constant danger of tripping herself up; she swung a cricket bat from one hand with a satisfied sort of glee that suggested she had heartily enjoyed the violence that had preceded her text.

I saw a blue, trailing mark tracing from beneath Athelas' ear to his collar and leaving a trail of white slime all the way down to his waist, glimmering on the houndstooth of his jacket.

"Flamin' heck," I said, impressed, as they crossed the street to meet us. "Looks like the siren managed to get a pretty good hit in!"

Abigail said sharply, "Ezri! Report!"

"Not hurt, boss," she said, her brows arching. I wasn't sure if she was amused or maybe just reminding Abigail that she wasn't supposed to be too worried about her subordinates—kinda the vibe that might have happened if you swapped me and Zero. "Met up with the siren, that's all. Turns out they're pretty persuasive if you've got your camera app open, even if you can't hear. Didn't you get the text?"

Athelas said placidly, "We weren't in too great of danger; the child is quite proficient with her cricket bat."

"Listen, grandpa: I'm not a kid, and I—"

"I really do advise against finishing that sentence, child," said Athelas silkily.

Ezri stopped, swallowed a bit, then jerked a thumb toward him and said, "He's the one that killed it; I was too busy trying to stop myself taking out my earplugs to do much until I dropped my phone and the app crashed."

"What do you mean, they're more persuasive through the camera app?" I asked. I could ask Athelas later about Ezri. It wasn't that I was jealous—or maybe I was, who knew? All I knew was that seeing them together, I had had a sudden insight into what it must have looked like to others when they saw me and Athelas.

It's not that I think of him as a dad or anything: you'd have to overlook a heck of a lot to think of him as a dad. But he was my weird uncle, and I wasn't used to seeing that he could possibly be anyone else's weird uncle—which was probably a bit hypocritical of me, because I'd been trying to push the psychos into realising that I wasn't a special human. That any human was worth loving and protecting.

It was just a bit jarring to realise that they actually were capable of seeing like that, and to realise that maybe a time would come when I wasn't as important—special? Unique?—to them because there were other humans to fill that gap. Not just Athelas but Zero—and Jin Yeong.

"Ah, this is *interesting*," purred a voice in my ear, and I caught a whiff of Jin Yeong's cologne.

"Get off," I said irritably, hunching my shoulders and inching away from him.

"I am not touching you."

"You're standing too close!"

Jin Yeong's brows winged up, and I saw a touch of amusement darken his eyes. "What is wrong?" he asked. "You became spikey again."

"Let's wait until your big boy and the others get back," said Ezri to me, striding ahead with her shoelaces flapping. "I don't want to tell this fifty times, you know."

It was really hard not to stick my tongue out at her retreating back. Technically, I'm too old to be doing that anymore, and I try not to do it at anyone but JinYeong these days, but it was a struggle at that moment. Reckon Ezri knew it, too. I don't think she could have swaggered more if she'd been JinYeong.

Luckily for my patience, Zero and Palomena were already with the rest of the group when we got back. The group itself was none too easy to see, making me aware that someone had fiddled with a tricky bit of Between to separate them all from the human world by a whisker. That was probably a good idea: siren aside, it wasn't the best idea to let the world at large get a good look at all of us together. There were still a few too many people out and about who shouldn't know that we were colluding with humans.

Heck, what was I saying? *I* was a human.

Ezri was still bright and sauntery as she joined the group in the park. She grinned around generally and asked, "You lot have as much fun as we did?"

"Fun, she calls it," said one of the blokes on Abigail's team.

"Just tell us about it instead of skitein' about how much fun you had," another said. "You met the siren?"

"My lord," said Athelas easily, cutting them out to make his report directly to Zero. "The siren is rather more problematic than I'd anticipated. We may perhaps need to find another way to hunt—and the humans will certainly need more protection if we're to continue together."

"Yeah, but I didn't die," Ezri said. "And what do you mean about continuing together?"

Athelas was talking to Zero—pointedly so—but I noticed that he'd made sure we could all hear. More mildly still, he added, "I would suggest some personally applied magic rather than the item-based, impersonal armoury they're currently using."

"Our armoury has kept us alive pretty well until now," Abigail said, distrust immediately springing to her eyes. "Why would I let you put any sort of personalised spell on us?"

"You can do as you please," Zero said briefly. "The offer is there if you choose to avail yourselves of it. If not, continue on as you've been doing."

"I'm gunna do it," said Ezri, her chin sticking out. "I don't see how it's any different from us having magic brooches and stuff that weren't ours to start with. Maybe they won't be so glitchy if they're made for us."

"Fae magic—" Abigail began.

Athelas murmured, "It's all fae magic, is it not?"

To my surprise, that made Abigail flush a deep, brick red. It didn't seem to surprise Athelas, though: he gazed at her for a little while longer—enjoying her discomfort?—then looked away, smiling faintly. Zero flicked a look at him but didn't make it a long one.

He asked, "Did you find the nest?"

"There was no nest in sight, my lord. The siren that accosted us seemed quite comfortable, however, so I would have assumed that its nest or friends were in close proximity."

"Friends?" Tuatu said sharply. "What do you mean, friends? You said we were dealing with one of them!"

"You said we have to find the nest," I said to Zero, my mind running on a different track for the time being. "You reckon that's why it was strong enough to worry Athelas: it was connected to its nest?"

Was there a shade of approval in Zero's gaze when it lit on me? "I suspect so. Athelas?"

"There was something attached to it," agreed Athelas. "Not a homing thread as such, but it felt as though there was a connection through which it was gaining power. I would have liked to test the idea, but our young human friend here was quite...useful with her bat."

"You blaming me for not being able to do something?" demanded Ezri.

"I would not dream of it," said Athelas.

"This little one is spikey, too," murmured Jin Yeong in my ear. "I think you lost a sister."

"I think you should belt up," I muttered, jabbing backwards with my left elbow. There was a soft huff of air and a faint cough as the elbow connected with his diaphragm, but I didn't have to look over my shoulder to know that he was grinning again.

"Well excuse *me* for saving your dusty patchwork jacket!"

"I did, however, have time enough to ascertain that we are indeed dealing with more than one siren," Athelas continued, unperturbed in the face of Detective Tuatu's further perturbation. "The creature was certainly communicating with another."

Flamin' heck, I thought, growing cold. I exchanged a slightly guilty look with Abigail. We'd just been walking around without our earplugs in because we had assumed, along with the others, that there was only one siren.

"I saw you on the app," Tuatu said, interrupting my thoughts. "You popped up for a few seconds, music and all. If there are *more* of these things—"

"What were they playing this time?" I asked him.

He looked fed up. "'How'zat?'"

Reckon Ezri and I were the only ones who knew enough about both cricket and music to appreciate that. Did sirens know enough about cricket culture to recognise a cricket bat *and* pick a song that was a sly cricket pun, or was that just part of the magic?

"Perfect," I said. I didn't try to hide my grin, though it faded quickly enough at my next thought. "Oi, so whatever they're doing, it simultaneously streams to the internet, overlays a track, and does a sireny little thing to make the person who's making it do what they want them to do?"

"That's about it," said Ezri. "Felt like I *had* to dance, and I can't dance. The music was in my head, and I could see exactly how I could dance right down the end of the pier. Found out the pier was a fair bit shorter than I thought it was once I was free from whatever that needing to dance was."

"I'd like to know how they're influencing you through sight," said Zero, frowning. "Sirens aren't particularly well known for their abilities to influence people through sight. They're usually auditory predators."

"My earplugs weren't in properly," Ezri admitted. "But when I opened the app to look around, I had a really strong impulse to take 'em out altogether, so I reckon they're doing something else as well."

"Flamin' wonderful," I said. "Looks like today's a bust, then."

"Wonderful," muttered Tuatu, echoing me. "What am I supposed to put in my report, that's what I'd like to know? I was here officially today."

I stared at him. "That's what you're worried about? I wanna know how we're supposed to stop ourselves from jumping over the edge of buildings—"

"Dancing, more like," said someone from Abigail's group.

"—or dancing over the edge of buildings while we're looking for these mongrels. Or right off the edge of ships," I finished. "If they're still able to get to us using things other than sound, how are we supposed to protect ourselves? It's all right for you three—"

"Might I demur, Pet?" enquired Athelas. "I confess that had I been looking at the phone when the child was, I might have had some difficulty myself. I don't know what has been done with the aid of electronics, but I would have said that their influence was magnified to a dangerous degree."

"We did all right," protested Ezri. "You didn't try to take a nosedive into the water, and after I got the app closed, I did all right as well. The earplugs are good enough, we just need to figure out another way to see stuff that doesn't involve camera apps."

Zero, ignoring that aside, asked, "You're certain you didn't see anything that could have been a nest?"

"Nope," said Ezri. She sounded disgruntled, but then, I hadn't ever heard her sounding really gruntled either.

"I'm afraid not, my lord," echoed Athelas.

Zero looked around at the whole group and asked more loudly, "Did anyone find a nest?"

All of us shook our heads or muttered a *nope* into the ground.

"It is strange," said Jin Yeong. "There should be a nest. If they are not at home, there should be a nest. We already did the measurements."

"What measurements?" asked Abigail.

"Sirens can only get so far from salt water before they're in danger of drying out," Athelas explained. "That much we know for sure. The detective also managed to find us an area of influence that showed the furthest reach of their power by plotting the attacks onto a map. We covered that area today and found a single siren."

"So we need to know how come they aren't nesting," I said, nodding. "What if they've got extras? Extras like what they're doing through the camera app to give themselves a bit of visual persuasion?"

"We don't know of anything that could do that," Abigail said. "And we've got a few useful things, these days."

"I know of nothing that could do it," agreed Zero. "Off-hand. I'll do—"

"—some research," I finished for him. "Yeah, but what are we going to do today?"

"Cordon off the waterfront," said Tuatu, already dialling a number on his phone. "And get a few of the special officers down here to enforce it."

"At least we killed one," Abigail said grimly. "That's one less to kill when we find their nest, I suppose."

A babble of agreement rose around us, but Zero sent Athelas a considering look I had no trouble interpreting. "You killed it?"

"I very much doubt the creature is dead, my lord," said Athelas, his gentle voice somehow cutting through the others.

"It was a bloody mess when it went into the water," opined Ezri. "If it lives after that, I don't want to know what it'll take to kill those things."

"It was undoubtedly injured, but it managed to fall into the water, and I do believe that sirens are known to have water-healing properties, are they not?"

"It's suspected so," agreed Zero. "I'll do some research when we get home. Pet, where did you put the *Behind Kinds* book last?"

"It's in my room," I said. "I'll get it for you when we get back home. What are we gunna do now while the detective's doing his thing?"

"Regroup and return with a plan," Zero said. "We still don't know exactly where the creatures are hiding, but we do know they're harder to fight than we first believed, and we now know there's more than one. We can reckon on them knowing we're coming next time, too."

"They also know a lot about how human electronics work," said Abigail, a frown creasing her brow. "How have they managed to link themselves with the internet, and *how* are they opening apps and projecting themselves through them?"

"Might as well ask us how they're layering tracks of music over stuff and running it live on an app," I told her. "I mean, we've got someone who might know, but that's about it. Oi, Tuatu, you better make sure that none of your lot gets too close to the waterfront while it's being cordoned off—or make sure it's a few of the ones who know about stuff like this."

He nodded, still on the phone, and I heard him say something about *hallucinatory drugs* and *appropriate PPE*.

"We'll see if we can figure something out to keep ourselves safe," Abigail said to Zero. "*Before* we come out with you again."

"I'll say," muttered a couple of the humans behind her.

"You can come home with us and figure it out, along with our next move," I said. "If that's it for the day, that is?"

I looked up at Zero enquiringly, but it was Abigail who spoke first.

"We're not going anywhere with that lot," she said, with finality.

"Okay, no tea and bikkies for you," I said. "You've got Ezri to debrief, anyway. I'll text or call later if there's anything else you should know."

"I'll text or call if I come across anything, too," she said.

I thought at first that she meant she'd call or text about anything Ezri told them that she thought we might not know. It took a second or two before I realised that she was looking straight at me, and that she was talking about the records I'd asked her to look through.

"Thanks," I said, with significantly more sincerity than I would have otherwise felt. "Catch you later."

The humans didn't do the melt away thing that my psychos do, but it wasn't far off. They weren't more than a few steps away before they sorta flickered between the trees and were gone.

Palomena, very carefully not watching them, said, "I believe I've fulfilled my duties; perhaps I should go before I see something I'd rather not see."

She disappeared with a lot more finesse than the humans, but there was something similar about it despite that.

"Flamin' heck," I said. "The humans really have got a bit of hardware, haven't they?"

"They have," said Athelas thoughtfully. "It's terribly interesting."

"Yeah?" I gazed at him. "Why's that?"

"Humans with fae paraphernalia," he explained. "What else? For humans who have such a chip on their shoulder against the fae, they certainly don't seem to be worried about making free with fae goods."

"Staying alive is a strong motivation," said Zero. "Are you ready, detective?"

Detective Tuatu pocketed his phone and said, "Good to go. I hope you lot have a good explanation for this, because it's not going to be easy to keep people away from the waterfront, even with everything blocked off. Ironically, it probably would have been easier while Upper Management was still running the station: they'd have known the real risks."

"They *are* the real risk," I said, unimpressed. "C'mmon, you lot. Time for tea."

In our house, it's almost always *time for tea*. That's a useful thing when one of your housemates doesn't technically need to sleep at all and the other two only need to sleep a few hours per night: it makes everyone sit down and rest.

Or, in this case, discuss the business at hand.

"I really hope you three have something up your sleeve," said the detective, half an hour later.

He sounded a bit sour; maybe I should have put some sugar in his tea. Still, he looked pretty comfortable on the spare chair; he wasn't trying to fit on the couch with Zero, which would have been far less comfortable. I would have put him next to me again, but JinYeong had already taken his usual spot by the time I got out of the kitchen with the tea tray, and it looked like Tuatu was pretty happy with the spare chair, anyway. Maybe I'd have to relabel it *Tuatu's chair* instead of *spare chair*.

"We'll contact the merman," Zero said.

Tuatu stiffened a bit, but that was just because he'd had bad experiences with mermen in the past. "What merman?"

"He's our tech guy," I explained. "He's good at fusing magic and electronics."

"How do you know he's not behind this?"

Athelas' eyes danced a little. "To be absolutely honest, we

don't know for certain," he said. "However, the merman knows it's in his best interests to help us, and I believe he may even have a motive of his own for assisting to the best of his abilities."

"If it's the one I think you're thinking of, you're wrong," I said, narrowing my eyes at him.

"No doubt we all have our ideas upon the matter," he said mildly, and his gaze was on Jin Yeong. Maliciously, I was pretty sure.

Jin Yeong snarled very faintly, more tooth than sound, and said, "We will ask him. If the earplugs are not enough—"

"And they are certainly not enough," interjected Athelas.

"—then it is necessary to find something that is enough."

"I'll visit the merman," said Zero, with a very faint emphasis on *I'll*.

"I wasn't offering," I said pointedly, and to my surprise, that made him grin.

"Are you rebelling?" he asked.

"No more than usual," I said. Maybe I'd been spending too much time with Jin Yeong: I was getting to be pretty malicious. Mind you, it wasn't as though Zero hadn't gone behind my back and corrupted the bloke—or in this case, merman—I was keen on.

I didn't know if he'd done it in order to get what he wanted or to prove to me that I couldn't trust behindkind when it came to being affectionate. I wouldn't put either motive past him: I've never been able to say Zero doesn't protect me, it's just that I've often had a few things to say about the *way* that he does it.

These days, I wasn't exactly sure why he was protective—wasn't sure if Morgana was right about him liking me as a woman instead of some sort of useless little sister—but I did still often have a big problem with how he expressed that protection. In Marazul's case, Zero had done exactly what he thought was the right thing to do. He'd decided that Marazul was a weak link, and he had set out to exploit that link. It was just a shame that he'd been right. Reckon it would have been easier to be blasé about it if he'd failed to corrupt Marazul.

He'd done the same thing with JinYeong—had tried to, anyway, because with JinYeong, Zero hadn't been right. JinYeong had actually gone against everything Zero had told him to do, in order to be next to me as a friend when I really needed someone.

By way of being just a bit more malicious, I put a plate of biscuits closer to Detective Tuatu, careful to make sure I put them on top of a pile of files that we definitely shouldn't have had. They weren't police ones, but they definitely had a bit of info in them that they wouldn't have had if it wasn't for police reports.

Tuatu looked suspiciously at the files but took a biscuit. "Have you been raiding the police station again?"

"Raiding is a strong word," objected Athelas. "We do, after all, return the files after we're finished with them; I dare swear we make better use of them than the police department do, if it comes to that."

The detective looked as though he really wanted to negate that suggestion but couldn't think of how to do it justifiably.

To make him feel better, I said, "These ones aren't yours, anyway. They're from the humans."

"They've got police files?"

"You've got a really suspicious mind," I told him, pointing at him with a teaspoon. "They're *not* police files, they're records from the humans you met today: they've been making their own records for a couple hundred years now. It's just that they have a few extra bits that might have come from the police station. You know. *Originally*."

"I thought you said they were dying out and that's why they want me to keep their little cache for them," he objected. "It seems to me like they're doing pretty well, and have been for years!"

"How do you think we've still got the records?" I pointed out. "They've been making sure stuff like this gets kept safe for the next time a group forms; they die out pretty often, by the sounds of it."

"This is how I end up being trapped in my own home by a tree that changes size and helping out with investigations into sirens along the waterfront," he complained. "I always want to say no, but there's never anyone else saying yes."

"Yeah, there are," I said, forgetting that what I was about to say was hardly convincing. "They're just mostly dead."

"Yeah, thanks, I feel much better."

"You've got a dryad, though," I said encouragingly. "You'll be safe enough. And you've got the North Wind at your back."

"And who's going to protect me from her, I'd like to know?"

"Fair point. But at least you'll stay alive long enough to figure it out."

"What are you looking for in these records, anyway?" asked the detective, after a disgruntled sort of silence.

"Kids like me," I said. "Turns out there's quite a few of them, and they're all pretty important."

Detective Tuatu sent a narrow look around the room. "Important to what?" he asked. "Because from what you lot have told me, the world is going into a kind of Ragnarök, and if these kids are going to make things harder—"

"They won't make things harder for you," Zero said, his eyes a shade bluer. "Well...tangentially, perhaps, but no more than that. They're more likely to make life extremely difficult for my father and the King Behind; by definition, their existence will propel the worlds Behind and Between into civil unrest, but once the change is made, the human world should return to normal."

"That doesn't sound tangential to me!"

"That's only because you're not aware of the full extent of the unrest in the worlds Behind and Between," said Athelas, smiling faintly.

The detective didn't say anything else, but he looked thoughtful, and that was enough. If I knew Abigail, she'd already made sure she had a way to contact him again. I was pretty sure she'd get an affirmative answer out of him the next time she asked him to look after her stash.

It wasn't like he didn't already have an object around his neck that was similar to the things he was being asked to look after. And thinking of that necklace...

"Oi," I said to him. "You said you got that necklace off your grandma. Givus a look at it."

"I'm not taking it off around them," he told me. "Sorry. I trust you, not them."

"Rude," I said. "Your grandma tell you anything about it other than that it was a good idea to wear it all the time?"

Detective Tuatu's lips pinched in and rolled out. "She told me a lot of nonsense."

"Bet it doesn't seem like nonsense these days," I said. "Like the widdershins thing."

"Maybe not," he said. "But it still doesn't make a lot of sense."

"She alive or dead?" I asked curiously. I'd been assuming dead, but you never knew with people who knew about anything to do with the worlds Between or Behind.

"I don't know," he said. "She disappeared a long time ago. It's why I became a cop."

"Heck!" I said in surprise, staring at him. "Look at you being all silent and strong with your trauma."

"I'm not traumatised," he said. "I might have been if I hadn't come to think she disappeared on purpose, though."

"Maybe you should talk about that with Abigail and her lot as well, then," I told him. "They know a few people I wouldn't have expected them to know, so you might get lucky."

"Lucky isn't something I've been since I met you," Tuatu said. "I'll think about it. In the meantime, can we please come up with a plan for next time? I can't keep the waterfront cordoned off indefinitely, and the markets will start up again in two days."

CHAPTER SEVEN

It wasn't quite dawn when I called Morgana. I hadn't slept, and I didn't think I was going to drop off any time soon—not with JinYeong's cologne seeping under the door and into my room like it had legs of its own. I suspected that he was sitting out in the upper living room instead of his own room, which was to be expected given that Athelas and Zero were both out of the house. I didn't poke my head out to check because if I did, he would have seen me, and I was feeling a bit too weird about everything to have him looking at me at this time of day.

Usually, it's rude to call your friends before the sun's up. Zombies don't sleep, though.

Sure enough, Morgana sounded wide awake and completely coherent when she answered the phone; she answered it pretty quickly, too, which was a relief. She'd only just started talking to me again after finding out she was a zombie, which was understandable: I'd been the one who had to tell her what she was, after all. It's pretty hard not to resent the person who brings the world you think you're living in crumbling down around you.

"Pet," she said. "Are you all right?"

"Yeah," I said. "I mean, I've got something I want to talk about, but it's not like I'm in trouble or anything."

I could almost picture the sharp, interested look on her face, the *moue* of black lipstick. "Let me guess: someone tried to kiss you?"

"You're flamin' terrifying," I said sourly. "He didn't try, he *did* it. Kissed me and told me he loved me. Then he dared me not to fall in love with him."

"Wait!" said Morgana sharply. "It was the vampire? The vampire did that, right?"

"Yeah." I would have wondered how she had guessed it was JinYeong I was talking about, but when I thought about it, I knew that if someone had told me one of the psychos would do it in that particular way, I would have known exactly which one they were talking about, too.

"What about Zero?"

"What about him?"

"He hasn't...I don't know. Made a move?"

"Nah, Zero's been patting me on the head."

She sounded surprised. "Patting you on the *head*? Good grief, how old is he!"

"Yeah, but at least he hasn't made a move on me."

"I don't know," she said. Her voice seemed disappointed. "Some men are like that: the fatherly kind. It's a move for some of them. I wouldn't like it much, but Daniel likes it."

"What, he likes patting you on the head?"

"No, he likes *being* patted on the head."

"That's not surprising," I said. Daniel was our—well, Morgana's—resident werewolf.

"He doesn't like people thinking of him like a dog. He says he's not a dog, he's a human. It doesn't stop him getting all floppy and relaxed when I pat him on the head, though."

I grinned, the constriction that had been in my chest all evening vanishing. It was familiar and yet somehow new to be talking to Morgana again properly; I'd known that I missed her, but I hadn't realised how much.

"Wait!" said Morgana. "We're supposed to be talking about Zero and JinYeong, not me and Daniel! What else did JinYeong say? Does Zero know what he's done?"

"Good grief, no!" I said hastily, answering the last, most pertinent question first. "And he's not going to know, if I have anything to say about it! I'm not having the two of them trying to sling each other through walls again."

Morgana sounded a bit brighter. "That's very promising!"

"Yeah, promising for a fight," I said sourly.

"Well, if it is, that's a good sign!" Morgana argued. "I was surprised when you said he'd been patting you on the head, but if you think he'd be jealous enough about little vamp boy making a move on you—"

Hastily, I said, "I didn't say that! I said it'd mean a fight: Zero doesn't think it's a good idea for humans to be mixing with behindkind."

Heck, I'd just got to feeling more comfortable around Zero again; there had been a kind of uncomfortable insecurity every time he patted me on the head or stood just a bit too close to me, prompted by Morgana's certainty that he loved me, or liked me, or whatever it was she had thought. I liked to think that he'd just become a bit more demonstrative, even if I didn't know exactly why. Unlike JinYeong, Zero hadn't tried to do anything that I could have construed as romantic in nature, and I'd started to feel more comfortable around him again by degrees. Not enough to hug him as often or freely as I'd used to, but enough to make me less likely to try and dodge every time he went to pat me on the head. He hadn't said so, but I was pretty sure it had hurt his feelings when I did so. Since he was only just starting to acknowledge the fact that he *had* feelings, let alone figure out how to use them, I didn't want to discourage him.

And I would definitely have had to discourage him if he was really in love with me.

"Why?" asked Morgana, and I realised I'd said the last bit aloud. "I mean, I know you've rejected the vamp, but why would you reject Zero?"

"Heck!" I said, startled. "Didn't mean to say that out loud. What do you mean, you know I've rejected the v—Jin Yeong?"

"He's too pretty for you," she said. "You're not the sort that goes for pretty boys, are you?"

"It's not his fault he's pretty," I argued, taken by surprise. "And he's a good fighter, anyway, plus he listens when you tell him no— actually, he *listens* to me in general, which is more than I can say for—"

"I'm confused," complained Morgana. "Have you rejected him or not?"

"Of course I did! I was just surprised that you knew it without me telling you."

"Trust me, I watch a *lot* of dating shows, and—"

"Good grief, *why?*"

"Don't interrupt, Pet," she said imperiously. "This is *important*. I watch them because it's a good study of human nature, and—"

"Only of weirdos!" I protested. "You don't think normal people go on those shows, do you?"

Morgana sniffed. "I thought you said you wanted to talk about it?"

"I already feel better." I said it flippantly, but the truth was that I did already feel better. I asked, "How are you doing lately, anyway?"

I asked the question tentatively, unsure what reaction I'd get. I hadn't wanted to risk asking it at all, but I didn't want Morgana to think that I wasn't concerned about her. It was pleasant just being able to talk to her again, and if I had to forever ignore the issue of her being a zombie to be able to do that, I would. I hadn't had a female friend before, and I only had two in my life, if you could count the North Wind as a female friend.

"I still haven't changed my diet, if that's what you're asking," she said bluntly. "And I still don't plan on it."

"Okay," I said. "Just be a bit more careful at the moment, all right?"

Morgana's voice sounded unusually sober. "I know," she said. "Daniel told me about the cycle. He says I might be important to the...the way things turn out from now on. I'm not going to fight in the Trials, but—"

"You're an Heirling," I said. "And the king doesn't like us Heirlings much: you might have to fight whether or not you want to. If someone tries to force their way into the house, they won't just go for you—they'll try to take out Daniel and the kids. Someone just went after someone like you and burned the whole house down."

"Don't worry," she said, and there was a thread of darkness in her voice that was a deeper black than her lipstick usually was. "If someone tries to get into the house—if they try to hurt the kids —Daniel won't need to go to the kitchen to get me something to eat."

Maybe I was comforted by being able to talk things over with Morgana, but I'm more inclined to think I was comforted by knowing what a gothic little battler she was. Hopefully, she'd never need to put that attitude to the test, but I hoped I was there to see it if she did.

I managed to get to sleep after that, which was a pleasant surprise. I meant to sleep for just a couple of hours, then get up early and drag Jin Yeong out with me to follow up my lead at the post office before Zero and Athelas got back home. They probably wouldn't cause a fuss if they knew we'd gone out together, and we could probably do something case-adjacent while we were out to make it look good.

Unfortunately, by the time I got downstairs, Zero and Athelas had returned.

I hesitated for just a moment, then decided to push through anyway. I didn't want to wait any longer.

"Pet," said Zero, as I pulled on my hoodie more from force of habit than actual need, "where do you think you're going?"

It wasn't like I could tell him—not just yet. I did want to be open about my secrets, though, if it was possible. Jin Yeong had said as much the other night: it was getting dangerous for humans out on the streets, and for me in particular. So long as the others knew I was out and when I was expected back again, there was a better chance of me surviving...all of this. I wasn't prepared to tell them exactly what I was doing, but I was prepared to let them know that I was up to something.

I said, "There's something I need to see about. It's personal. If you're not using Jin Yeong, I'll take him with me."

"I shall come," said Jin Yeong at once, before a baffled Zero could say anything about it.

"You're...not going to try and push into the case?" he said, as though he didn't quite comprehend any of the words—or maybe their meaning when all together. "You want to go somewhere with *Jin Yeong?*"

"What a startling circumstance!" marvelled Athelas.

"It's not as startling as all that!" I protested. "I've gone places with Jin Yeong before: actually, I'm with him as much as I'm with either of you! Anyway, we know it's sirens, and you lot have already been out today, so I figured you know what you're doing next."

"Us knowing things doesn't usually stop you from trying to stick your nose into our business."

"No, we just disagree about what's my business," I said

promptly. "It looks as though you're doing a good job all on your own, and—"

"How delightfully condescending," said Athelas. "It's good of you to admit as much."

"We will go," Jin Yeong announced, ignoring both Zero's amusement and Athelas' sharper-edged version of the same. "*Hyeong* does not need me."

"I didn't say that."

"*I* said it," said Jin Yeong. He pinched my cuff between thumb and forefinger and tugged me gently toward the front door. "We will go."

He released me once we were outside the front door, which made me suspect that he was trying to annoy Zero, but a sparkle came to his dark eyes when I said, "Right: Hobart P.O. You're up for vamping a few humans, aren't you?"

"Ah, this will be fun!"

"No unnecessary vamping," I warned him, stepping down from the patio and marching toward the road. "Just enough to get us a look at the records and find the bloke's real name, and maybe the security cameras if we know when he came last."

"I am very useful, am I not?" said Jin Yeong, his step a swagger. "I can do all of that, and I will also buy coffee."

"Okay, but only if you get the good stuff," I said. His eyes grew brighter, and I looked up at him in distrust. "What are you grinning about, anyway?"

"I am not grinning," he said, his nose lifting slightly. "I am looking forward to our date."

"We're not on a date," I said flatly, as we followed the street. "Don't try and trick me into stuff like that."

"You told *Hyeong*," he pointed out. "You chose me. Now I shall buy coffee."

"Yeah, because I don't want the others to know what I'm up to. I wasn't asking you out on a date. I would have just said it if I was."

"Hm," said JinYeong, narrowing his eyes at me. "How would you ask?"

Before I could think better of it, I said, "I wouldn't ask, I'd just—hang on. Stop grinning at me. We're not going to talk about this; we're supposed to be working."

"Very well," he said, slipping his hands into his pockets. "It is not a date, but we will have coffee. That old *halabeoji* is following us again."

"I know," I said. "He's been following us since we got past the wheelie bins next door. He must be hungry again. Maybe I should try to set him up with Vesper to get a square meal every couple of days."

JinYeong sounded unconvinced. "Hm. He is dirty."

"You're worried about Vesper's chairs?"

"That little lady is too small," said JinYeong. He sounded sulky, but I was pretty sure he wasn't. "Dirty things shouldn't be allowed in her house."

"You're *worried* about her!" I said in amazement, stopping in the middle of someone's driveway to stare at him. "You're worried he's going to bring trouble into her place."

He scowled. "I am not worried. She can poke trouble with her knitting needles."

"You're allowed to be worried about people, you know," I told him. "It's not a weakness."

JinYeong's shoulders hunched just a little. "It is a weakness," he said. Before I could open my mouth to disagree again, he added, "I did not say it is *wrong*, I said it is a *weakness*."

"You sounded just like Athelas then," I said, but I couldn't help sneaking another look up at him while he was looking away. All of my psychos had changed to some extent since I'd known them: I had always thought that Zero had changed the most of all of them, but right now, I wasn't so sure. I couldn't picture the JinYeong I'd first met—the one with bloody eyes, always trying to jibe Zero into fighting tooth and claw, the one who had seemed as though he would happily tear my throat out—worrying about a small, defenceless old lady.

Jin Yeong only sniffed, which made me add, "You can be human every now and then, you know. It's not forbidden."

"But I am not human," said Jin Yeong, with a curious dissatisfaction in his voice. "You said I am dead."

So that still rankled, did it? I'd said it to him thoughtlessly one day—maybe even more than once—and I hadn't realised it would hurt him so much. I certainly hadn't thought he'd still be thinking about it.

"You're not dead," I said. I'd been doing a bit of reading since then—Zero's impressive book collection wasn't for the faint of heart, and it definitely wasn't light reading, but it did come in handy for a girl who was trying to stay afloat in a dangerous world of behindkind—and I'd learnt a lot more about the virus that turned people from humans to vampires.

Unlike Morgana, who was technically both dead and alive at the same time, Jin Yeong was alive and functioning. He just had a very good grip on his internal systems due to a virus not unlike the one that made Daniel turn into a werewolf at will—one that required blood transfusions regularly to keep the system up and running.

That's a very polite way of saying that his DNA had been savagely rewritten to prioritise blood over everything. Blood to heal, blood to live. He didn't need to breathe because he could oxygenate his own blood without the use of his lungs. Didn't need to make his heart beat unless he wanted to because the blood already knew its way around his body.

Kinda creepy but also very cool.

Also technically not dead.

And now that I knew how seriously the insult got under his skin, I wouldn't be able to use it again. Waste of a good insult, that.

Jin Yeong didn't quite smile, but it seemed to me that his stride became looser, more relaxed: he sauntered along by my side with his hands in his pockets and his face turned slightly toward the sun as if soaking in the warmth of it.

He was still a bit sauntery as we went up the post office steps, almost purring. I elbowed him in the ribs to remind him not to dazzle everyone in the place, but he just rubbed his ribs and grinned a bit as the girl at the counter blinked in amazement and hastily called us forward.

"G'day," I said to her, and was ignored for my troubles. I could have just said hi, but it wasn't like she was paying attention to me, so it pleased me to be as okker as possible. "Got a couple questions for ya, mate."

"We wish to know the name of the man who owns this box," JinYeong said, his voice soft and persuasive. He took the bit of paper I had scribbled on and passed it to her. "And his phone number. Also his address."

"I can get his name and email address," said the girl, leaning close to the front of the counter with her arms folded. Smiling up at JinYeong, she added, "People don't need to leave a phone number or an address—just their email. So that's all we've got. I can give you my number, though."

"Heck, that was smooth!" I said, startled. "Oi, we just want his email address; you don't have to give us your number."

She shot me an annoyed look and turned back to JinYeong. "Just a second, I'll get that for you."

She typed and clicked away on her computer for a few minutes, then angled herself away from me slightly as she wrote on the back of a parcel card. I didn't have to see to know that she was writing down her number as well.

It annoyed me a bit, so I leaned in JinYeong's direction to crane my head around and see the screen. I saw the name, and below it an email address. *maddogjonny@tafe.com*. That really was all there was: no address, no number. There wasn't even a name.

The counter girl couldn't angle the screen away from me

without turning it away from JinYeong as well, but I saw the annoyance in the way she pressed her lips together. She recovered quickly enough to smile at JinYeong as she passed the card to him, though.

He took it from her, nodded in acknowledgement, and towed me away by the sleeve. Outside, he tore a strip off the bottom of the card and tossed it into a nearby garbage can with a grimace.

"What?" I said, not exactly sure if I was amused or...relieved? Perplexed? "You don't like girls making the first move?"

"*Ani*. I do not need that bit." He looked at me from beneath his lashes and added provocatively, "I will like it *very much* when you make the first move."

He left me gaping at him from the stairs and strolled away up the street toward the mall.

"Oi!" I said, catching up with him. "I wouldn't be making the first move because you already did it! Gimme that card!"

He passed me the card, grinning, then shoved his hands back into his pockets. He was far too pleased with himself, I thought sourly.

"All right," I said, my voice purposely cold to show that we were going to be talking *business* and nothing else, "we can guess that the bloke's name is Jonny. And this email address is a student one. It belongs to someone who's going to the TAFE here in Hobart."

"Ah. We will go to see this Jonny," said JinYeong, as if he hadn't just been trying to flirt with me. "I will...talk to him."

"Okay, but no biting," I said, hurrying after him.

There weren't as many Jonnys as I'd expected, and as soon as I mentioned the *mad dog* part of the email to the receptionist there, her eyes lit with amusement.

"Ah yes," she said. "That will be Jonny Campbell: they call him Maddog Jonny."

"Sounds like a fun bloke," I said. "He around today?"

She looked me up and down in a way that was about as

pointedly business-like as I'd been earlier with JinYeong. "I'm afraid I can't tell you that," she said. "The privacy of our students—"

"Pretty rich, after you just told us the bloke's name," I pointed out.

That might have been a bit mean of me.

The receptionist faltered, frowned worriedly, and said slowly, "I did, didn't I? Why did I do that?"

"Because I asked *very nicely*," said JinYeong, leaning his arms on the counter and observing her with dark, liquid eyes. "You will forget you told us, anyway. You should tell us what we want to know."

"Oh," she said. "Well, by the computer, it seems that Jonny has a pattern-cutting class right now. You should be able to find him in Block C, room 42. You'll need to be quick, though: class finishes in fifteen minutes."

"Thanks," I said, feeling a twinge of guilt. It was far too easy to do this to people; no wonder JinYeong had gotten into the habit of it. I wondered if I would have ended up the same way if I'd been a vampire.

JinYeong looked at me sideways as we walked, and said eventually, when we got to Block C, "This one did not give me her number."

I couldn't help the small snort of laughter that came out. "Yeah, I noticed that."

"You are still...prickly. Why are you prickly?"

"Dunno," I said, shoving my hands in my pockets. "I just don't like doing that to people."

"Ah," he said, thoughtful and lingering. "That. Even if I wished to stop it, I could not. It became familiar."

"Oh," I said. So it really did bother him sometimes, did it? "You really can't help it."

"I can help it a little bit," he said, reminding me of what he had once said about Marazul and his merman form. "And I can make it stronger; but some of it just happens, even if I do not wish it to happen."

"And sometimes it just doesn't happen," I said, grinning. "Like with me. That's gotta be annoying."

"*Ani*," he said, and once again the word lingered. He shot a look at me beneath his lashes and said, "Sometimes you are annoying. That—it is not annoying."

"You're confusing," I said. "Oi, this is the room."

JinYeong followed me into a light-filled room that was over-stuffed with scraps of material, wafting bits of pattern paper, and bolts of cloth. A dressmaker's dummy or two poked out of the mess, headless and eerie, with unfinished garments pinned to them. The mess of material at one end of the jumbled set of desks that had been pushed together turned out to be a bloke, slumping face-forward.

He was probably only a few years older than me, maybe early twenties, and either he didn't care about wasting the money he was spending on attending TAFE or he was just too tired to care, because he was fast asleep. I might have thought he was dead, but he was snoring, and let me tell you *that* was a nice change up for the books. Maybe his teacher had given up on him as a bad job, because he was the only one in the room.

JinYeong gave a small sniff of laughter and kicked the desk leg closest to him, jolting the table and, by extension, the bloke.

"Jonny!" I hailed him in a friendly sort of way, sitting down on the desk beside him as he flailed a bit and sat up. "We need to have a bit of a chat."

For a second, I thought he was actually gunna run for it. JinYeong must have thought the same, because he grabbed Jonny by the collar before he could do more than start to push away from the desk in a confused jumble of limbs.

"Okay, if this is about my rent, you'll get your money tonight, promise!" he said, staring at JinYeong and then at me.

"It's not about the rent," I said.

"And I'm not due in court for another two weeks, *plus* I didn't do it, so if that's what it's about, you can tell the old goat I'll see him in court!"

"Nope," I said. "We want to have a chat about that P.O. Box you own."

He slumped again, visibly relaxing. "Oh, is that all! I can't tell you about that; it's private. I get paid to not talk about it."

JinYeong leaned over, startling Jonny into jerking backward, and said into that frightened face, "I think you should talk."

"Look mate, you don't have to get nasty; I didn't do anything wrong!"

"Didn't say you did," I said. "We just need you to answer a few questions—and I reckon you better be pretty flamin' truthful, 'cos my friend doesn't like liars and he's *very good* at figuring out when people are lying. Tell us about your post box."

"Look, it's not *my* post box—it belongs to the bloke who hired me."

"Someone hired you to go and rent a P.O. Box for them?"

"Yeah. I told you: it's not mine, not really," he babbled. "I get sent money to cover the cost every year."

JinYeong leaned a little closer. "Who hired you?"

"This is probably gunna sound weird," said Jonny, trying vainly to move further back in his chair, "but—"

"You can't remember his face?" I suggested.

"How did you know!" he said, awed. "It doesn't make sense, but no matter how much I think about the bloke, I can't remember his face—can't remember his voice, either."

"How can you be working for someone you can't even remember?"

"I don't know, man," he said. "I just took the job to earn a bit of money. It's not like it takes a lot of energy, and I get paid every week."

Indignantly, I said, "You could have been working with drug dealers!"

"I don't know that," he said. "You don't know that. All I know is that I get paid fifty bucks a week to go and check the mail. There's hardly ever anything there, anyway—he's lucky if he gets something once a month. Anything that comes gets forwarded to him."

I met Jin Yeong's eyes. "What do you mean, forwarded?"

"Not in the mail," he said. "That'd be stupid. I drop stuff off into a letterbox round about here. It comes from the post box to me and then stops there."

"Who owns the house?"

"There is no house," said Jonny. "It burned down years ago. The letterbox and a few trees are about all that's left. I'm surprised no one's tried to redevelop it. Mind you, it's got a bit of a creepy feel, so that might put people off."

"I'll bet," I muttered. "Oi. Write down the address for us."

He looked from me to Jin Yeong as he scribbled a note on a scrap of pattern paper. "You're not gunna get me in trouble?"

"We're not the cops, if that's what you're asking," I said, grabbing the paper before he could get rid of it.

"But if you tell anyone that we came to see you," said Jin Yeong silkily, "you will be in *very much* trouble."

Jonny swallowed. "Right. Not a word," he said. "Oh, and if you're hoping to find this bloke, you might be out of luck: I don't think he checks his mail too often. Sometimes the stuff I put there is still there the next time I go. I reckon he switches up his days so that he's harder to catch if someone like you comes along."

"We will take care of that," Jin Yeong said. "You: *forget* what we talked about and go back to sleep."

Jonny, his eyes suddenly heavy, yawned and stretched, then laid down on the desk again. Before I had a chance to open my mouth, he was asleep and snoring faintly.

"Flamin' heck!" I said to Jin Yeong. "That was quick."

"He is no more use to us," he said, shrugging one dismissive shoulder.

"Fair enough," I said. "Right. If we can't find out who it is this way, we'll find out another way."

"Ah," JinYeong said thoughtfully. "We will send a mail to ourselves?"

"And people think you're just a pretty face!"

"I am a pretty face. I am *also*—"

"All right, all right," I said hastily. "You reckon it'd do much good to just put something in the letterbox at the empty block ourselves?"

JinYeong didn't hesitate. "No. It will need that thing—a postmark. And perhaps that person will know if this boy doesn't deliver it."

"That's what I thought," I said, faintly gloomy. "Right, I suppose it's back to the post office for us, then."

We went back out into a surprisingly warm sunshine; and maybe JinYeong was enjoying that more than vampires are supposed to enjoy sunshine, because when we got back to the post office he stopped at the outside pillars, just a few steps away from the sliding glass doors.

I stared at him. "What? You don't wanna go in?"

"I will wait out here," he said, and propped himself against the wall. "There is nothing I need in there."

He was waiting for me when I got back out. He yawned, catlike, and asked, "Are we going home?"

I caught the faintly malicious gleam in his eye as he explained, "*Hyeong* will be annoyed if we are gone longer. He does not approve of me."

"What do you mean, he doesn't approve of you?"

"He doesn't approve of me loving you," JinYeong explained. The gleam was slightly more pronounced now, and I didn't like that.

"You already told me that. Don't go using me to needle Zero," I told him directly. "If that's why you like me—"

"That is just a bonus," he said, grinning at me. "Are we going home?"

"Well, you're gunna be pretty pleased to find out that we've got somewhere else to go first," I said more cheerfully, wriggling my phone at him. It wasn't that I was pleased, but I was satisfied that I wasn't going to be used in JinYeong's constant push to annoy Zero. "I need to get some info off Abigail."

JinYeong frowned. "About your family?"

"Maybe. Hopefully. They've got a lot of history there that I haven't been able to find anywhere else, and I figured they might know something about my great-grandma Anne. You blokes reckon that to be an Heirling, humans have to have a bit of behindkind blood somewhere as well as human, and she went out of state, just like me."

He hissed in a breath, thoughtful at once. "Ah. You think she went Behind?"

"Yeah. And I think there was something I read in one of Abigail's books earlier—now that I know my parents knew about Behind, it makes sense that my family would show up in history from humans who also knew about it."

"You should be careful of the humans," JinYeong said.

I stared at him. "Look at you, getting all behindkindy."

"I did not mean that. I meant that they are too much like *Hyeong*."

"I know," I said, but I couldn't help shooting an approving look at him.

He grinned. "I told you. My pretty face is a bonus. We will go, but if they ruin my suit, I will be *very annoyed*."

CHAPTER EIGHT

THERE WAS no one outside when we got there, so we showed ourselves in.

"They need to get themselves better security," I said to Jin Yeong as we walked cautiously down the hall. It was nice to be able to get in easily, but it was a double-edged sword: if the humans were too startled at seeing us with no notice, there was a pretty good chance we'd get shot by a crossbow—or at the very least take a cricket bat to the side of the head. "Now that I know what sort of magic they've got running around the place, it doesn't take much to get through."

"They are probably not prepared for something like you," said Jin Yeong, with a laughing glitter to his eyes.

"Watch out who you're calling a thing," I said, a bit more softly. We were getting closer to the area where we might find people: just a bit further down the hall was the office they seemed to use as a meeting room. Hopefully we'd find Abigail before anyone else.

It took me a moment to realise that Jin Yeong had stopped walking. I turned an enquiring look on him, and he said, "I will wait. I think they will talk more if you go alone."

"You're basically a fixture today," I told him, but I left him there to pace in the hallway like a slightly erratic pinball and headed on into the room.

Abigail was in the office digging through a box of what looked like someone's garage sale items when I walked in, with Ezri sitting on the desk beside her, legs crossed and lifting a fringed jacket out of the box.

"You lot need to work on your magic defences," I said.

Abigail dropped the paperweight she'd been holding in one bandaged hand. "Pet!"

Was I mistaken, or did her eyes flare with panic?

"What are you doing here?"

"Came to see you about that thing I asked you about," I said. "Didn't feel like talking about it on the phone. Don't know who's listening, half the time."

"I'd be more worried about the friendly listeners than the unfriendly," she said, rather grimly. "Look—"

"No time to talk?" I guessed. She still looked vaguely uncomfortable, but that could just have been because I came back again to the headquarters after everything that happened between us a little while ago.

I had almost not come back again: a tacit way of way of saying, *I know you don't trust me so I'll pretend that I don't know where you live.* Actually, I was a bit surprised that they were still in the same spot: I would have expected them to move after finding out that I had, as they thought of it, betrayed their existence to my three psychos. I'd figured they wouldn't trust me not to tell Zero where they were.

Apparently I was wrong. That was a pleasant surprise.

Still, Abigail didn't look too comfortable to have me here, and I shouldn't let myself be offended at that. It was fair enough.

"I can come back another time," I said. "Or you can text me a place and I'll meet you there."

"You're here already," she said. "We'll just have to go to the conservatory. The offices are both occupied at the moment—we're having a computer upgrade tonight and there are wires and stuff everywhere. Follow me."

The conservatory turned out to be a bit in the building where there was no roof. The rainfall and sunlight that had been allowed in through the hole had created a patch of greenery that boasted a few trees and a few small shrubs, and someone had put a couple of chairs underneath one of the trees where you could rest your legs in the sunshine and your upper body in the shade.

"Heck," I said, impressed. It looked almost like a bit of Between—if there had been enough of Between itself to it. I saw a flutter of shadow that was probably JinYeong following at a distance in the hallway, and sat down next to Abigail with the comforting sensation that I had backup if I needed it. I didn't think I would need it—never wanted to need it when it was the humans I was dealing with—but it was nice to know I had it.

"This is my favourite part of the building," Abigail said. She seemed pleased by my delight in the space. "Hang on, I'll get out the book; I've put in some bookmarks to make it easier to find the right parts, but I also wrote a few notes down."

"I can just take pictures with my phone, can't I?"

"You can try," she said, grinning. "Don't expect it to work, though: Blackpoint rigged this all for us, and he laid in a *lot* of security."

"Old-fashioned it is, then," I said, taking the lined page of notes she passed to me.

"There aren't too many Annes," she said, flicking the book out of her phone the way she'd done once before. It solidified in the air and dropped into her lap, and she turned carefully to the first of the bookmarks I could see sticking out of the top. "And I can't promise you that the mentions we found are *your* Anne. The records were made before the days they started worrying about who could find their names, so there's a bit more to go on, but I don't know how helpful it's going to be."

"I thought you didn't believe in the names thing," I said.

"I don't," said Abigail. "I'm just mentioning it because of how it affects the searches. The most recent Anne that could still be yours is this one: appeared suddenly in Hobart; they found her along the rivulet in the twenties. No mention of how old she was —just called *young woman*."

I let out a breath. "Not the same one, then. We're after someone who disappeared later in life—it sounds more like that one escaped from Be—Faery. My great-grandma disappeared in the thirties: left a one-year-old kid behind and just vanished."

"Then there are these two. There's one with a birth record from the turn of the century, so she'd be the right age for having kids in the twenties or thirties at the latest, which seems early. The other one was about fifteen in the thirties, so depending on when your great-grandma started having kids..."

"Don't know that," I said regretfully.

"I thought you said you came from Queensland," Abigail said, frowning. "Or is that another part of your memories that you don't have? Wouldn't it make more sense to be looking for stuff like this from a group up there?"

"Nah, the family came from Tasmania originally," I said. "Mum's side, anyway. Mum moved back to Queensland with Dad early on when they got married; she always said he came to Tasmania just to find her."

We'd ended up in Tassie again pretty quickly, though. Must be something about the place.

"Maybe he did," Abigail said dryly. "I mean, your great-grand-mother—well, whether or not they're the same Anne, almost all of the Annes I've seen in the records have... impressive histories. Impressive or depressing."

"Yeah," I said, remembering the entry I'd seen in Abigail's book. "Like that one that vanished out of state—the pregnant one."

"Exactly. I wrote a note for her, too, but she's a bit early for your great-grandma, I would have thought: that was in the eighteen somethings."

"Yeah," I said reflectively. "That's a bit early. Oi, you reckon my dad already knew about all this stuff when he came down here?"

She shrugged. "You'd know more about that than I do. But you're pretty well-trained, and I don't think you can claim it's all from the big white fae."

"Some of it is," I said. "The fighting part of it—well, it's from him and Athelas and Jin Yeong. The other stuff...yeah, my parents taught me a few things."

"You're lucky you had them for long enough to learn stuff from them," she said, and I heard the note of distant regret in her voice.

It made me ask, "How did you end up here? I know you said it was *City Fae*, but what happened to you specifically?"

"Specifically, my husband and daughter were killed in the crossfire when the fae came after me," she said, her eyes glassy and hard.

Heck. That regret wasn't distant enough for how big it was. I'd had longer to process and accept what had happened, and I was nowhere near healthily recovered.

"Sorry," I said, digging the toe of my boot into the mossy floor. I already knew she hated Zero and Athelas, but I hadn't realised exactly how hard it must be for her to work with them. Heck. What was gunna happen if she ever met Blackpoint and figured out the extent of his betrayal? He hadn't meant it as a betrayal, but there was no way she wouldn't see it as one.

Just the very fact that he was fae and had concealed it from her would be enough.

"You figure that memory out?" she asked suddenly. "The out of state one?"

I shivered a bit. "Yeah."

"Did it help shake anything else out?"

"A bit," I said. "Not enough, though. We're working on it."

"Just make sure they're not working on you while you're working on it," Abigail warned me. "And watch out for your boyfriend, too. He's a bit friendlier with those two than I thought he was."

I couldn't help grinning. "No need to worry about Jin Yeong," I said. "He wears his heart on his sleeve, anyway."

"Yes, I can see that," she said. "But there's something about him that isn't normal. You might want to make sure he is what he says he is."

"He's very honest about that, too," I remarked. "Don't worry about me. I'll be all right in the end."

I wished I could believe that, because the thought of what was going to happen in the future—near or far—still worried me a lot.

"Have you thought any more about joining us?" she asked.

It shouldn't have surprised me, but it did.

"Figured you lot wouldn't want me anymore, actually," I said, glad to find something I could be completely honest about. "Not after what happened last time."

Abigail hesitated, then said, "Let's just say that I've started to appreciate your position a bit more recently. We'd be stupid not to want you, anyway. By and large, I still think that humans should stick with other humans, and I've...got a feeling that your big boy would let you go if you asked. Just think about it again, anyway."

"I'll think about it," I said, with an unsettling feeling of déjà vu and something else that I couldn't qualify.

"Just don't leave it too long," she said. "Look, Pet, I don't want to be rude, but I have to get back to the setup in there: I don't dare leave it alone for too long in case something happens. I've noted down everything that has to do with Annes for you—just make sure you don't lose the paper. We'll see you the day after tomorrow when we go after the sirens again."

"Day after tomorrow, yeah," I agreed. Heck, Zero and Athelas must have figured out a way to protect everyone, then—*and* messaged Abigail. Rude of them not to tell me before I left today, but maybe they would have if I hadn't just run away with Jin Yeong.

I grabbed Jin Yeong on my way back through the house, and maybe he knew that Abigail had been trying to convince me to join the humans again, because he seemed a bit preoccupied—or maybe annoyed—when I rejoined him. It wasn't until we left the house well behind that he broke his silence, and then what he did say surprised me.

"This—" he gestured widely and vaguely back in the direction of the humans' headquarters. "This is necessary, why?"

"Don't know," I said. "But my great-grandma was part of the stuff that Athelas got the detective to look for, and I reckon it's important. Wouldn't you do it if it was JiAh?"

Jin Yeong went very still for a moment. "JiAh is...different."

"Yeah?"

"I already know everything, but it helps *nothing*," he said. "If I had not known, perhaps it would have been better."

"Yeah, but would you have let someone else decide that for you?"

He sniffed. "*Ani.*"

"Exactly. And speaking of things I don't know, I should probably try to get Athelas to help me with some memories again today."

"There are more?" he asked, one brow going up. "You already found some that day. You were not happy."

Not happy was a pretty big understatement for the state in which Jin Yeong had found me.

I shrugged one shoulder; it wasn't as if I didn't already know that—or as if there was anything I could do about it. I said, "Yeah, but there are more—there *have* to be more. I've been making myself forget stuff for years now; I think my parents thought it was the only way to keep me safe, but it's made everything flamin' hard recently. I know...well, I don't know, but I'm pretty sure I saw the murderer the night he killed my parents. I just can't seem to remember more than finding them that night."

"You should wait for me," said Jin Yeong. "I—when I am upset, I do not want to be touched. I think you need to be hugged when everything is too much. *Hyeong* is the same, and—"

"I'm not accepting hugs from you," I said suspiciously.

"They are *free hugs*," he said coldly. "I will not...*expect* things."

I looked across at him. "Oh. Thanks."

"Or," he said, more persuasively, "you could stop playing games with that twisty old man. Then there will be no need for hugs unless you wish to have them."

"Not until I find out what happened to Mum and Dad," I said. A small memory or two had popped out as I went about my everyday life, lately—perhaps a remnant from the sessions with Athelas and the encounter with Zero's dad, perhaps just a natural sort of healing after the big blockage had been removed and my mind's own normal flow had begun again, sweeping away other debris. I didn't think it would be long before that blockage disappeared entirely, and I wanted to be as ready for it as possible when it happened.

Maybe that way, I'd be able to mitigate the damage I was almost certain it would cause.

"Heard we'll be ready to go after the sirens again the day after tomorrow," I said to Zero when we got back. Jin Yeong and I had come back to the house to find Athelas sitting in his chair and flicking through a book that must have been magic-adjacent, judging by how the illustrations didn't seem to be quite tied to the pages. Zero had been in the kitchen, doing magic at the table on a series of small, plastic items. Some of them had melted into the table, which was going to be a pain to clean up; but most of them seemed to have turned out fine, so when I'd chopped up the beef and added all the spices to my pot, I leaned on the kitchen island, edging around JinYeong to see Zero, and pointed at the mess.

"I suppose that's stuff to stop the humans getting tricked into taking out their earplugs," I said, since he'd only grunted in reply to my first question. "What's it going to do for the problem with the camera app?"

"The merman is working on something for us," Zero said briefly. "Don't interrupt, Pet; I've already ruined too many of these. They have to be ready for the electronics tomorrow."

"Got it, sorry," I said. "JinYeong, shove over, I need this space for tea."

I pushed him aside without thinking about it, but instead of allowing himself to be pushed as he always did, JinYeong's arms moved just a little, then stopped. I was jerked to a surprised stop, far too close to being nose-to-nose with him for comfort. He moved his head back just enough to make a small air-kiss in the direction of my nose, his eyes dark with laughter.

My eyes flew to Zero, and my heart dropped when I saw that his eyes were on the both of us.

He said icily, "What do you think you're doing, JinYeong?"

I stood up straight at once and said to JinYeong, "Stop doing weird stuff!"

His eyes danced; he turned to face Zero and shrugged one shoulder. "It is only natural, isn't it?"

"What do you mean, it's only natural?"

"*Kobaek haesseoyo*," said JinYeong. He sounded pretty cheerful for a bloke who had been very definitely turned down after a declaration of love. *Or* for one who was on the point of being tossed through a wall—*again*.

I would have glared at him, but I wasn't sure he wouldn't take it as encouragement.

There was a moment of silence before Zero spoke. His voice wasn't a rumble this time: it was a piercing, icy chill. "You did *what*?"

"I told her that I loved her," Jin Yeong said, his voice crystal clear and resonant with mockery—and maybe a bit of challenge. "I told you I would do so."

"I told *you* that if you tried anything else, I would personally take you apart and—"

"Don't take anyone apart in the kitchen!" I told Zero. "I'm making chilli, and if you think I want to try and differentiate between what's blood and what's chilli, you're flamin' wrong."

Zero's blue eyes turned on me for a brief second before flicking back to Jin Yeong. He said, "Come outside."

"Heck no!" I said firmly. "It's bad enough having you throwing him through walls: I'm not gunna have you throwing him through the fence, as well."

Jin Yeong turned a more-than-usually-smouldering look toward me, then a provocative one on Zero. "She does not want you to hurt me, *Hyeong*."

"I just don't want my house wrecked. Pretty sure the new neighbour is already scared of you, too, Zero: for blokes who are meant to be blending in, you're not doing a real good job of it at the moment."

Zero's eyes flickered across to me. "I told him that he wasn't to make any overtures toward you, and I told him exactly why."

"That was pretty flamin' rude of you, then," I said. "If I don't want him making—good grief, did you say *overtures?*—toward me, I'll tell him myself! Actually, I did tell him myself, so you can stop trying to pick a fight."

"*Nep*," said Jin Yeong, his nose lifting. "She told me already. We will work it out between ourselves."

I turned back to Zero. "Also, are you keeping secrets from me again? Why isn't he supposed to make overtures?"

"I can't—I can't tell if you're being sarcastic or not," said Zero, looking genuinely perplexed. "Don't you know that—"

"This is my business, *Hyeong*," Jin Yeong said. "I will listen to you in other things, but—"

"*When?*" demanded Zero, as if at the very end of his patience. "I would like to know when, because I don't remember you doing much listening in the past *or* the present!"

"He's got a point," I told JinYeong.

JinYeong pursed his mouth. "I am very good when people ask me nicely. You should try to ask nicely, *Hyeong*."

Zero very carefully put the pieces of plastic that he was trying to enchant back down on the table.

"JinYeong—" He hesitated, then said exasperatedly, "Just go and check on the officers that the detective has at the waterfront! They're not allowed to have their phones on them to avoid the danger of beguilement. If you can't be useful around the house, you might as well be useful elsewhere."

"*Ye, Hyeong,*" said JinYeong primly.

"And stop saying yes at me!" Zero said grimly. He added, as if unable to stop himself and annoyed that he couldn't, "Don't go too close! Stay on this side of the perimeter they've set up. It's not safe to go further until we're better armed."

It must have amused JinYeong, because I heard the laughter in his voice as he said, "*Ye, ye, Hyeong,*" and faded away through the wall and into Between.

"We'll discuss this later," Zero said to me; and, sweeping up all the bits of plastic that weren't melted, he marched away upstairs.

"I didn't agree to that!" I yelled after him. Grumpy old fae. He was as bad as Athelas sometimes.

Since Zero didn't seem inclined to engage any longer, I left the chilli simmering in the kitchen and went to see if Athelas needed some tea. Perhaps I hoped he might be persuaded to help me look for a few memories, too, but tea always helped to grease the wheels with him.

"Are you here to enliven my day as well?" asked Athelas, as I approached. "How delightful! I would prefer a cup of tea, however."

"You can have tea," I told him. "No enlivening. The house is flamin' perky enough without that. I want to do a bit of spelunking."

"I see," he said, closing the book he was reading with one finger as a bookmark. "Then I really do insist upon tea—and you might consider espresso rather than your usual, perhaps."

I threw a look at him over my shoulder as I headed for the kitchen. "You want my heart rate up?"

"I believe it would be useful."

"All right," I called. "But if I can't sleep, you're going to be the one I'm annoying."

The jug started boiling then, but I was pretty sure he murmured, "A regular day in the life, in fact."

He had put away the book he was reading when I got back with the tray of tea and biscuits, which gave him a moment to drink his tea.

Over the rim, he said, "I trust you're not cooking anything that can burn, Pet?"

"Already gave it a bit of a stir," I said. "I can stir it again later. Some of it might stick to the bottom if I'm gone too long, but it won't burn. What, you reckon we'll be gone for a while?"

"It's likely," he said, finishing his tea with terrifying speed. "Time can be fluid when one is dealing with matters inside one's mind."

I had wanted to do this, but I still had some uncomfortable memories from last time, and there was a nasty little pit in the centre of my stomach. "Sure you don't want a couple of bikkies and a refill?" I prompted him.

His grey eyes dwelt on me for a moment before he said, "You may refill my cup."

"You're not doing me a favour," I said in some annoyance, but I got up and refilled his cup anyway.

"No?" he asked, his eyes on the stream of tea. "As before, Pet, once we begin, there will be no stopping. Are you sure you wish to begin?"

"Dunno what you think you're gunna do," I said to him. I stuck my nose in the air a bit, too, because I didn't want him to know that I was already feeling sick and vulnerable. "I already know better than to let you into my mind again, and that little worm of yours isn't gunna do much good when I'm not scared enough to—"

"Might I remind you, Pet," said Athelas, his voice terrifyingly cool, "that I have not yet done more to you than meddle a little with the inside of your mind? Might I *also* remind you that—"

"No thanks," I said hurriedly. "You already killed me six times, so you can count that toward the things you've shown me."

"I do not intend," Athelas said silkily, "to kill you. I can do nothing with a dead body. Now. Shall we begin?"

He didn't give me much choice about it: he leaned forward over the tea tray and had me by the wrist before I knew what was happening, and if his voice was silk, his grip was iron.

"Oi," I said. "What are you up to? I thought you were gunna try to get in my head again."

"I thought we might try something a trifle more...tangible than that," he said. "You seem to be able to grasp at things you should not be able to grasp at, so perhaps it would be best not to give you something to grasp at."

Something cold and painful pierced my ear, but I had no time to worry about that, because all of a sudden, the living-room walls flickered and displayed Zero's face, close and terrifying. I felt a flicker of the memory within me—it was the first time I'd actually met Zero, and he had choked me to within an inch of my life. What was it doing up on the wall?

That was all I needed: my memories plastered on the wall for everyone to see. I definitely didn't like this turn of events.

"Oi!" I said indignantly. "That's not an important memory! What are you messing around with that one for! And how the heck did you get it up on the walls?"

"Who's to say what's important and what's not?" Athelas

asked, gazing at the walls. "If you would like to see something more interesting, make it happen."

"I'm *trying*," I said through my teeth. Mostly I was trying to figure out how on earth he was projecting memories onto the walls of my house. Once I'd done that, I could try and get the right ones out. "But you keep pulling up the wrong memories!"

"Make them the right ones," he said. "And stop blaming me for your own inadequacies."

"Inadequacies, my foot!" I said wrathfully, and somewhere within the turmoil of my mind, I felt a familiar little gnawing. "You put that worm in my head again, didn't you? How did you do that when we're still outside of everything?"

"That is for you to decide," he said. "But after all, you did ask for your memories to be examined."

"I asked for you to help me find the missing ones," I snapped. I threw a look around the room, trying to find the focal point of the magic that was dragging memories from me, but every point of magic in the room seemed to go toward a different source, and it took me far too long to realise that they weren't going toward different sources, they were going to different *ends* and *coming* from a common source: me.

Everything was connected to me: my house, Between, the worm, the display of memories. And Athelas was using those connections against me—using my own house against me to power the worm, his control, the display of memories. Using a magic so familiar that I had never realised, until this very moment, that it was actually magic.

"Oh, that's not on," I said, because it was *my* house. All the power and protection in it was *mine*, and he had no right to make it turn against me. Not for petty little memories that didn't matter, anyway.

"Then stop me," he said, cold and amused. "Or shall we go onto other memories—there is one there that seems to be surrounded by a great deal of protection. Dear me! is that the *vampire*...?"

I gritted my teeth and tried to find where the worm had gone, but all I could feel was the tug of the memories as they were dragged from me, and Jin Yeong's face, very faintly flushed from kissing me, segueing onto the walls.

Oh no. *Heck* no. That was not going to be displayed for Athelas' distantly amused eyes.

I fought it, hauling back on the memory to prevent it going out, but it slipped away from me, faster and faster, and the worm chewed faster and faster. Panicked, I saw the next part of the memory infuse itself into the wall, and I could do nothing about it because we weren't inside my mind, where I could control that sort of thing.

This time, we were outside of my mind.

A surge of rage welled up in me, pushing me to fight, to strike out. To push Athelas and the worm out of my mind altogether. But that wouldn't work here, outside my head, so instead, I let Athelas further in. I found the tug that pulled out my memories and followed it down into my own mind, leaving behind the outside of moving walls and bodies. I sank, and as I did, I dragged Athelas down with me until there were no walls or structure. No barriers. I used the magic of the house, the connections that all clung to me, to take us deeper and deeper, until we had followed the worm all the way down and back to its source: Athelas. He was connected to me, too—because everything was. The worm came with me, too, and I set it free.

I saw a flash of despair in those grey eyes, but I couldn't pull back. The worm burrowed deep into his mind in an instant, and memory flooded over me. I think...I know...I wouldn't have pulled back even if I could have. I pushed forward instead, right into memory, until the memory was no longer a flat display but a world of its own; and this time, it wasn't my memory.

This one was Athelas' memory. I was Athelas, and before me

was Zero's dad, bright and deadly. His eyes pinioned me and I couldn't move; I felt the slither of something familiar and dreadful in my mind—a little worm that knew how to search for what it needed to know.

"I did as you asked, my lord." I felt a brief scuttle of memory within the memory: blood and heat and a wet, choking gurgle that Athelas' mind smoothly pushed beneath the surface where it couldn't be seen.

"So I see," said Zero's father, and the cold calculation in his voice made me understand that he'd seen that memory too: Athelas had allowed it to come to the surface in order to prove that he had carried out what he had been ordered to do. "Your second assignment—"

"My lord, you have other servants, I believe."

"It is not a request; it is an order."

I felt so tired, because this body, this mind knew exactly what was coming, and knew it had to say the words anyway. "I'm aware, my lord. I must refuse."

"Yes, so you said. I believe you were concerned about the effect on my son."

"Losing his brother—"

"—who was already plotting against him," interrupted Zero's father.

"My lord, I can't take from him *again*. After tonight—"

"Must I remind you again what will happen should you not obey?"

I felt the stillness that came over Athelas' face: the stillness of his limbs—almost a stillness of heart. He said, with a cold stab of despair, "My lord—"

"Then I will take from you," said Zero's father, his smile beautiful and fearsome, "in blood and pain. And I will make sure that you pay for your disobedience anon."

I lost track of the memory in a sudden, hot and cold flush of desolation, and lost myself in Athelas' mind for an aching, bewildering span of time that couldn't have been more than a couple of minutes but felt like an eternity. When the memory came back, it came in pieces.

Every breath hurt; every movement was fire. I still breathed, but barely; in my peripheral was the blue wetness of blood that pooled around my temple and stung my eye.

"Now," said that voice in a whisper in my ear, "I will attend to it myself. And I will take my time attending to it."

The sound of my breath—of Athelas' breath—and blood bubbling in our lungs. The sound of a distant bell. Not church. Not here. An old-fashioned sound. A summons, said approaching steps beyond vision. Still, all I could see was blue, and all I breathed was blood.

"Father." That was a voice. It seemed old and whispery, but it had to be Zero's half-brother, didn't it? It made our hand twitch as if it really could move, could do anything to help. It was only a twitch. This body knew what was possible to do and what wasn't possible: it was not a body used to helping people. There was no use.

The air was stifling, so why could we hear the screaming so clearly?

Sound was trapped, and I was trapped and we were trapped and the screaming—

The screaming—

The edges of the memory fluttered away like burning parchment, and I fell, sobbing. The screaming followed, torn into pieces and searing my mind as I fell into another memory.

I looked down into my own face, the sight of it alien and not quite right. It took me a while to realise that the not-quite-right-ness to it all was the fact that I was seeing myself from a higher field of vision than usual. The thin face; the dark, messy hair and big grey eyes that put a twist in the heart of this body I was in.

"I do want it...very much," Athelas said, through my lips. "Don't tempt me."

I felt the longing in him: the sick, hopeless longing to be safe, to be cared for, to rest. The longing to be free from a darkness so horrible—a darkness so filled with blood and terror and death—that he couldn't even think about it in a straight line.

But I knew none of that showed in his face, because I could see it reflected back in my own grey eyes. I could remember from my own point of view.

I would have followed that memory back where it went, but I was too late—or perhaps Athelas was just in time. Something seized me by the nape of the neck, or where it would have been if I were in my body and not in someone else's mind, and fairly *hauled* me away.

"Out!" said Athelas' voice, grey and worn to a thread of itself.

"I'm sorry!" I said, sick and horrified at how easy it had been to force the memory from him. "I'm sorry!"

Maybe I hadn't been speaking aloud, because the next moment I was on the carpet, and there was nothing in sight but the ceiling and a kaleidoscope of colours and movement. The shadows were all wrong, but I wasn't sure if that was because it was so much later in the day than it should have been or because the shadows themselves had decided to make their own minds up about where they preferred to be.

"Where's Athelas?" I asked, slurring slightly. I wanted to apologise properly, not inside his mind where I had forced myself and from where I had taken memories I had no business taking. All I could see was the brilliance that was JinYeong and the cold, thready movement of my house around me as it bent and wove around the Between in the room.

"Athelas is…taking a moment," said Zero's voice from the huge mass of icy-blue movement and shadow somewhere across the room. "What in heaven's name did you do?"

I stood, staggering, but JinYeong was there to prop me up, edging his arm against my back. He didn't try to put the arm around me, which was good. I probably would have tried to do something about that, and I would probably also have fallen over while trying.

Athelas was nowhere in the room, but I was pretty sure he was still somewhere around the house: there was a big mass of silver and steel somewhere near the back of the house—maybe the patio—that assured me he was still alive, at least.

I drew in a small, shuddering breath, and said, "Reckon something went a bit wrong with the magic Athelas was doing," I said.

Only nothing had gone wrong with it. I had just figured out how to use it against Athelas instead of him using it against me. It was mine, and using it, I had taken from him what he would have taken from me.

With a sick feeling in my stomach, I realised that the memory I had been looking at must have been the other side of the events Zero had told me about. Somehow that old distrust of Athelas that I had felt, cropping up again, had brought forth this memory as a result. Zero had said that he found Athelas barely functioning just after his brother was killed: had said that he was so far injured that it was impossible for him to have killed Zero's half-brother in that state.

"Sit," said Jin Yeong, pushing me toward the couch. "Sit. We will have coffee, and then a talk with that old man."

"Saw the night your half-brother died," I said to Zero, allowing myself to be pushed into the couch and staring without seeing at the cold teapot of tea and the abandoned biscuits. Jin Yeong seemed satisfied, because he disappeared into the kitchen. "Reckon you need to have a chat with your dad."

It had never occurred to me that the injuries Athelas had sustained that night had been because he refused to kill Zero's half-brother. Or that it had been Zero's father who did the deed. Ordered it, yes. Done it himself? No. But I'd definitely heard Zero's dad killing *someone*.

Zero's face could have provided ice chips for a party full of people. "You shouldn't have done that," he said.

"I didn't do it on purpose," I muttered, but I couldn't help the pang of guilt I felt. The memory had been buried away carefully: deep and quiet, where it couldn't easily be called to the surface by a curious worm or a smaller memory or two. If I hadn't been distrustful of Athelas once again, I don't think I would have been able to get to it, either.

"I trust this puts to rest your suspicions," said Zero. "I came upon Athelas mere moments after giving chase to the murderer—him and my old human nurse together. She was old, but she shouldn't have had to die in that way. I found them together in what seemed like a sea of blood: Athelas knew she'd been with me since I was born, though she was just a child then. He was fond of her in his own way, and I suppose he wouldn't kill her either. I would very much like to know how you were able to access that memory, because I'm certain he didn't let it go willingly."

"He didn't," I said. "I figured out what he was doing with the house magic and turned it back on him—he sort of did it to himself. Maybe I can do that to your dad next time he tries to pick stuff out of my brain."

Zero opened his mouth but closed it again. At last, he said, "Before this moment, I would have advised against that. Now I'm not sure."

"Don't know how you lot lived without me," I said. "Isn't it fun when all the stuff you thought you knew might not be true?"

"No," he said, but his eyes lightened with laughter. "But at least I have the comfort of knowing that my father has that particular surprise ahead of him."

CHAPTER NINE

ATHELAS DIDN'T COME BACK INSIDE for the rest of the night. He sat on the back patio instead, drinking tea and gazing out at the backyard with one leg crossed as elegantly over the other as always. He didn't refuse me whenever I brought a fresh pot of tea out; he didn't speak to me either, though. Just before I went to bed, I wriggled in between the back of his chair and the wall and wrapped my arms around his shoulders for a few minutes.

Athelas allowed that, too; I felt the brief pat as one of his hands touched mine lightly.

He said, "Well done, Pet."

After that, I felt as though I might be able to sleep, so I gave him one last squeeze around the shoulders and went to bed.

The next morning it was as though nothing had ever happened—nothing with Athelas, at any rate. When I came downstairs to make tea and pancakes, I passed him as he sat in his chair, elegantly, eternally awake. He seemed peaceful and rather more cheerful than he had been the last week or so. Jin Yeong, on the other hand, was still prancier than usual: inclined to annoy Zero in a way that was as obnoxiously cheerful as his usual attempts were obnoxiously offensive.

I made pancakes, which pleased everyone except Zero, for whom they were really made. I didn't take offense at that because Jin Yeong was already doing a pretty good job at trying to rile Zero, and I didn't blame him for having other thoughts on his mind. At last, to get a bit of peace, I made a batch of blood pancakes, which seemed to delight Jin Yeong so much that he gave up trying to annoy Zero in order to enjoy them, and I was able to sit down without fear of a food fight starting in my clean kitchen.

"What are we gunna do after we clean up the sirens?" I asked Zero, plopping a few more pancakes on his plate. "You blokes said that stuff just keeps getting worse during the cycles—are we just gunna be trying to keep the streets clean? 'Cos that doesn't leave us much time to be getting ready for the Heirling Trials, and your dad isn't the only one circling the blood in the water."

"Only until the Heirling Trials begin," Athelas said. "Once they begin, human life will again be safe—or as safe as it was previously. Things may be a trifle different this time, however, as it's been rather longer than usual since our last king changed."

"How long, exactly?" I asked. There was a lot I didn't know about the politics of Behind—and more that I *did* know and just didn't understand. "All I know is that he killed the Heirlings the first cycle after he took control to make sure he could keep reigning."

"Five hundred years or so," Athelas said, settling back with his cup of tea. "Cycles are long by human standards in most cases, but they were never meant to be so long. The standard length is more in the region of two hundred years or thereabouts."

I stared at him, then at Zero. "Good grief, are you *that* old?"

"I am not," said Zero, his eyes lightening in amusement. "Neither is Athelas. I was born near the turn of the twentieth century, and he was born some thirty years before."

"Flaming *heck*," I said, very distinctly. "Wait until I tell Morgana. She's gunna *love* this. Older bloke, my eye!"

I caught them all looking at me and said hastily, "Never mind, it's not important. Does that include the twenty years that your dad kept you in stasis or whatever?"

"Those twenty years were in the nineteenth century, previous to my birth," said Zero, unmoved by my awe. "I thought you were aware that fae live longer than humans."

"Yeah, I just didn't know *how* much longer! You're older than a lot of Hobart!"

"I," said Jin Yeong primly, "am young."

"The heck you are. Younger, yeah. Young, no."

He just grinned and went back to his pancakes, but was interested enough to say a few moments later, "I will live longer."

"Yeah, but will you ever grow up? That's the real question."

"Perhaps I will, perhaps I will not," he said. "You will have to watch me and see."

"Flamin' fantastic," I said, but there was no edge to the words. "Hang on, then: who killed everyone before this murderer started, that's what I'd like to know. You know, after the king's first Heirling group murder but before you started chasing the murderer."

I was too full for more pancakes, but I dipped my finger idly in the maple syrup and licked it anyway, unwilling to get up and clean while there was still discussion to be had. Athelas, eyeing me in disfavour, said, "We have considered the question, Pet, I can assure you."

"It's just that if you two were born nearly four hundred years after the current king started reigning, and there have been unsuccessful cycles before now, it doesn't make sense for it to be anyone but the king doing it, right?"

"The current king came to the end of his natural reign some three hundred years after he began," said Athelas. "Longer than most, but not quite as long as some. I'm told that the cycle he pre-empted was in the early nineteenth century—the eighteen twenties, I believe."

"Was the next cycle after that when Zero was supposed to be born?"

"By the human calendar, it would have been roughly 1880," said Zero. "My mother was stolen around that time, but I rather fancy my father had underestimated how difficult it would be to join the Heirling cycle when the king already had enough power to see that the previous cycle didn't happen. He capitulated and aligned himself with the king. Hence the delay in my birth."

I squiggled my finger through the syrup again, fizzing with a sudden thought. "Is that when the king's Enforcers got all tangled up with your dad?"

I didn't miss the look that passed between Zero and Athelas, and it annoyed me.

To my surprise, Jin Yeong gave a rude sniff of laughter and said, "Even I knew as much, *Hyeong*. Are we stupid?"

"What he said," I said, pointing my syrupy finger at Jin Yeong. "It's obvious that your dad would try to get the Enforcers on his side from the inside if he was still trying to get someone from the Family as king. He'd need the info, and it'd mean allies next time a cycle came along."

"I'm not sure my father quite understood that killing other Heirlings would prevent the cycle from starting if he did it early enough. I rather think he thought if I was the only one left, it would still begin."

"So you reckon it was the king and then your dad, hiring someone out?"

"Let's just say that those are questions I've asked myself," Zero said. "At any rate, we need to catch the murderer first to find out."

"Heck," I said. "So you don't know, either."

"We know that the king was responsible for the first cycle that failed," Athelas said. "Whether he did it himself or commissioned the work is another matter, but we know it was at his behest. The others are less...settled."

"So by the time you were a kid, your mum was dead and your dad had his finger in every pie around Behind that had a bit of power."

"What a charming way you have of expressing things, my dear," said Athelas.

"I'm a naturally charming person," I said. "Oi, Zero: is that why your dad got you into the Enforcers? He wanted a bit more of a presence there?"

Zero turned a put-upon look on me, but it was mingled with amusement. "I never told you that my father put me in the Enforcers."

"You can't tell me he didn't pull strings—or that he wouldn't have tried," I said frankly. "Of course he would: what better way to show that you're the king's man and not planning on doing any funny business! Anyway, it's not like you're not always talking about him being the one behind the Enforcers trying to get you back; it's a flamin' easy conclusion to come to. Oi—reckon the king put your dad up to killing the Heirlings 'cos he knew better about what stops a cycle?"

"No matter how many possibilities you throw at us, we still don't know the answer," said Zero, with a touch of exasperation. "It's likely, but it's just as likely that my father did it himself in the hopes that it would leave me alone to challenge the king."

"But you quit being a cop instead and went rogue with your human friend who didn't like other humans being hurt," I said, nodding. "That must have been pretty annoying for him."

"If the results are anything to judge by, one presumes so," murmured Athelas.

I narrowed my eyes at him. "Where were you while all of this was going on, then?"

"Reporting to my lord's father, of course," Athelas said. "Very, *very* carefully."

Zero's blue eyes flicked over at him and then away again. "I thought you were very carefully keeping away?"

"That too," said Athelas, with a faint smile. "I didn't want to learn too much, after all! You know how your father likes to know all the details."

Zero nodded silently and went back to his pancakes. Someone who didn't know him might have thought that he was merely unwilling to talk, but I recognised it for what it was with a touch of sadness. Zero was grateful, but he didn't want to say so.

"You lot know you can say *thank you*, right?" I said, staring around at them all. "And that it's okay to admit that you need each other every now and then?"

"It's not all right," said Zero, while Athelas said mildly, "I believe I must disagree, Pet."

Jin Yeong threw me a melting look and said, "I need you."

"That was *not* what I meant!" I said, flustered. "All right, if we're going to be cleaning up messes for a while before the Heirling Trials begin, shouldn't we be getting this lot done as soon as possible? Why are we waiting?"

"We're waiting on the merman," said Zero, pushing away his empty plate. "And once we have what we need from him, I'll need some time to prepare for the humans' inclusion."

"One needs to make allowances for the humans in one's group," Athelas said, smiling gently at me. "Does not one? It shouldn't be rushed."

I snuffled a laugh and said, "Fine. What should I be doing today, then? Dinner's already in the crockpot, and all that's left is the dishes."

Zero threw a look in Jin Yeong's direction as he rose and said to me, "Come with me, Pet. I think Athelas could do with a bit of a rest today and Jin Yeong needs to readjust his attitude."

Jin Yeong's brows went up, but he looked more amused than anything.

Athelas said mildly, "I do assure you that I'm quite capable of functioning at a normal level, my lord," but he seemed pretty happy to sit there with his teapot. It could have been just a twinge of guilt that made me think so, but he seemed tireder and greyer now, after breakfast. I put out biscuits for him as well, which he

BETWEEN DECISIONS • 165

accepted with a faint, almost mocking smile, and I found myself agreeing with Zero that he needed rest.

When we left the house, I said to Zero, "You reckon he's going to be all right?"

"Of course he'll be all right," Zero said. "Athelas has suffered a great deal worse than anything you could inflict upon him."

"I know," I said quietly. "But he's already had someone messing with his mind—I didn't mean to do the same thing to him."

"I think you'll find that Athelas is quite proud of you."

"Yeah?" He had said *well done* to me, but I still remembered the dreadful understanding in his eyes as I sank into his memories, and I wasn't sure if I could forgive myself for having become a person like Zero's father to him, even for a moment. "Oi, where are we going?"

"Café," said Zero briefly. "The merman has another meeting today, so we've agreed to meet along Elizabeth Street at the Mago Café."

"Nice," I said, very pleased. That might give me a few minutes to go and check on the Librarian while Zero was close enough to help and not too close to stop me doing what I wanted to do. A sort of unimpressed safety net that would scold me if I got too stupid.

Marazul was already at a table when we got to the café, his wheelchair taking up one side of the small wooden table and leaving the fixed seat for Zero and me. I let Zero sit down first because I wasn't planning to stay long anyway, and maybe Marazul took that as a bad sign, because there was disappointment in the hazel eyes that had looked up at me with a cautious sort of hope a moment before.

I leaned against the table next to his, nodding at him in a friendly sort of a way, and Marazul seemed to let out a breath.

"Pet. It's good to see you. Hunting many goblins these days?"

I couldn't help grinning, which put a glow into his eyes that would once have set my heart fluttering. I said, "Nope."

"Have they got you a new computer yet? I've got something that might be useful for you."

Zero's eyes flicked over the messenger bag that was on the table beside Marazul, the flap very slightly askew.

"Is that what you brought? You didn't need to; I only asked for the program for our phones."

"No," said Marazul, readjusting the flap of the bag so that nothing could be seen. "It's just something I agreed to do for another hacker. We've been working on it for a while and I didn't want to trust it to a delivery person. I took the main bulk of it to the location yesterday, and I'll take the rest today."

He looked a bit shifty to me, but maybe I was just a bit suspicious when it came to him these days.

Zero didn't seem to take it in any sort of way—except maybe as none of his business. He only asked, "Did you get the program finished?"

"Done and dusted," said Marazul. "I hope you've been working on something to bind it to, though: I wouldn't try to attach it to the phones themselves. The program will have an effective range of a metre in each direction, so you'll need to keep your phones on your person—and the benefit is that someone else's phone won't be able to be used against anyone wearing the program if they're within a metre of the wearer."

"You'll have to show me how to attach it—and I'll need to know what material will best suit it. I prepared plastic at home, but this...I don't know what this is, and if I have to work with it—"

"That's the electronic signal," said Marazul. "Don't try to touch that. Just work with the magic in it; leave everything else alone. As for materials, something plastic will be suitable to—"

Before they could get too deep into discussions that I was

pretty sure I wouldn't understand, I said hastily, "I'll go for a bit of a walk, all right? Got something I want to check on."

Zero flicked a look at me, but to my gratification, he only asked, "Where?"

"It's all right, I won't go far," I promised. I just wanted to see if the alley was still there—or at least, the Between version of it. I wanted to know if the Librarian was still there in his library, looking down at the streets every so often to turn up his nose at the ugliness of them. "Not even down to the end of the block. I want to check on something on this side of the road."

To my surprise, Zero didn't argue; he simply nodded and said, "If you're not back in half an hour, I'll come for you."

That felt good, and I was very nearly as prancy as Jin Yeong by the time I had walked the half block to get to the alleyway entrance. It didn't stop me being as cautious as I should be, though: once I got there, I hovered around the entrance for a few minutes before taking a tentative step in.

To my surprise, my foot fell onto brick without a problem, and the next two steps were easy, too.

"Flamin' heck," I said beneath my breath. I hadn't actually expected to be able to get back in: I hadn't expected him to leave it open. Had he, like the other fae I knew, completely underestimated humans to the point that he hadn't expected me to come back, or had he simply thought that I was under the thumb enough—or just not stupid enough—to try and get back in?

Well, if so, the joke was on him, because I was *definitely* stupid enough to come back in.

I edged myself in carefully, for all that. I didn't want to be stuck in here, and I didn't want the Librarian to find me poking around if he hadn't expected me to come back. On the other hand, if he hadn't expected me to come back, he should have made sure I couldn't get back in: that was a good defence, at least.

I wandered past the tables and set my foot on the first step of the corrugated iron staircase. There was a clear line of sight to my right that showed the way I'd come; another directly behind me that showed the way I'd left the alley the first time. I could see the street through each, and that was a bit of a comfort, even if it was a dangerous sort of comfort to rely on.

It wasn't until I was on the first landing that I found myself wondering, what if it *had* occurred to him that I would come back in? What if he had let me in on purpose?

"Flamin' fae," I muttered. "Always so flamin' tricky."

I took another step despite that, and then another. If he'd meant me to be in here, I would have seen him by now: seen him or felt him, whichever was the more important one. I wanted to see the library again. More than that, I wanted specifically to see the windows again. The Librarian hadn't seemed to think that I'd be able to see anything but the human world through them, but the roc I'd seen hadn't come from any strictly human part of the world, and I was pretty sure it was too big to be skulking around Between. I was also pretty sure that the landscape I'd seen was nowhere in my own world.

If that was the case, there were a few places I wanted to see— or at least a few things I wanted to test if the windows would let me see.

I was still pretty careful about entering the place, though; I stopped short at the uppermost landing, too, just before it turned to wooden floorboards. I couldn't feel anything or anyone, and I definitely couldn't see anyone, but it was still hard to step over the threshold. Maybe it was the very real danger of poking my nose in where I technically hadn't been invited. Maybe it was just the difference between the cold steel beneath my feet and the warmer wooden boards that felt as though they could almost be living. Either way, I didn't intend to stay longer than I had to, and I would be running for my life at the first sign of trouble.

I took that final step over the threshold, and it was easier after that. I still kept a good eye on the library around me, but I didn't feel as crawly with dread as I had, which made me suspect that there was a prohibition sort of spell on the entrance that I'd managed to overcome.

"Tricky," I murmured, and stopped by the nearest window—the one through which I'd seen the underwater landscape. I couldn't help shooting another look around the room as I did so: it remained empty and silent, and even my scraped nerves couldn't sense the smallest disturbance to the essence of Between around me.

I wondered momentarily what this building looked like when it wasn't half Between, but that thought seemed likely to make it hard for me to keep seeing things in the way I needed to see them, so I pushed it away and concentrated on the window instead.

The Librarian had advised me to think about something I wanted to see, since the windows would most likely show it to me.

I thought about Ralph's house first—just a fleeting idea that passed through my mind before the actual place I wanted to see—and for a moment I was shocked to actually see the second-floor sitting room from where I had once caught a brief glimpse of the world Behind. Did that mean I was now looking in through the window I had once looked out of? Maybe. Probably.

It occurred to me a moment later that it probably wasn't safe for Ralph if I dwelt too long on his house: if the windows had anything like a search history in a computer, it wouldn't be too safe for me, either. I hesitated a moment longer, but my past experience with behindkind in general and fae in particular suggested that it was extremely unlikely that any such thing yet existed. Of course, it was probably something that Marazul or Blackpoint would want to create, if they heard the idea. Both of them were very good at using magic and technology in conjunction, but the two of them were anomalous enough from other behindkind to cause me to worry less.

I took in a quick, sharp breath and let it out again. Then I let the thought that it would be nice to know what Zero's dad was up to, and where he was, float to the top of my mind. I didn't know where that was, so I just focused on the idea of Zero's dad in my mind, and that must have been just as good as knowing where I wanted to see, because although the window grew cloudy for a few moments, it cleared soon afterward.

At first, it was hard to tell what I was looking at. There was so much colour and movement that it was hard to believe I wasn't looking at a Van Gogh; a moment or two later, it was obvious that I was seeing a dance where ladies in bright, gaudy ensembles danced with men in even more gaudy outfits. Despite the general melee, it was pretty easy to spot Zero's dad—mostly because he'd grown a canopy of flowers and moss around and over him. He was indoors, too, so it was pretty rude of him; the grass even extended into the dancefloor.

No one seemed to find it too rude of him, though. Most of the other attendees avoided him entirely, and the ones that did approach him all looked as though they were equally powerful.

Was this Zero's childhood home? I wondered. Or was Zero's dad attending a party somewhere else in the world Behind? The fact that he was comfortable enough to be growing flowers and grass that intruded on other guests' space made me think that he was in his own home. I'd have to ask Zero if his childhood home had a huge golden ballroom with stars for a ceiling and ice for the floor—once I'd actually told him how and why I knew about it, that is.

I would have liked to have been closer to the fae. It wasn't easy to see him from where I was, and I felt I might have been able to lip-read enough to know what he was saying if I were only a little closer, despite the lack of sound.

Did that mean this was the closest window available? I didn't think so, because I could see others that looked much closer. It was more likely that this was the only one that didn't have protection spells on it.

I shivered, realising that I'd have to make sure Zero had

similar spells on the windows of our house. It wasn't that I thought the Librarian was necessarily evil, it was just that I didn't trust him or his house not to spy on us if needed.

I didn't trust someone else with the same kind of setup not to do it, if it came to that. I already knew that behindkind had the same kind of surveillance capabilities as humans did: they just did it by magic instead of technology. Bugs that were really bugs, for example, and long-distance critters that looked like bats with long range hearing. I'd met one of those a little while ago.

I couldn't help grinning. I'd almost forgotten about Big Ears: I'd found and set him free from a human who had had access to Behind and who had been murdered by—we assumed—Upper Management. He'd given me the equivalent of a wish—call on him once, and he would help me. I wasn't sure how helpful he could be for anything other than intel; didn't even know if he would make good on his promise. Still, it was a nice thought. Maybe I'd try to call on him one of these days, just to see if he'd actually turn up. Add him to these windows and you'd probably have a really good surveillance system.

Hm. Should I call him now? Was now better than never, or would there be another time that he would be more useful to me? This was the sort of thinking Athelas excelled at; I wasn't sure that I had his talent for it, and I dithered for a little while.

What would Athelas think about this setup, anyway? "Very useful, I'm sure," he would probably murmur. Which reminded me that I was here in the library specifically because it had occurred to me that the windows were likely to be useful to me.

"All right," I murmured. "Show me the king."

The window flickered a bit, then blanked into being just a window with shutters behind it. Reflected, I could see myself and the library behind me; it was a soft reflection, but the worry in my face was clear to see, and so were the books.

Well. That was flamin' portentous.

I shivered and said to the window, "You got it wrong, mate.

I'm not the king. Got no intention of being the king, either. Show me the king."

The window did another bit of a glitchy fit, but instead of changing and showing me something else, it became more reflective and mirror-like, the shutters on the other side of the glass vanishing and my reflection growing certain.

I dunno. Maybe it had always been a mirror and had only been pretending to be a window for a while.

"If you're gunna be creepy, just go back to what you were doing," I told it in disgust. "I don't want to be playing silly beggars with a piece of glass."

I left it at that because I had already been gone a good twenty minutes, and Zero aside, I didn't particularly want the Librarian to come back in here and catch me looking through his windows —if they really were his windows and not the windows of some shadowy master. It was a shame that I hadn't been able to do what I came here to do, but I'd been able to get into the place, and that was already further than I'd expected to get when I arrived.

I went softly down the stairs and back into the courtyard, passing humans who sat at the tables there, not quite in the same plane of reality as me. It wasn't that they looked faded or fuzzy or anything like that; they were just...not quite interacting with all that there was to interact with here. I had to stop myself from reaching out to see if I could spill someone's tea here, and if that would make me visible to them, because I was pretty sure none of them saw me.

I felt a bit more visible when I got back to Elizabeth Street, but that was mostly because a Pomeranian tried to bite me as I passed the table he was sitting at. His owner glared at me, too, so I was definitely back in the human world. I hurried past them both and into the Mago Café again, glad to easily catch sight of Zero's bulk across the room. The Librarian's windows being able to see people as well as places had left me feeling oddly *watched*, as if now that I was gone, someone else could very well be there, watching me. Hopefully, the Librarian used his windows for good.

Actually, hopefully he didn't know that they could see people and not just places. That didn't seem likely, but a human could hope, couldn't they? Sometimes hope is all you have to keep you going.

Marazul smiled at me as I approached the table, but it looked like he was already getting ready to go. Both he and Zero had an empty mug in front of them, but the takeaway cup next to them had me fooled for a few moments before Zero pushed it toward me without a word and I caught a whiff of coffee. I took it happily; for a few moments, I'd thought they were doing some shorthand version of the behindkind contract they'd enacted the first time they agreed to work together without me in between them.

Nope. Zero had just remembered to get me a coffee, too. That was nice.

"It's time to go," he said, while I was still enjoying the scent of the coffee. "We've got a lot to prepare for before tomorrow."

Oh well. There was time to drink it on the way home. I was still gunna savour it.

CHAPTER TEN

JINYEONG and I ended up needing to visit Abigail and the humans the next day. It would have been nice to be able to text or call them, but whatever Zero had done to our phones with Marazul's program had limited the signal to a very specific area, and a very specific group of users.

That very specific group was the four of us—or at least for now.

"The merman says that once the humans are set up as well, we'll be able to connect to the same network, but it won't necessarily be the human network," Zero said.

"Pretty sure he said it's human network *plus*," I corrected him. "It's still ours, it'll just have a bit of Between to it. That's how 'Zul works."

"Dear me!" said Athelas. "It would seem that you've become comfortable with the merman again, Pet!"

"It'd be a bit unfortunate if I couldn't be," I pointed out. "You want me to be going 'round ignoring people we need to work with?"

JinYeong looked as though he would have liked to have said yes, but managed to restrain himself. Zero smiled very slightly and said, "I believe he said something like that. The sirens shouldn't be able to interfere; nor should anyone else, human or behindkind."

"He's made us a private network," I said, nodding. "That's gunna make it hard to let Abigail know where and when to meet us tonight. Shouldn't we have done that before we linked our phones up to the network?"

Athelas and Zero exchanged a look and had the grace to look exasperated with themselves.

"No worries," I said. "I could do with a walk. It's probably better if we don't do too much over the phone at the moment, anyway. If you're done with those little gadgets, I'll take 'em round. I'll let Abigail know where we're supposed to meet, too—though I s'pose we're safe to contact her after they join up to the network."

"I shall come too," said Jin Yeong at once, turning a bland look on Zero when Zero narrowed his eyes at him.

"Tell them we'll meet them at eleven tonight," Zero said, looking away. "Somewhere away from the waterfront to start with —make it the park at the top of Salamanca Place."

"St. David's? All right."

"We'll split them into three groups after that: one with Athelas at Brooke Street Pier, one with me starting from the opal shop, and another to go with you and Jin Yeong and start at the ship, since you're apparently inseparable these days."

"Perhaps you could be good enough to ask the humans to contact the detective while you're about it?" suggested Athelas, while I was still trying to protest the *inseparable* comment. "Thus saving my lord or myself a journey from the house?"

"Why not?" I said sourly. "Wouldn't want to work you two too hard when you're so flamin' old."

Zero's gaze lifted to the ceiling for a noticeable amount of time. I thought I heard him murmur, "I knew that would backfire."

Still, he didn't try to stop JinYeong coming with me to the humans' headquarters, which I suppose was nice. He did give me a pretty close look as I went past, though; I couldn't decide if it was a *make sure you behave yourself* aimed at me or a *make sure he behaves himself*.

I said, "Yes, Dad," at him by way of a parting shot, anyway, and I'm pretty sure he laughed, even though he tried hard to hide it. If he didn't know by now that I was keeping JinYeong at arm's length, he ought to. I'd already told him that I'd rejected JinYeong, and it wasn't as though we were going to be doing anything but business while we were out.

That business took a little less time than I'd expected, too, because the humans were a shifting mess when we got there. There was also a fair bit more Between to the place than I was used to when JinYeong and I headed for the usual back office, skirting the most affected areas as best we could. The sunshine had been bright outside, and it was hard to see as we moved along the hallway; even JinYeong moved a bit more slowly than usual, though I wasn't sure if that was because he was wary of the bits of Between fluttering in the hall.

At the doorway to the office, I squinted and tried to clear the glitter from my eyes, unwilling to step into a darkened room even if it was a room belonging to my allies.

To the movement within the room, I said, "Oi, are you in there, Abigail?"

"Don't step on that!" said a sharp voice, and Abigail emerged from the darkness, her red hair a beacon.

Fortunately, my eyes were beginning to clear by then, and I could see what she was talking about. Ignoring the Between that wanted to be seen, I gazed around at the writhing mess of cables and furniture, catching myself in the doorway. JinYeong gave the lot of it one look, raising a brow, and propped himself against the doorframe.

"Good grief!" I said. "You really weren't kidding when you said you were updating! Reckon I'll stay out here."

"That's probably best," Abigail said, with a touch of gratefulness. She turned a glare on someone in the depths of the room and added, "We've already had someone trip on the wires *four times* this morning, and if anyone else does it, I'm going to start removing appendages that aren't useful again."

I didn't see who she was glaring at, but I wouldn't have liked to have been the one on the receiving end of that glare.

Someone in the room—probably Ezri—said more quietly, "Yeah, and if you think she's talking about the cables, you're wrong. She's talking about your—"

"What's up, Pet?" asked Abigail, turning back to us. "You lot lose your phones?"

"Not exactly," I said. "Made a few gadgets that might help with the job tonight, but we've got a bit of a temporary situation where we can't call or text anyone except ourselves, so we came in person."

A touch of amusement lit her eyes. "On purpose, I suppose? I assume it's got something to do with the sirens?"

"Our mate worked us up a private network and signal jammer sorta combo for our phones," I told her. "Yours, too. Apparently they'll work just fine if you pin them to your clothes; reckon I'd put 'em somewhere a bit safer than that, though."

She hesitated, and I could see the old distrust still working behind her eyes.

"The mate that made this stuff isn't fae," I told her. "If that helps. Zero had to attach it to stuff to make sure it's wearable, but the magicky, techy stuff wasn't fae-made."

"I'm gunna use it anyway," said Ezri. I couldn't see her, but I could see one of her boots over the top of a couch further in the room. It waggled a bit as she talked—probably because she enjoyed being contrarian to the rest of the group. "I'm not looking to die tonight."

"That makes a difference," Abigail said reluctantly. "Are you vouching for them, Pet?"

"Yep," I said, without hesitating. That was one thing I was sure of: Zero and Athelas wouldn't let the humans die if they could help it. Not when they were actually our allies now. They definitely wouldn't do anything to hurt the humans' chances of living.

"And all we have to do is have the gadgets on our person? Pocket, phone, anything like that?"

"So long as it's not somewhere easy to grab," I agreed, pinching the plastic baggie of plastic badges that Jin Yeong pushed at me and slinging it into Abigail's waiting hand. "They've got a little pin on the back to keep 'em on, and it's pretty heavy-duty."

"In case the sirens get the idea that they're what's making it hard to get to us? Makes sense. We'll have our own kit as well."

"Makes sense," I said, echoing her. "The more the merrier. Oi: reckon you can let Tuatu know what's going on before you take those outta the bag? We can't call him, either. There's an extra one for him in there."

I saw the gleam that returned to her eyes, and guessed that she had just realised she would be able to bring up the favour they wanted him to do for them. I let her think about that without calling her out, even if I might have been grinning a bit.

I said, "Anyway, we're on for tonight at eleven. Zero says we'll split into groups of three: I reckon he's hoping to—"

"Surround them," she said, nodding. "It sounds like we'll be drawing in the boundary. What about drunks?"

"Hopefully, they'll all stay in Salamanca Square," I said bluntly. "The waterfront is still going to be cordoned off, and I'm pretty sure someone has made it hard for people to get through."

"Drunks aren't exactly normal people," Abigail said, unconvinced. "All right, that sounds good. See you then."

"Right, we'll leave you lot to it," I said, taking the dismissal with another grin. To the group of humans I could vaguely see in the sprawl of technical equipment, I advised, "Don't lose anything you're gunna need later."

That was met with good-natured jeering from the office, which we left behind pretty quickly. When we got outside, Jin Yeong said, "They are doing something."

I looked up at him in surprise. "You reckon? There was more Between around the place than there usually is, anyway. What do you reckon they're up to?"

"I do not know," he said moodily. "But something is different. Perhaps they are doing a dangerous thing they do not wish us to know about."

"Yeah, probably," I said, slightly cheered. It wasn't like the four of us weren't doing dangerous things that Abigail didn't know about. "At least they have a bit of magic to help out—and once we're done with the sirens, they'll have a bit more. Zero'll let 'em keep the badges, won't he?"

Jin Yeong shrugged but said, "We would have no use for it. Unless *Hyeong* does not wish for this sort of thing to be with the humans, why would he ask for it back?"

"Yeah," I said, but I wasn't quite content, so I just kept walking.

I didn't mean to take the long way around to get home, but somehow I found myself heading more toward the city centre than our house. Jin Yeong must have noticed, but he didn't say anything, and it wasn't until we were nearly at the mall that I realised where I was going.

"Flamin' heck," I said, stopping in front of the pizza shop on the corner. "Oh well, since we're here, we might as well get something to eat. You want pizza or bao buns?"

Jin Yeong's left brow winged up. "You will buy me food?"

"Nope; you're gunna buy me food. I was just giving you the chance to pick what you wanted to eat."

"I am *very confused*," Jin Yeong said.

"I haven't got any money," I pointed out. "Spent it all on groceries."

"That is not my meaning."

"And it's still not a date!"

"Ah. Then I will buy you food," he said, and pulled me into the bao bun shop.

"Zero and Athelas, too," I added, just for good measure. "It's gunna be pricey."

He just threw a look at me over his shoulder that suggested he knew I was trying to annoy him, so I settled against the wall to wait for our order, happy to be so well understood.

We took the long way home, too—back along Barrack Street to turn onto Bathurst—but this time it was deliberate. I wanted another look at the Librarian's alley. Actually, I wanted another look at his windows, but I didn't dare to actually try and go in there again. Twice was risky but understandable; three times was downright stupid.

Still, I couldn't help lingering as we passed, enjoying the smell of fresh greenery floating out onto the dusty street. Something clicked in my mind, and a memory floated in along with the scent. I had been here before—not this week, not this year, but years ago. Years ago, when I had found odd, Betweeny, delightful, dangerous things nearly every day and had made myself forget them as soon as they were out of sight.

I breathed in the scent and memory both and felt the tingle of delighted surprise that always came with discoveries of Between when I was a kid. I'd stopped here once on the way back from a trip to the lolly shop further up the road; I was supposed to meet Mum in Elizabeth Mall when I was done, but the refreshing smell of growing green things and the flaring of Between around the alley edges had caught me, body and soul. I had curled my fingers around the hard-edged covers of the book I'd brought along to entertain myself with while Mum had her meeting, and stepped toward the alley instinctively. I don't know how long I stood there, gazing into the alley where I could see two realities sitting on top of each other. I might even have gone in and out very quickly, but if I did, I didn't remember it. Not properly. I remembered tiny moments of sitting at a sunny table in a courtyard far away from road noise and drinking sarsaparilla cordial and smiling up at someone's face while I read aloud to them, their face lost in a sunburst. Then, in the memory, I was outside again, smelling the same scent of greenery but warmed by the sun instead of cooled by the breeze, my fingers still tight around my book.

Someone had grabbed me by the arm and I had wrenched myself free, shoving them away. A smelly, dirty body went stumbling backwards, and I followed them, apologies tumbling out. It was the old mad bloke: perhaps drunk, perhaps just always loopy.

He bristled his beard at me as he found his feet again. "No," he said, wagging a finger. "Bad human. This is a behindkind place, I can smell it. Always trust your nose!"

I wrinkled my own nose a bit, because it was pretty rich for him to be telling people to trust their noses when he stank to high heaven, but all I had said was, "You hungry today?" and that had made him grin at me.

"*Hajima*," Jin Yeong said, pulling at my sleeve and drawing me back to the present. "That is not a good place to be."

"I know," I told him, allowing myself to be pulled away. "Just wanted to see if it was still open for people like me to wander into. You reckon they would have fixed it after this long."

The look he threw over his shoulder was amused. "There are no other people like you."

"What about the old mad bloke?"

Jin Yeong opened his mouth, then shut it again. After a moment or two, he said, "He is a little bit like you."

"And what about Sarah?" Sarah was the North Wind's protégé —or family. At any rate, she was a kid who had been Behind and escaped again, thanks to North's help. Sarah also tended to be able to do a lot of the same things that I could do.

"She is also a little bit similar—do not make a list at me! I will not listen."

I cheerfully irritated him all the way home, just to warn him what life would be like if we really were dating, with time off in between to pinch bao buns out of the bag and eat them. Jin Yeong had been resilient to my glares; likewise resilient to my outright declaration that I wasn't going to date him. The one thing I could think of that might be effective was to start annoying him as much as I'd done when we first got to know each other and hope that would be more effective. Jin Yeong in love with me was far too soft and inclined to be injured—physically and emotionally— and I still had the dark remembrance of him nearly dying twice to help me. There was no way I was going to let that happen again.

Jin Yeong was far more cheerful by the time we got home, despite my efforts; he sauntered into the house without opening the door and tossed the bags of bao bun onto the coffee table in front of Zero.

Zero stared at me and then Jin Yeong. "What's this?"

"Got distracted," I explained. "So we brought back bao buns. Yours are the ten in that bag; Athelas' are here with ours because none of the rest of us eat ten bao buns at a time."

"Athelas isn't here," Zero said, his eyes growing lighter in amusement. "And if we're going to be carping about portion sizes, I'm roughly four times your size—you should only be eating two and a half bao buns, and I can see three there. Not to mention the one you probably ate on the way home."

"I'm having a late growth spurt," I said, narrowing my eyes at the grinning Jin Yeong, who knew that I had, in fact, eaten two of the bao buns on our way home. "Oi, where's Athelas, then?"

"He decided he'd go to see the detective, after all."

I wondered, my suspicions rising, if Athelas had gone to get Detective Tuatu to do more for him. I couldn't help wondering if it would have anything to do with the records and documents he had gotten Tuatu to gather for him, too.

"I'm still worried about Athelas," I said, sitting down and reaching for my own food. "How come he's nicking off right now? You can't tell me he didn't trust the humans to send a message to Tuatu—I mean you can, and he probably doesn't, but I wouldn't have thought that would get him out of the house."

Jin Yeong shot me a considering look as he sat down beside me, but Zero only said, with a touch of exasperation, "Pet, if you're going to start suspecting Athelas of—"

"I didn't say I *suspected* him of anything, I'm trying to say that I'm worried about him!" I said indignantly. "You know—his state of mind. He's been mopey for the last couple of weeks. I don't reckon he's healing properly."

"You are worried in a friendly way," said Jin Yeong, nodding. He delicately unwrapped one of his bao buns. "You should not do that."

"Yeah? Well, maybe you blokes should all stop warning me about getting too fond of the others."

I didn't miss the molten look that Jin Yeong turned on Zero, or the cold one Zero shot back.

"It's mostly Athelas warning me about you two," I informed them. "Well, and himself. And *don't* go ruining his best tea again, Jin Yeong, or I'll put something nasty in your kimchi."

Jin Yeong closed the mouth he had opened with a very distinct *click* of teeth.

"Athelas," said Zero pointedly, "is not wrong."

"You shouldn't pat me on the head, then," I pointed out. "Isn't that against the rules or something?"

"I was told that one should pat a pet on the head," Zero said, his eyes light and bright. "I'm within the rules."

"Put something in his pancakes," said Jin Yeong provocatively.

"Heck no!" I said. "I've gotta stand behind him until the Heirling Trials are over. I'll put something nasty in his pancakes then, when we're all still alive to annoy each other."

JinYeong bared his teeth and grabbed another bao bun with a distinctly irritated lunge.

"What are you gunna do afterward?" I asked Zero, ignoring JinYeong's mutterings. I was supposed to be annoying him, not encouraging him, after all. "When the Heirling Trials are over and you're either on the throne or not?"

"I won't be on the throne," Zero said bluntly. "I might not even be alive. I'll think about it when the time comes; until then, I'll try to stay alive."

"I shall open a shop," said JinYeong darkly.

"Not if you're gunna lure in humans to eat," I told him.

JinYeong looked at me provocatively over his bao bun. "You will have to stop me, then. Come every day to my shop and we will—"

"Hang on, what kind of shop?" I demanded. "You've never said you wanted to open a shop before."

"You did not ask. I shall sell clothes."

"I didn't ask because we've been too busy trying not to die, and—"

"Everyone will buy my clothes," he said. "And for that little old lady there will be a place to knit."

I stared at him. "What, for Vesper? Weren't you just saying before that—"

"Are the humans prepared?" interrupted Zero.

I don't know if he was just trying to remind us not to count our chickens before they were hatched—or out of the slaughterhouse—or if he really did want to clarify things.

"About as much as they can be," I said. "They took the stuff, but it's a good thing I could tell 'em the badges they're going to be wearing aren't fae workmanship."

JinYeong wiped his fingers and shot me a mocking look. "What will they think when they know about behindkind?"

"Don't know," I said frankly. "And I hope I don't have to find out, either. But they don't hate behindkind right now—just fae. So technically—"

"It's hard to keep people safe when they don't like the way you do it, isn't it?" said Zero, entirely emotionlessly.

"Rude!" I said wrathfully. "I'm not lying to them, I'm just not telling them all of the truth! And they've still got a choice about whether or not they use the stuff; I'm not forcing 'em to take it."

Zero's eyes lightened just enough to let me know that he'd been laughing at me all along.

"Fine time for you to be growing a sense of humour *now*," I said sourly. "You could at least have admitted that your way of keeping people safe and mine are poles apart when it comes to things like consent and personal wishes and—"

"I admit it, I admit it!" he said hastily, holding up his hands. "I'll also admit to doing things that I regret—*occasionally*—and that have sometimes not been the wisest in hindsight. In my own defence, however, you're an infuriatingly difficult pet to look after."

"Look at you, being all soft and approachable!" I said in wonder.

Zero looked away. "I am neither soft nor approachable, and I object to—"

"Better not get too soft," I said mischievously. "Athelas is just about to walk through the door, and he wouldn't approve!"

That got the both of them looking at the door just in time for Athelas to walk through it and for me to pinch Zero's last remaining bao bun.

"Good heavens!" said Athelas mildly, in the face of that scrutiny. "It would seem as though you have been waiting on my arrival. Might one presume that the morning went well?"

His eyes dwelled momentarily on the bao buns, then rose enquiringly to me.

"Oi!" I objected. "What are you blaming me for? I saved you some!"

"Thank you I'm sure," he said wonderingly.

"Anyway," I said hastily, "we weren't staring at the door and waiting for you, we were just talking about what we're going to do after the Heirling Trials are done."

"We were not," Zero said, beneath his breath.

"What are you gunna do afterward?" I asked Athelas.

Athelas stared at me. "Dear heavens, what a question to ask!" he said, and wandered into the kitchen. I heard the jug boiling a moment later or I would have got up and made him some tea. When he came down into the living room a few minutes later, I repeated the question, but he'd gone cold and irritated by then, so he must have had an annoying time with the detective.

At any rate, he crossed one leg over the other and said in a chilly sort of voice, "I have a feeling that I shall be otherwise occupied. Far too busy to be running after a little pet."

"You do not *have* to run after her; I shall run after her," Jin Yeong said coldly.

"No one's gunna run after anyone," I said, sorry I had forced Athelas to answer the question when he obviously didn't want to. I had an idea that he and Zero still had to have a conversation with Zero's dad about who owned Athelas, and how free Athelas was. I s'pose that would make anyone's tea taste a bit sour. "That's the whole point of getting past the Heirling Trials—no people chasing us, no people trying to kill us. I flamin' refuse to have people chasing me when everything's over."

"You may run after me instead," said Jin Yeong graciously. He sent a small, slow smile in my direction and leaned forward very slightly. "I will run slowly."

Zero threw an empty mug at him, swift and hard, but Jin Yeong, his eyes alight with laughter, was swifter again. He tumbled over the back of our couch and landed lightly, then leaned against the back of it behind me, arms folded across the top and his chin just grazing the top of my head.

"I will not," he said maliciously, "make myself slow for you, *Hyeong*. You will have to try harder than that."

Athelas looked down into his teacup and sighed, but I'd already seen the glow of laughter in his eyes. "Perhaps we could refrain from rehashing old history," was all he said as he went back to his tea.

"I'm attempting to do so," Zero said grimly. "Jin Yeong doesn't seem inclined to assist me in that endeavour."

"Maybe if you talked properly instead of riddling, he'd understand what you're talking about," I said bluntly. "Because I sure as heck don't."

"I understand nothing," Jin Yeong said, but there was a careful innocence to his voice that I didn't even slightly understand. "You should be more clear, *Hyeong*."

"If I were any clearer, you would be passing through several walls right now," said Zero. "However, since the pet insists that she doesn't care for that kind of clarity, I'll refrain."

I felt a glow of warmth. It was the first time I could recall him taking my wishes or preferences as any kind of guide. "I'll make you pancakes again tomorrow," I said.

Zero laughed quietly, surprising me, and said, "Wait until we see what tomorrow brings."

"Make me kimchi fried rice tomorrow," Jin Yeong said at once, his fingers gently plucking at the back of my hoodie as though remembering that he wasn't supposed to be getting so close to me but unable to stop himself in time. "Tonight will be tiresome."

"It cannot possibly be more tiresome than a vampire in love," said Athelas, and the gleam in his eye said that it was more of a barb at me than Jin Yeong.

"No shortbreads for you, then," I told him, and retreated into the kitchen to make coffee and cool my cheeks.

CHAPTER ELEVEN

I₸ wasn't cold outside, but I still felt a bit shivery as we waited for Abigail and her lot to meet us at the park. Maybe I hadn't been in enough situations like this to get used to them. Heck, maybe I'd been in too many. Either way, I couldn't help the heel of my left foot bouncing just a little as the humans finally arrived and filtered through the gate, light and shadow rippling over them as they moved along the bitumen path and into the park.

I grinned at Detective Tuatu, who was with them, and saw the deep blackness of shadow just behind him that had a dark blue sheen to it.

"G'day North," I said, nodding. Well, this was promising: the only thing better than having my three psychos to face up to sirens was having North along for the ride as well. If the literal North Wind couldn't give us the upper hand, it was hard to know what would. I didn't see her being beguiled away by any siren, no matter how winsome.

"Pet," said North, by way of greeting.

Zero gave the smallest of bows in her direction, and North returned it.

"Look at that," I said cheerfully. "Everyone getting along! Isn't that nice?"

"It's suspicious, is what it is," Tuatu muttered, receiving North's reproachful look with an unconvinced one. "You don't have to babysit me, North!"

"Sirens," said North, as though they had already had this conversation many times, "are beautifully persuasive. I want to make sure they don't lay a scaley finger on you."

Athelas, who had been quiet the entire afternoon since he got back from visiting the detective, said, "Protecting what's yours, in fact?" with a gleam of real amusement to his grey eyes.

"Let's begin," Zero said, with a touch of impatience. "Abigail; detective?"

"Here," they said. Tuatu added, "The men who were guarding the waterfront will meet me down there. I'll let them know what they need to know."

"There's not much to know," said Zero briefly. "We'll split into groups of three and approach from different directions. Keep your earplugs in and your badges on you at all times. Use your camera apps only when necessary and try not to touch your phone unless you're messaging someone in one of the other groups. The badges should stop you being compelled to take your earplugs out from any electrical impulse, but if you take them out while the siren is nearby, their auditory power will still work on you. You'll —yes?"

"We had an idea," said Abigail, who had cleared her throat very loudly. "You said that sirens have a sort of boundary they can't go past, equidistant from their nest?"

It annoyed me to see the gleam of amusement in Zero's eyes. At least he was polite when he said, "Yes. What did you have in mind?"

"They'd head there if they were threatened, wouldn't they?"

"Our research suggested as much," said Athelas. "That's where the injured one went, I should assume."

Zero asked briefly, "What's your idea?"

"We brought along something that might be useful," Abigail said. "It's an emitter: it gives out specific high-frequency sounds when you attach it to speakers."

"Sirens are...susceptible to some frequencies of sound," Zero said slowly. "High frequencies in particular. How did you know that?"

"You're not the only ones with friends on the side," Ezri piped up. "We were told that if we played this kind of frequency through speakers, we might be able to sorta herd the sirens and catch them that way."

"At the very least," said Abigail, "we might be able to drive them back to their nest—which, providing we can find it when they're there, would be pretty useful. We just have to give each person a portable speaker."

"I suppose you brought those along as well," Zero said, his eyes a shade lighter.

"Of course," said Abigail, reaching into her backpack and drawing out a small red speaker.

"Too risky, my lord," Athelas advised. "They'll turn it to their own use."

Abigail wasn't so easily persuaded. "Even if our device can only emit one particular frequency of sound? Even if we've already got in our earplugs?"

"They could amplify themselves enough through the speakers to draw in crowds from the pub-crawlers tonight," Zero said. "Especially if the thing you brought malfunctions."

Abigail hesitated, then asked, "What if it's fae-made?"

The four of us stared at her; reckon the humans already knew, because they didn't seem surprised.

Zero said, "I beg your pardon?"

"What if it's fae-made?" she asked, lifting her chin. "Particularly for problems like this, I mean. And what if we attached one of the badges to it to make sure no one can get in? Everyone who has a speaker would already have a badge; we just need to secure the emitter and put it somewhere that can't be easily got to."

Zero thought about it for a solid two minutes, and everyone let him do it. That's what happens when you've got an air of authority and about twenty sharp objects belted to your chest, I suppose. Must be nice.

At last, he said, "We'll try it. Do you have a way of stopping them if something goes wrong?"

"Low-level EMP emitter," said Abigail, nodding. "It's attached to each speaker already."

"Heck," I said, staring. "You really were doing up some tech this morning!"

"Well, we were already getting the computer in," she said, and I saw the gleam of her teeth in the shadows for a brief moment. "Seemed like it was worthwhile."

"What if the sirens can still use them?" asked Zero, but he asked more thoughtfully.

Ezri grinned and held up a hammer. "Then we'll do it the old-fashioned way," she said. "Smash the hardware. We already have earplugs, so it's not like there's too much of a risk."

I saw Zero and Athelas exchange a look: a look of mixed amusement and respect. Zero said, "Very well. We'll do it your way. We'll still take groups of three, but we'll spread out. Where's your frequency emitter—the base?"

Abigail passed him a small box with metal housing that looked to be pretty heavy. It also looked like it would take a bit of damage without being too worried.

"We'll need one more badge," Zero said. "We've got one for every speaker that's going with a person, but none for the emitter. Who's going to stay with the emitter?"

Jin Yeong took his badge out of his pocket and gave it to Zero.

"Heck no!" I said firmly. "Put that back in your pocket you flamin'—"

"There are already not enough people," Jin Yeong said. "This is a good chance. They can not hurt me: I am more beautiful and more persuasive."

To my irritation, Zero only nodded. "Keep your earplugs in," he said. "Don't do anything stupid. Break into three groups; we'll spread out in our groups from different directions and drive inwards—"

I scowled at Zero as he sorted the humans into three groups, and then at JinYeong. "All right, but you better stick close to me; I'm not having a siren talking you into taking a dive."

JinYeong looked far too pleased at that, so I added shortly, "If I want you in the drink, I'll shove you in myself."

"No, I am in my—"

"Yeah, yeah, you're in your best suit. You always say that."

"It is because my best one is always ruined, and then my *next* best one becomes—"

"Are we going to get going, then?"

"Yes," said JinYeong, as our group formed rather lopsidedly. He still sounded far too satisfied with himself. "From now on, I will stick very close to you."

Lucky us, we ended up with Ezri in our group. She must have been feeling pretty mellow, though—maybe it was the bandage around her hand. Come to think of it, most of the humans looked a bit battered: several had been patched up around the arm or leg, and I was pretty sure one of them was missing an ear, too.

"Someone been having a go at you again?" I asked her, as we threaded our way down through Salamanca Place through the late-night bar-hoppers. We were the closest to our starting point, so we'd stayed in the park the latest.

She grinned down at the bandage. "It was all in a good cause. We're all a bit banged up at the moment: it's worth it, though."

"What, because you killed a few of the other side?"

"That's always a bonus," she said. "Good grief, why are there so many idiots out on a Friday night! Do they want to be killed?"

"Believe it or not, some people have a normal life," said someone from behind us, in a disgruntled voice.

"Mugs, all of 'em," opined Ezri. "There's no fun in being normal—look at that one, he knows. Maybe he's trying to make a break for life with a bit of an edge."

Just to our left and further down the road, I spotted the drunk, not too steady on his feet and making a beeline for the cordoned-off waterfront, toddling along under the shadow of the *Aurora Australis*.

"Ah," said Jin Yeong, clicking his teeth. "So annoying."

"Flamin' heck," I said, below my breath. "Maybe he won't be able to make it over the—nope, there he goes. Oi, Ezri: you and your lot get going with the herding. Take my speaker; reckon I'll have my hands full—me and Jin Yeong will go and get that idiot out of trouble."

"Gotcha," she said, plugging one of her ears. "Good luck. Message us when you're coming back and we'll make room for you."

I gave her the thumbs up, blocking my own ears as we parted ways, and Jin Yeong drew very slightly closer to me. It would have been disconcerting any other time, but today it was comforting: if he got too far out of my radius, he'd be out of range and unprotected from any electrical interference. So I didn't hunch away when our arms swung naturally beside each other, and I didn't complain when the backs of our hands occasionally brushed, either.

The drunk, tottering along under cover of the *Aurora Australis'* red hull, seemed to be heading in the direction of the silver gangplank—who the heck had left that out?—and Jin Yeong's pace increased.

I gently pinched my fingers around his wrist and pulled back very slightly. *Go slower. Let him get ahead*, that pinch said. The drunk was already enthralled, and if I had a guess, I would have said that wherever he was going was closest to where the siren he already heard was waiting for him.

JinYeong slowed, and we followed a bit more cautiously while the drunk made a parody of going up the gangplank twice before he managed to get aboard the ship. We were still ten or fifteen metres away when the silver aluminium gangplank was summarily drawn up and disappeared over the edge of the deck, with barely a flutter of blue uniform.

"Flaming heck!" I said aloud, furious with myself. The sirens must have seen us following along behind, and now we were going to lose the bloke because I'd let him walk into danger.

I looked around hastily, my breath caught in my lungs, hoping to see another gangplank—or a rope, or a bit of wood—*anything* that could get us onboard and to the hapless bloke who was stumbling to his death.

This time it was JinYeong who seized my wrist: he pulled me along the dock until we were opposite the gap in the ship's railings and then put his hands briefly on my shoulders to turn me to face him. I stood where I was put, uncomprehending, while JinYeong took a few long, light strides away across the dock. I didn't understand, in fact, until he dashed at me, laughing, tie flying. A laugh caught in my throat, and I opened my arms. Wiry arms caught me around the waist and rolled with me, and then we were flying, or almost flying, in a tight coil that whisked us breathlessly through the air and curled into a swift, light landing.

I emerged from that landing in a swirl of cologne, on the run, and took off after the vague shadow that was the drunk. Ahead of him was the movement of cloth in a very familiar shade of blue, but the drunk didn't pursue that flutter: he turned at the stairs with a funky little wobble and headed upward at an impressive turn of speed.

I caught myself up at the base of the stairs, turning too fast, but JinYeong had something else in his sights—there, on the deck toward the bow, was one of the uniformed staff members we'd seen the day we came on board for the first time. The one who had looked confused when we didn't reply to him. Only now that staff member didn't look quite so uniformed. Now he looked...scaley.

I snatched at Jin Yeong's suitcoat as he dashed for the siren, hauling him back within range of the badge I wore, my muscles straining. He turned to me and I saw him shake his head; he released himself and pushed me toward the stairs again, then took off at a run toward fore of the ship, leaving me caught between rage and terror.

There was no time to think: Jin Yeong could look after himself, and the human couldn't.

Jin Yeong had *better* be able to look after himself, or I was going to—

I didn't know what I was going to do, so he better be able to look after himself.

I turned back to the stairs and took them three at a time, regretting the lead the drunk had on me. There was no time to text, no time to call anyone. I just ran, my eyes on the tottery legs moving up the stairs far too quickly ahead of me, gasping with the effort of the stairs. I lost sight of him somewhere around the fourth or fifth level and stopped briefly, panting, only to catch sight of a shadow, wobbly but quick-moving, to my left.

I took a chance and sprinted out onto the deck, chasing the shadow. It wasn't until I'd followed it around fore that I saw that I'd been chasing exactly that—a shadow. The drunk himself, real and tottery and beatifically smiling, was one deck above me.

Ah heck.

He was moving toward the railing, too, phone in hand, shoulders moving to music that only he could hear, and when I threw a look down at the lower deck, Jin Yeong whirled in a fast, furious back and forth with the siren we had seen when we boarded. A moment of searing relief shot through me: his earplugs must be doing the trick, then.

Only if he was fighting the siren we had seen at first, *why was there another one looking up at me from the lower deck?*

There were two of them here.

Of *course* there were two of them.

Their flaming nest was probably here—and they were being driven toward their nest.

The drunk's shadow lengthened and stretched out into the darkness of empty space, and I looked up sharply.

Yep, there he went. One idiot climbing over the railings while the siren who had bewitched him watched from below, a shadowed, mysterious smile on his face.

If I could draw attention away from the drunk for just long enough...

"Oi!" I yelled at the siren.

Its eyes did a weird vertical blink that had to mean it had an extra set of eyelids, and it looked away from the drunk and over to me for just a moment. Above my head, the drunk wobbled on the railings, arms windmilling, and the siren's gaze snapped back onto him. I saw its mouth open. Ah heck.

A flurry of movement behind the siren bowled him over, and I saw a small, bright spot of orange tumble through light and into darkness. Jin Yeong rolled effortlessly to his feet and lifted one hand unerringly to his ear. I saw him snarl, then strip the second earplug from his ear and hurl it into the darkness after the first as the two sirens sprang to their feet.

Their mouths opened, one toward Jin Yeong, the other toward the drunk and me, and for a brief moment, I heard something.

"Do not look at me!" Jin Yeong snapped, the words bursting through my earplugs with a filigree of Between as if I was really hearing them instead of being fed the translation through Between. "Do not look at me with your beautiful face! I do. Not. *Like*. It!"

But I saw his foot step forward as though pulled by a string, and I didn't hesitate: I swiped my finger across the screen of my phone, opening the camera app. Hopefully someone was watching on the app to send out an alert to Zero. Otherwise, I was probably going to take a long drop with a sudden stop that wouldn't be too healthy for me, and Jin Yeong wouldn't be far behind.

Unfortunately, it looked like there wasn't any other way of distracting the sirens for longer than a few seconds. I unpinned my badge and dropped it at my feet; then I took in a deep breath, took my earplugs out and said softly into the camera, "Oi. Do you wanna dance?"

I don't know whether the song was already there in my brain or if it came as a result of my challenge, but it was threaded through every thought before I could breathe in. It ran through my blood like vampire spit and fizzed through my sinews, pulling me into a dance that was The Dance. Light and shadow, the trill of notes along the breeze, and the deep bass twang of small waves slapping against the ship as another siren leapt lithely from the water and onto the deck.

Even the shadows danced and sang, and it wasn't cheesy; it was life. Life, and breath, and blood fizzing through my body.

Oh heck, said the bit of me that was still able to think. *Oh heck. What do I do now?*

I couldn't see Jin Yeong, but I couldn't see the ship any longer, either. All I could see was the music and the dance, and the road that I needed to turn to melody beneath my feet.

Pretend it's the little worm, suggested my brain as my feet mashed potatoe'd along a surface that was pretending to be much bigger than it was.

The worm.

But if it was a worm, where was the thread that led back to its source? I needed that to do anything. I pony-trotted to slow my forward momentum, and looked down desperately into the camera app, searching for the source of the compulsion.

I saw a face not my own, but not entirely unfamiliar. Perhaps it was my own face idealized and made beautiful with the kind of behindkind sort of beauty that's almost terrifying. But it was the source—or at least the medium for the source. I found the tug of Between that was attached to me in fibrous filaments that were almost too small to see, and pinched them a little, slowing the flow of the magic and hoping it would affect the potency of the call that gripped me.

It did; I couldn't stop dancing, but I was able to turn my pony-trot into the Charleston, which allowed me to move back for every move forward and kept me in the same spot long enough for a desperate look around.

What I saw chilled me to the bone. I didn't remember dancing over the railing somewhere on the fourth level of the ship, but I was already out past it and dancing my way toward the lip of the deck past that—and then to a drop straight down onto the deck if I was lucky enough to avoid shish-kabobbing myself on the various metal projections on the way down.

I tried to stop the Charleston, too, but I wasn't strong enough. Now that I knew what the tug felt like, I could feel the tug of the other two sirens on deck, even though they were turned on JinYeong instead of me. Then a fourth, feeble tug came from the side of the ship that ran along the dock, and I turned my head in dread.

Deep in shadows that gleamed only with reflected light from the glass of the specimen capsules, water dripped. And as it dripped, it grew smooth and firm and...humanoid. And then the water stepped down onto the deck, scales rippling down to hide the nakedness of its body.

The capsules. The capsules were the nests. Whatever else the expedition had collected from Antarctica, they'd also brought back sirens.

I tried to slow down my back-and-forth Charleston to at least text the others, and for a moment, the dance and the music didn't align. A ripple of dissonance swelled through my phone as the siren realised I wasn't dancing appropriately for the song—dissonance, and then a stronger, sweeter call that filtered through even the Between fibres I had pinched and wrapped itself around my heart again.

This is the you that the world will see, whispered a voice. *The real you. The you that can dance on air and live forever in minds and hearts. Join us. We are beautiful and we will make you beautiful, too.*

I caught my breath in delight and my feet moved forward again: forward toward delicious death and terrifying freedom.

I didn't even feel myself fall, but I felt the force of the sudden deceleration as my hoodie sleeve caught on something. It should have hurt when my shoulder dislocated, but all I could feel was frustration.

I reached up to unhook myself with my other hand, and a tickle of breeze brought scent to my nostrils, causing my nose to wrinkle involuntarily. I hesitated, dangling from thickly woven cotton that wasn't thick enough to prevent itself from tearing slowly, and the fresh evening breeze swept up and around me. I smelled JinYeong as if he stood next to me, and the sudden, shocking brightness of relief that he must still be alive cut away the threads that had held me.

The deck swayed below me. I gave a yelp and grabbed onto that spar for dear life just as my cuff gave way, and the momentum of that desperate movement sent me swinging wildly, the metal cool and slippery within my whitened fingers. I caught sight of the deck below my swaying feet, sickeningly far away, and two figures facing each other at the very point of the bow.

They didn't move, but I saw the threads, the fibrous filaments that clung to every part of JinYeong and tugged him toward the siren, who sang a song I couldn't hear because it wasn't directed at me.

I screamed at him, but JinYeong, his voice molten with rage, said in the most terrible whisper I had ever heard, "I am the most beautiful thing on this ship and *I will not allow you to be more beautiful*. I will do as I please: go away!"

The siren shut his mouth in shock, and swayed. He said, in a tremulous voice that carried up on the breeze, "You reject me?"

"I do not need your beauty," Jin Yeong said through his teeth. "I am already beautiful. You have nothing I need, and I will not come with you. My heart is already full."

The siren wailed—a high, bitter keening of loss that was suddenly, ear-shreddingly audible—and I saw the gleam of ice in his hand just seconds before he plunged that icy knife into his own chest. I wasn't past feeling vicious satisfaction as he folded in on himself and flowed downward into a brief wave of water that splashed against the deck and then melted away into nothing. That would teach him to try and kill Jin Yeong.

The others ran in fear, wailing, which would have amused me if I hadn't been so cold and tired—sirens who had stood up to Athelas' viciousness, running from Jin Yeong's beauty—and he let them run.

They vanished into their nests like water, but Jin Yeong didn't even watch them go: he looked up at me and lifted a hand to point at me.

"You," he said to me, blazingly autocratic. "You will *not let go* because otherwise you will have to turn vampire."

"Don't reckon I could if I wanted to," I called down to him, my voice thin and weary. "Heck. My hands are *cold*."

And then I let go.

Someone *bit* me. It hurt as much as the deck hitting me had hurt, and pushed away the swarming, painless darkness, enraging me. Every part of me hurt, from my skin to my hair ends: a deep, bewildering pain that would have crushed a scream from me if it hadn't taken away my voice to do so.

Shadows and a pounding of feet. Wind, high and furious and chilling.

Screams and the warmth of something pooling around me that

would have itched if I had any senses that weren't raw with pain. Glass smashing.

Wailing.

Feet twitching, trying to dance.

Wailing cut short in a roar that seemed to shake the deck beneath me.

Another bite, deeper and more painful than the first.

A cold, hard voice that commanded, "Give it to her!"

Jin Yeong's voice, nearly as cold, saying, "No."

That woke me a little, and I found myself beneath a shadow of blood and silk.

"I will *drain you myself and feed it to her*!"

The shadow above me that was Jin Yeong snarled "*Wait!*" without politeness, without compunction, and covered me more thoroughly.

A whisper of voice fluttered through my mind. "My lord, I advise listening to the vampire. It will be soon enough to reassess when we return to the house. Must we discuss the matter here?"

"I'm not dead," said a dreadful, grating voice. The sound of it vibrated through my nose and bones, and I heard myself moan again, sharp and high like a dog that had been hit by a car. I tried to say, "Can you lot shut up and take me home now?" but I'm not sure how much I managed to say before I sank into darkness and scent.

There was a buzz of light and colour in my mind even before I opened my eyes. I breathed, and that didn't hurt, so I moved, and somehow that didn't hurt either. Something that had popped out of place in my shoulder last time I was awake was back in place.

"You said," said Jin Yeong's voice accusingly, "that you would not let go."

"You said you wouldn't bite me again without my permission," I said, without opening my eyes. How was it that I could see the room without even opening my eyes? How was it that I could see everything in glittering strands and shadows again, shifting between what they could be and what they were?

I rolled up into a sitting position, my eyes snapping open, and nearly fell over to the side.

I felt good. Life felt good. That was nice, but also funny, and I laughed into the ridiculous complexity of the room around me.

"Who's been decorating?" I asked, lurching around to look at the deeper intricacy that was Jin Yeong.

"You should not get up," he said, pushing away from the wall and crossing the room.

"Heck!" I said, staring at the sheer bulk of his shadow stretching up and over the wall as he approached. I managed to find the carpet with my feet and stood, swaying. "What's going on with your shadow?"

Jin Yeong sniffed a laugh and said, "Ah, you are drunk again!"

"I'm not drunk!" I said indignantly, and fell over.

He grabbed me by the arm and lifted me away from carpet that was moving in a way that carpet shouldn't be able to move. "*Hyeong*, I *told* you—"

"Can you *please* tell the carpet to stop moving?" I muttered. To the glittering, icy part of the room that drew around Zero, I said, "Oh, there you are! Did you try to make Jin Yeong turn me into a vampire?"

Jin Yeong managed to get me upright, so I saw Zero's face, splashed with dry, green blood and taut with worry, as he said, "You nearly died."

"Nearly dead is not all dead," I told him. I was feeling far too alive and fizzy, and that made me worry that I might really have been turned into a vampire. I tilted my head back into Jin Yeong's chest and said accusatorily up at him, "You better not have turned me into a vampire."

Jin Yeong surprised me by giving vent to a bloody sort of

chuckle. "I think I couldn't. You are too determined to be a human. I would not try."

"You have a remarkable tolerance for vampire spit," said Athelas' voice. "And I very much doubt it's entirely due to your, er... continued exposure, either. Well, perhaps it is in part, but that doesn't account for all of it."

Zero sat down wearily on his couch as if he'd been standing for the last day. He scrubbed vigorously at his face with both hands, but emerged just as weary and grey as he had been, to say, "It's very puzzling. You should have at least a bit of fae blood in you, but you don't get sick."

"I'm special," I said, grabbing Jin Yeong's arm again to stop myself from falling over.

He grinned and steadied my head with his other hand. "You are certainly drunk."

"Don't grin at me," I told him. "I'm not going to date you because you're cute."

"Yes, but I am cute. It is a bonus."

"I'm gunna chuck up on your shoes."

"Do not throw up on my shoes!"

Feeling argumentative, I said, "You can't stop me. I'm allowed to throw up where I want to in my own house."

Jin Yeong sighed. "You are making a ridiculous argument where there is no need."

"Yeah, and I'm allowed to do that in my own house, too."

This time, he hissed with laughter, and that made me laugh, too. We sat down on our couch, giggling like little kids while Zero looked at us kinda sideways, resigned to the stupidity. He might not have actually been sideways, but it looked that way to me. Maybe I was drunk, after all.

"How much spit did I end up with, anyway?" I asked Jin Yeong, since Zero seemed to be getting less taut.

Jin Yeong stopped laughing straight away. "You lost *a lot* of blood. Never do that again."

"I'll be sure to tell the behindkind trying to kill me not to be so rough next time," I said, sober enough to start feeling sour about that. "Should we go back to the ship and get them while I'm hopped up on spit again? I know where their nest is now—"

"There's no need," said Zero. "They're all already dead."

"Oh," I said. I was starting to feel less buzzy and more...sleepy, though still in a pleasant way. "Didn't you need to keep some of 'em alive to find out who gave 'em the stuff they were using?"

"We tried," Zero said, with a certain dryness to his voice. "It seems that sirens are sensitive to rejection. Three of them killed themselves before we could stop them, and one died in a...sudden windstorm."

"Oh," I said again, yawning. "That's nice. I'll just sit here, then. How did you know where the nest was, anyway?"

"You told us," he said. "Over and over again."

"In my defence, I was half dead at the time," I told him, blinking heavily. "They've got green blood, eh? You should clean that up: don't you know that *blue and green should never be seen?*"

"Go to sleep, Pet," Zero said. He looked tired and drawn, and for a bloke as pale as Zero, that's saying something. "I've already seen you nearly die once tonight; I'd rather not see it again."

"All right," I said, hunching up against JinYeong without thinking about it. The brief fizz of energy was fading quickly, but I didn't like seeing Zero so drawn and grey. I said through a yawn, "But tomorrow we're gunna have a talk about trauma and the fact that it's okay to hug someone who didn't die if it makes you feel better."

JinYeong made a small *psh* noise of discontent, so I patted his shoulder and rolled my head back to yawn at him. "Thanks for not turning me into a vampire. I'm not going to fall in love with you, though."

There was another sniff from JinYeong, but this time, the *psh* sounded much more content, which was weird.

"You're all flamin' weird," I mumbled, and went to sleep.

CHAPTER TWELVE

IT SOUNDS stupid to say that I felt disgruntled to find Jin Yeong absent from the couch when I woke the next morning, but it was true. Zero must have gone out early, too, because I couldn't feel him anywhere in the house, and I was still pretty fizzy and extrasensory from the huge dose of vampire spit yesterday.

"Hang on," I said to the ceiling. "Did Zero try to force Jin Yeong to turn me into a vampire yesterday?"

"I imagine he thought you were better off as a vampire than dead," said Athelas' voice.

I tucked my chin into my chest to level my gaze on him and saw that he was sitting back in his chair, one leg crossed politely over the other. His chin still tilted up a little, as though he'd been staring at the ceiling, too, but his eyes met mine.

"Sounds like he's got a habit of that," I said. "Isn't that how Jin Yeong got turned, too?"

"It seems that each of us are inclined to repeat the same mistakes over and again," said Athelas, and perhaps he sighed a little.

"Well, at least you know that I'm not fae enough to be worried by it," I said, sitting up. Heck. All I could smell was Jin Yeong's cologne. Bad-temperedly, I pulled on my hoodie and zipped it up as far as it would go to cover my cologne-soaked clothing. "Where's Jin Yeong?"

"I'm sure I don't know. What are you doing, Pet?"

"Trying to get rid of the smell," I said crankily. Jin Yeong had no business making me smell like him and then vanishing in the morning without a word. We had *stuff* we needed to do.

I allowed myself a few minutes to ruminate balefully on the things I wouldn't be able to do today because Jin Yeong wasn't there before puffing out a breath and moving on to what I could do instead.

To Athelas, I said, "Oi, I reckon it's about time that we had another session with your little brain worm."

"The results were not stellar last time," he said, after a brief pause.

"The heck they weren't! I learned a lot—and you don't need to worry about me trying to get your memories again. I'm just trying to get my own. That was an accident."

"A remarkably proficient accident."

"You afraid I'll pull stuff outta your brain that you don't want out? That's flamin' rich!"

"Let us say rather that I am unwilling to try today," said Athelas. "There will be time enough for that in the very near future."

"There won't be time for much in the near future if Upper Management and Zero's dad have anything to say about it," I pointed out. "And if you think the king isn't gunna start paying attention when everyone and their siren is out making trouble on the waterfront, you got another think coming. We still don't know who was behind that, either."

Athelas' grey eyes rested on me consideringly. "You are supposed to be resting and recuperating. Kindly stop bouncing on the couch."

"I have too much energy," I complained. "And excuse me for

feeling a bit antsy while the world is trying to end and take everyone with it!"

"If you want to use some energy, perhaps you could make tea," he suggested, an edge to his voice that warned me not to push my luck.

"I don't want to make tea, I want to try and figure out my memories," I said. There was a heavy, restless feeling in me that weighed me down with all the anxiety of the world that shifted around me, spiralling ever closer to the certainty of the Heirling Trials. "Zero's dad is getting a bit too nosy, and Upper Management is doing everything they can to throw us into the new cycle —when that stuff starts happening, we aren't going to have time to deal with the murderer. We'll just be trying to stay alive. Anyway, Zero is gone, which is the perfect time to—"

"Today is not the time," said Athelas, his voice silken steel: absolutely unyielding. "I would like to drink tea without the prattling of a pet to distract me. Remove yourself."

I sat back in shock, my fingers instinctively curling in on themselves. I hadn't heard that tone from him in a very long time, and it was still capable of withering my heart in my chest. Today, he could almost be the Athelas who had been captured between floors—the Athelas who had killed me without hesitation six times. What the heck was going on with him? Had Zero been doing the equivalent of throwing him through walls for getting too close to me in his own way?

"All right," I said quietly. "I'll get you some tea. Got some nice bikkies for you, too."

He didn't answer, so I left him to gaze at the ceiling in peace and retreated to the kitchen.

I boiled the jug and grabbed the shortbreads, sliding glances toward Athelas and then turning my eyes away again each time. Did he feel the keenness of the shortness of time, too? Was that what was eating at him lately? I felt it in the world around me— the movement of Between; the growing threat of Zero's father;

208 • W.R. GINGELL

the ever-hovering presence of the King of Behind, always just out of sight but not out of mind; the ratcheting tension in my own house—and behind that continuous, bothersome sensation was the reminder that once it was all over, I would be alone again.

Zero would be king—Athelas by his side, probably. If I lived, I would be here in my house, alone. Jin Yeong would be...

Jin Yeong would be elsewhere, of course. I'd already told him that I wasn't going to date him: he wouldn't hang around after that. Once he was away from me, he'd remember how beautiful he was, and how appealing he was to other women—he'd appreciate someone who was easier to get along with.

I was feeling pretty raw and gloomy myself by the time I brought Athelas his tea. He was caught in his own thoughts still, so I poured tea and laid out the biscuits for him. No need to disturb him right now.

As I went to slip away between Athelas' and Zero's chairs, making for the staircase, my hoodie sleeve caught against the brushed tweed of his sleeve and that faintest of friction slowed me down. I hesitated, stopped.

"You don't need to listen to everything Zero says," I told him, without looking at him. He seemed to want to be alone, but there was no need for him to be miserable and alone. "It's all right to want to be around other people. It's all right to be nice to them while you're with them, even if you're only going to leave in the end. You should at least enjoy the time you've got left."

He didn't really answer me, but I thought I heard him murmur, "Should I?" to himself, and sniffed a small laugh down at my feet as I climbed the stairs.

Grumpy old man. Whatever the reason that he was having a bad day, he would probably be better left alone with good tea and biscuits. When he felt better, I would go back downstairs and try again.

In the meantime, if Athelas wasn't going to help me, I would do it myself. Little things had been wriggling out of the woodwork of my mind ever since I first started working with Athelas—not much, but a bit here and there. I had a feeling that if I could recreate enough of that night, I might be able to prompt the memory to surface: those little bits and pieces that had worked themselves out of my memory had been a natural result of *déjà vu* and the disruption of the stifling of memories that I had been doing for so long. In fact, it wouldn't surprise me if the memories all came out naturally, on their own, in the end—but we really didn't have the time for me to let that happen.

I made my way to my room but left the bookcase-door open. I wanted things to be as accurate as possible, but I also didn't want to get stuck in my room with the Nightmare if I ended up actually conjuring that instead of my memory of that night. It had been suggested to me that the Nightmare wasn't just a normal sort of nightmare, and given the dangerous grip that reality seemed to have on a lot of my dreams, I didn't want to give it a helping hand to kill me.

I stood in the doorway of my room and drew in a breath.

First of all, I needed to put my pillow up at the right end of the bed. Since the night my parents died, I'd slept with my feet to the windows and my head toward the door, but I'd started out with my feet toward the door like a normal person. After a Nightmare starts standing at the foot of the bed, just waiting for you to open your eyes, you start trying to do anything that'll convince it to leave you alone. Changing up the direction I slept in had worked for a little while, and it was mostly habit by now, even though it hadn't worked for years.

It only took a few seconds to change the pillow; I didn't bother with the covers, though I did take off my boots. I try to keep my boots clean, but they usually ended up with stuff like blood and guts on them, and I preferred to keep that out of my bed if I could. Maybe that would have been an advantage today, but I figured I could work with things that were a little bit less physically present.

For instance, I thought as I let myself sink into the mattress, Athelas and his little brain worm were a pretty good prompt—not as good as Zero's dad, but I didn't particularly want a prompt that was likely to kill me—and there was no need to have the real thing, after all. If he were really up here, all he'd be doing was making soft, unpleasant remarks and leaving nasty surprises for me in the corners of my mind.

I could almost hear his voice—that soft, steel voice that I didn't like.

Hang on. I really could hear it.

It said, "You really ought to stop asking for things that will not make you happy, Pet. Life is so much more pleasant when one accepts what is on the surface of life and doesn't dig too deeply."

"Says you," I said aloud, and as I did, I felt the gathering of Between in my doorway: gathering, collating itself into one whole that was very nearly a real person. My eyes were still closed, but I knew when the figure finished forming itself and stepped into the room, not quite weighty enough to be real but terrifyingly present.

I opened my eyes.

He stood where the Nightmare always stood—Athelas, quiet, polite, and tidy—and perhaps it was that unpleasant fact that made the entire room shake and wobble in a twisting of reality and perception, before it settled back to normal. When it settled again, Athelas was there, almost solid and real, and instead of the room around me, my insides quivered a little.

"I don't like this," I said. I felt my chin crinkle and set my jaw to stop it. I had done it—I had to have done it, because there was no-one else here—so why did I feel so vulnerable and powerless?

"I believe I warned you," he said. "Things beneath the surface, and so on."

"You're always warning me."

"You never listen."

"I always listen," I told him. "I take it under advisement."

"Is that what you do?"

"I'm not dead yet," I pointed out, but a thread of deep discomfort still pulled within me, quickening my heartbeat and layering dread, tissue-thin piece by piece. It felt as though I couldn't stop it even if I wanted to.

Athelas took a step toward me, then another. "A remarkable circumstance," he said. "But all good things must come to an end, after all."

"That might be your philosophy, but it's not mine," I said. "Stay on your side of the room, all right? You don't need to come over here."

"I believe it may be time for you to sleep," said Athelas, advancing again.

"You're not trying to make me sleep," I said, my breath too fast and shallow. "You're going to try and kill me, aren't you?"

"I think it's time, don't you? I always did say that it was a mistake not to kill you."

His words shouldn't have been familiar, but they were: as if I'd heard him say something similar in the past and hadn't understood it at the time. Instinct urged me to get up and run, to tear aside the bits of Between that ran through my bedroom walls, escape to anywhere other than here.

But that wouldn't get me my memories. It would just get me to the real Athelas, who wouldn't help me, or Zero, who would protect me while smoothing over the surface that this Athelas was so concerned about preserving.

The problem was, I wasn't sure that getting my memories wouldn't end up killing me, and the Athelas up here was real enough to displace the air as he moved, sending wave after wave of panic over me in shivers.

"Did you?" I asked. "I don't remember that."

"Let us not lie to each other, Pet," said Athelas mildly.

If he could kill me—if this version of him could do it, if I could die here—I would allow him to kill me.

So while every thought and instinct screamed at me to fight back, to get away, I let him put his hands around my neck, his grey eyes gazing down into mine without any shade of regret.

I'm not sure I expected to feel the pressure of those fingers around my neck, or the confusing deadness spreading across my face as my oxygen was cut off. The face above me darkened, mottled with brown and mustard-yellow spots, and I felt my body spasm as it tried to do what I hadn't been able to make it do.

I don't know if I lost consciousness or if I simply went to sleep, but everything disappeared for the briefest moment.

And I remembered.

I woke in a sweat, the air heavy and hot and metallic in my lungs, in my mouth. Far away, in another world, or another layer of the world, I felt the flicker of my eyelids as they twitched; they were closed, but still I could see. I could see the room around me, with the softness of faint moonlight brushing everything in my room. The air felt thick in my throat, and the sheets were tangled around my legs with the light sheen of sweat the warmth of the night had brought out. I fought to free myself from the sheets, breathing in hot, salty air, my heart battering against the inside of my chest in a wild panic that had no reason or sense to it. I made myself take my time to detangle everything. Even when I finally put my feet on the ground, I didn't stand up straight away.

I don't know if I was still trying to control the beat of my heart or if I was so terrified that I just couldn't force myself to move, but the movements came slowly and stiffly. Sweat trickled down my back, but my feet were cold, toes curling beneath my feet.

There was something so dreadfully wrong, so absolutely alienly wrong, that I couldn't even find a way to acknowledge how frightened I was. So I stood and forced myself to move, little by little, until at last I was in the doorway of my room, loosening the latch on my secret door.

My first steps were tentative and jerky, lacking illumination from the streetlights outside, my eyes capable only of seeing the vague outlines of the room. The deep and abiding sense of dread that had spread over my limbs was so all-consuming that when I stepped on something sticky and soft, it took a moment for me to feel the wetness of it seep through my socks.

I stumbled on the wetness, then caught myself, and it seemed to me that the couch was lumpier than it should have been in the darkness. The dark horror in the back of my mind painted a head in the shadows above the backrest of the couch, just watching me and waiting for me to make another move. It could have been Dad or Mum, just sitting there in the darkness, having fallen asleep and not yet gone to bed, but in the chill of the moment, I couldn't make myself believe it.

I kept going, in tiny, soft movements that slipped and shifted beneath me, moisture seeping between my toes, until I was close enough to lunge for the light switch on the far wall in a panicked dive that seemed to claw at my shoulders with real claws.

I clung to the side-table that had bruised my hip in the dive and looked over my shoulder as the light flickered, brightened. Barely a thread of the carpet wasn't red; there wasn't a corner of the room that hadn't been dotted or splashed with dark red stickiness. I looked down at my socks, shivering so much that I could feel the teeth rattling in my head: the socks were stained red, too, the colour leaching up and over the arch of my foot to the ankle. Something trailed from my left foot; it had flung itself over the base of the side table in my last rush, too. I whimpered and wiped it on the carpet, but it wouldn't come off, and I couldn't bring myself to reach down and pull it off.

I knew what it was, though. My anatomy classes with Mum left me in no doubt that what clung to my sock was part of someone's small intestine. Everywhere else I looked in the room, I could see other parts of things I'd labelled and studied recently: stuff that wasn't meant to be outside of skin and somehow seemed elongated and misshapen in the lack of confinement.

When I had dreamed the memory, it had always ended right here, and I felt the desperate panic in the back of my mind—the same place from which I had felt my eyelids twitching—that tried to end the memory now, too.

I loosened myself from that part of me and gave myself entirely to the memory, allowing the terror and dreadful sickness of it to overwhelm me. I didn't cry, but maybe I would have if I hadn't been so cold and distant that even the terror had to sink through layers of ice to get to me.

The house seemed to shift around me, but I wasn't surprised; the other sense that I always forgot but that came back when I needed it, reached out to the Between part of the house and pulled at the edges of it as if it could be a warming blanket. I did it unconsciously, but something in the house saw, *sharpened*, and seemed to see me.

I heard, impossibly loudly, a footstep on the first step in the living room downstairs.

I gasped in a ragged, aching breath, sure beyond shadow of a doubt that something dreadful and deadly was coming up the stairs. I snapped the light off in an instant and ran back to my room, slipping and scattering slick innards as I ran, dragging the bookcase-door shut behind me with all the terror of not enough time.

I don't know how long I lay there under the covers, pretending to be asleep, before I knew that I was no longer alone in the room. The door didn't open, but I wasn't alone, and that was so many layers of not-right that my brain didn't want to acknowledge it. Instinctively, I stayed as I was: asleep. Just asleep. Not dangerous. Not awake. Can't see anything. I'm just asleep, you can go away now.

And then he said softly, "It really is no good pretending to be asleep, you know."

With dreadful inevitability, I opened my eyes, and there he

was at the foot of the bed: smaller than the Nightmare had ever been—but perhaps he had seemed bigger when I was smaller.

Smaller, and so much more familiar.

My vision swam, teeth almost buzzing in shock. I heard myself, my *present* self, whisper *Athelas*, but my memory self had no idea who Athelas was. He was here, but the younger me didn't know anything other than the fact that I was about to die. Gripping, terrifying, and merciless, the memory continued, and now I didn't think I could have stopped it if I'd tried.

"Who are you?" I asked.

Moonlight seemed to glow from within the knife he held, peeking out from the darkness of blood that still dripped on my carpet.

"Does it matter?" he asked, shadows and moonlight reflected on his face from that knife. The play of light and shadows made his eyes into depthless pools of grey, deeply shadowed beneath. He looked ancient and cold, almost skeletal. "You have no need for my name. It wouldn't do you any good to know it."

My younger self's voice trembled when I asked, "Are you going to kill me?"

"Oh, I think not," said Athelas. "We had a bargain, your parents and I: I asked them a question and got an answer. It would be...difficult to kill you."

"Are they—are they dead?"

He looked at me curiously. "I took them apart very thoroughly. You must have seen it."

I clutched my arms around myself, too cold to try and run, too cold even to cry, and my shoulders ached with the tightness of the grip.

"Why did you kill them?" I asked him, sick and terrified and somehow more bewildered than anything else. "They didn't—they didn't do anything wrong."

"They didn't," he agreed, and I saw the smile that flitted across his lips. "Very curious. I met only one other couple who

216 • W.R. GINGELL

deserved to be spared—neither couple could be allowed to live, of course. Not when they deserved to be spared. A delightful irony, don't you think? Are you glad to be alive?"

"I don't know what that means," I said, shivering in constant waves. "Why did they have to die? Why do I get to live?"

"I allowed them the choice," he said, and the hand that held the knife moved just slightly; a gesture of futility. "They wanted to save you—a very good choice, I thought. You, my dear, will cause significant problems, I think. Nothing I can do about it, of course! I am bound by my word."

"What word?"

"You should stay in the house," he said gently, and the gentleness with which he said it seemed to seep into my mind. "I really do advise you to stay out of sight as much as possible—in fact, you should try to stay in your room. You never know...*what* is waiting for you outside."

"I'm not going to stay inside," I said, as a vast heat of rage, fear, and tears grew up inside my chest. He had said he couldn't kill me, and even if that wasn't true, I was going to make sure someone made him pay for killing my parents. "I'm going to come out and find you. I'm going to make sure you die for what you did."

He smiled faintly, but there was a terrible greyness to his face. "Shall you? You'll forget soon enough, I should think. I believe you're already quite good at that."

"I won't forget," I said, but there was already a softening around the edges of what I could see. He turned, the knife sending two drops of blood arcing gracefully through the air, and he faded through the wall, then from my mind, before the droplets hit the ground.

Before they hit the ground, I broke free from the memory with a cry that should have been panic but was instead pain.

No, no, no. It couldn't be Athelas. It couldn't be him. It was just that I'd used his likeness to kickstart the memory, to shake it loose. Zero had said it couldn't be him. I had woken to find Athelas in the room when Zero and Jin Yeong were with the murderer—

I had *seen* him when I woke—

No, I had heard him. Heard him in the dark. Refrained from turning on the lights at his request.

I sat up, curling over myself to soothe the huge, aching pain that ate its way from my stomach to my throat. Not Athelas. It couldn't be Athelas, because I had learned to trust Athelas. I had learned to love Athelas.

But I had remembered his face—remembered it still, now, in horrible detail. *Athelas*, who was capable of ripping apart an entire floor of humans and behindkind who had kept him captive, who had left another mess for me to walk through with my eyes closed.

My pocket buzzed with a text, jolting my heart with the suddenness of it, and I pulled out my phone in a distant sort of a way, reeling from memories and terribly aware that the house felt suddenly still and dangerous.

I looked down at the phone for a good few minutes before I could make sense of what I was seeing, then registered that the text was from 541.

A smile, or maybe a grimace, trembled on my lips. How was that for good timing? Five was still looking into the paperwork Athelas had made Tuatu gather for him, which was pretty ironic right about now. The text said, *Kid. Got a name for you. Come see me when you can. Bring some of those little black things, I've run out.*

"No more liquorice for you," I said, and I didn't recognise my own voice. It sat uncomfortably in the air around me, and I felt again how dangerously quiet the house was. A shiver crawled up my spine, stirring up a wish that either Jin Yeong or Zero were somewhere near.

What was I supposed to do? Crawl out the window and find

them to tell them what I had remembered? It couldn't be true, but I had remembered it, and it *must* be true.

I wanted desperately, and feared as desperately, to ask Athelas himself if it was true.

I could go now—just walk downstairs and into the living room —and ask him what it meant. I made a small, stifled movement that stopped as soon as it had begun, and I knew then I wouldn't ask him. Because if I asked Athelas, he would tell me. And I knew, with horrible certainty, exactly what he would tell me.

I couldn't seem to move, one way or the other: not to get up and run, not to get up and go downstairs. Why couldn't I do something, or feel something other than a dreadful ache every-where? And *why* was the house so still?

I reached out to the Between underpinnings of the house, delicately and tremblingly. In the yawning dreadfulness of my too-full memory, I needed to know where Athelas was.

And then I heard it—or maybe I didn't hear it. Perhaps I felt it.

I heard Athelas rise from his seat downstairs: felt or heard the smooth creak of leather as he stood, the whisper of the carpet as he turned on the balls of his feet and faced the stairs.

I heard the first of his steps on the stairs and stuffed my phone back into my pocket with a shaking hand, paralysed with the need to run, but without anywhere to run that wouldn't leave me just as open to danger as I already was.

Athelas didn't know that I'd remembered. If I ran, he defi-nitely would know. If he looked at me, I thought, shivering, he would know.

I pushed past every instinct that screamed at me to run and forced myself to uncurl, to relax, to lie back down on my wrinkled bed. The upper landing outside in the living room upstairs cracked with the weight of a footstep, and desperately, I closed my eyes and tried to still the rise and fall of my chest as I breathed too quickly.

As I'd done all those years ago, I pretended to be asleep. I let my head sink naturally to the side that didn't face the wall: I couldn't bring myself to bare that additional point of weakness. Then I relaxed myself as much as I could, too late remembering that I was still facing the wrong way. I couldn't let the horror of it sink in, or I would have started breathing too quickly again, and I could hear Athelas moving across the upstairs living room now.

A breath of displaced air fluttered across the hand that was on top of my stomach, and I concentrated on my breathing. That would be Athelas at the doorway.

I don't know how long he stood there, watching me; how long I lay there, just trying to breathe deeply enough to seem as though I was asleep. I let myself move a bit, as if I was starting to wake up, then settled again.

"Ah," sighed Athelas' voice from the door. "Now this brings back memories, does it not?"

My stomach sank like a stone.

Ah heck. I didn't know how, but he knew that I knew.

Softly, he said, "It really is no good pretending to be asleep, you know."

My eyes opened, and I saw the memory of that night overlaid with the truth of today. Athelas, standing by the foot of my bed where the Nightmare always stood, with the words the Nightmare had spoken on his lips.

"What did you say?" I asked him, my voice a thin thread. He wasn't even trying to hide it—wasn't trying to convince me I was wrong—and that put the ice in my veins as nothing else would have. He was almost *pushing* the memory on me, as though he would have forced me to remember it if I hadn't already.

Athelas' lips smiled, but his eyes didn't. He said it again, exactly as he had before, word for word. "It really is no good pretending to be asleep, you know."

It was Athelas' face, but the voice was all Nightmare, and I saw the depths of shadow behind him for just a moment: shadows that had formed the Nightmare in my dreams.

"Don't stand there," I said, and there was a pull at my chin as it trembled briefly, because it was much too late. But I couldn't help the pleading tone in my voice, or the searing thought that if he tried to convince me that it hadn't been him, I would choose to believe it. "Don't stand there, Athelas."

He said again, "Come out," and there was death in his voice.

"Told you not to stand there," I said, my throat closing up. I should have been frightened—perhaps I was, just a bit—but mostly I was dazed and numb and achingly, gut-punchingly *desolate*. Desolate for my parents. Desolate that Athelas wouldn't even try to convince me that it wasn't him. Gutted to find that there was a warring thread of love within the aching betrayal: a thread that I couldn't unravel from the other.

I said, "You shouldn't—you shouldn't have stood there."

I was panting by the time I got to the end of the sentence, because it hurt *so much more* than I would have expected it to hurt. Maybe I could have understood if he'd been just the murderer, killing behindkind and the occasional human for some twisted reasoning of his own—or even for the king or Zero's dad. But I knew it wasn't just that. More, I knew who else had died by his hands—I knew so many people who had died by his hands.

"Reckon it was a mistake to come up here," I said to him, when I caught my breath. I sat up, and the room moved around me like it was on castors.

"So it would seem," he said, but he said it so calmly that I could have thought he had come up here for the exact purpose of forcing me to find out what I had just found out. "It's unfortunate that you couldn't leave well enough alone, Pet. I'm afraid I can't let you tell what you've learned to my lord."

"You said you can't kill me."

"I believe I said that it would be uncomfortable to do so," he said. "But that was some years ago: the situation is different now."

"Yeah? Want to explain that in a way that makes sense?"

He almost smiled, as if it was just a normal day of me being cheeky to see how far I could go with him, and that hurt, too. He said, "Ask the question, Pet."

"I don't have questions."

"That's very unusual of you."

"Why did you do it?"

I heard the barest breath as he let it out. "Ah, there it is. You'll have to be more specific, my dear—"

"Don't call me that."

Another emotion tried to cross his face and was ruthlessly crushed, leaving him smooth and expressionless. Breathtakingly harsh, he said, "Be. More. *Specific.* Pet."

"Why did you kill my parents? Why did you kill Morgana's parents? Why would you do something for the king or Zero's dad?" I waited, for just as long as a sob, but I couldn't help adding —almost begging—"It was because of Zero's dad, wasn't it? You had to? He made you do it to keep the throne for Zero, and you couldn't—"

"Don't attempt to make a good person out of me," he said sharply. "It won't work. I killed your parents—tore them apart piece by piece as you slept. The little zombie's parents, too. Ralph —the others. All of the others."

"Zero said you couldn't have," I said, through numb lips. "He said you weren't capable of killing his half-brother—I saw the memory myself! And you were *home* the day they found the freshly dead serial killer!"

"You are mistaken," Athelas said. "I certainly killed the boy— he was about to have my lord killed. My lord's nurse, on the other hand, I did not kill; it was very remiss of me and I would certainly not choose to be merciful again. The memory you stole from me —well, let us merely say it was fortunate that it was the one it was! Things could have happened...rather differently if you'd managed to pull out any adjacent memories."

"What do you mean, you killed him? I saw you—I *felt* the way you—"

"Don't imagine you know anything of me from a single memory! I had killed the Lord Sero's half-brother before that interview; the knife was given to me and duly left at the scene when I finished. I've never known who it was that my lord saw that night when he found me weltering in my own blood, but it was certainly not myself: I was barely conscious. If I find the person, they will receive the same kind of service that was performed on me to rid me of my disobedience—they would undoubtedly have implicated me with the placement of the knife, if my lord hadn't woken to see them."

"Yeah, I saw you get smacked around a bit," I said. The flippancy rang hollow, but I couldn't help it. If I hadn't said it, I would have cried, or screamed, or maybe howled with the sheer, aching *betrayal* that clawed its way up my throat and seared the backs of my eyes. "Zero's dad really did a number on you."

"I wasn't as obedient as I might have been," he said, shrugging. "I was still young and inclined to rebel occasionally. My lord's father simply made me aware of the consequences of so doing. He took his time with me, as he did with my lord's nurse: a timely reminder."

Athelas looked down at the bedpost again—and again I saw that faint smile. "It...informed my choices as to style, as it happens. As did the knife that was left with my body in an attempt to indict me of the death of my lord's half-brother: I use it only with certain people, you know."

"What certain people?" I asked, trying not to choke on the anger, or the tears, or maybe just the sheer terror. "People you really wanted to suffer? What did my parents ever do to you?"

"They had you, my dear," he said. "And your existence was an unfortunate thorn-in-the-side for two very powerful people. I did give your parents the choice, after all."

"You don't cut people in pieces because they're a problem to your boss. You said *certain people*."

"Still fighting," he said, the faintest of lines between his brows. "I wonder why you're fighting so hard when you remember it all?"

"You were with me," I said, through the dull pounding of my heart. "The night that Jin Yeong and Zero had an exploding body —they nearly caught the bloke, and you were *here with me*."

There it was, that faintly amused twist to his lips. "I think you'll remember that I didn't wish you to turn on the lights when you woke, Pet."

"But you were *there*."

"I was indeed there when you woke—covered in blood, I might add. It is fortuitous that Jin Yeong is so delightfully suggestible: if he had not sat down in my chair covered in gore, I couldn't possibly have accounted for the blood already there. I had to rig the entire body to explode just to give myself time to get away and obfuscate the vampire's senses sufficiently. That was...a very close call."

"Reckon that wasn't the only close call," I said. "You killed the wrong bloke across the road—twice."

"Remarkably bad judgement on my part," said Athelas. "And it was something of a shame to have to call in the Family to clean out the waystation—Upper Management had done a good job there, and it certainly would have made a nice little distraction. But I couldn't allow myself to be caught so early—not when there was so much work to be done."

"*Allow* yourself to be caught?" I choked. "Just like you were playing a little *joke* on someone? What, I suppose you were going to turn yourself in when you'd finished your work!"

"Of course not," he said. "Turning myself in would be a ridiculous thing to do: my lord will certainly kill me if he finds out what I've been doing behind his back."

"Did you kill Mr. Preston, too?"

"Good heavens, of course not. No doubt Upper Management

arranged for that—he was trying to turn whistle-blower, wasn't he? I don't concern myself with whistle-blowers."

"Just Heirlings?" I said bitterly.

"Indeed," he said, inclining his head. "Things seem to have worked out remarkably well in that direction: if I had really killed the old man, for instance, it might have cost us quite significantly. A happy accident, one might say. As it is, the Harbinger still sneaking around the house and favouring Lord Sero—if proximity is anything to judge by—is not a bad thing."

"Yeah, well he could be said to be favouring me, too," I said. "And you know what I reckon?"

"I'm quite certain you'll tell me," he said, with a quick, caught-in laugh that sounded nearly painful.

"Reckon you didn't kill enough of us," I said, with a vicious desire to wipe that smile from his face. "Turning humans into behindkind wasn't the cleverest idea you've had: reckon you're going to regret the *mostly* bit of *mostly-dead* that Morgana and Ralph are, too. I reckon you and Zero's dad are going to find out that there are still a few Heirlings out there who can stand up and fight."

He shrugged. "Stand up and fight, perhaps. Fight well? That is...less sure."

"There's enough to precipitate the Heirling Trials, though," I said. "And I don't think either Zero's dad or the King are very happy about that."

Athelas stilled. "Perhaps not. Still, on balance, I believe that my lord's father will consider himself quite satisfied."

"You probably want to start wondering about what Zero's gunna think," I said, and saw the smile vanish away completely.

"As I said," he murmured. "My lord would undoubtedly kill me if he knew what I've done. Oh, you can be sure he won't spare me, Pet! Take comfort!"

"Don't—" I stopped and started again. "Don't talk to me like that. We're not friends. You don't get to tease me."

"I had not forgotten," said Athelas, and he lifted his chin again.

"Yeah? I reckon you did, for a while?"

"I warned you, did I not? I warned you not to trust me. You have only yourself to blame if you've been taken in."

"I think you're the one who was taken in," I said, and I found that I was crying. "I think you got used to me. I think you started to l—"

I couldn't see him through the distortion of tears in my eyes, but I heard his voice, grey as stone, absolutely cold. "The ability of humans to deceive themselves is truly breathtaking."

"All that stuff—all the stuff you asked the detective to dig up —" No matter how much I thought about it, I couldn't force it to make sense in my head. I licked my lips and tried again. "You got him to dig up all that stuff about me and Morgana and—I just—"

"Pet, I fancy you are trying to buy time. I'm not so green as to allow my prey to lure me into speech so long that I'm caught, thank you."

I choked on a laugh, or maybe a sob, and wiped the tears from my eyes. "I'm your prey now, am I? Thanks a lot."

"You always were," he said, and his eyes were as hard as flint. "Don't flatter yourself that you were more to myself or my lord than a moment's usefulness. It is no longer convenient to my lord's father that you live, and I've been given a job to do."

"Is that what it was with my parents, too? You were supposed to kill me but you killed them instead?"

Athelas' eyes flickered away for the briefest moment. "They had the same choice as the others. Save their child or save themselves—they chose to save you. If I recall, they were one pair of only two who did so. I had to abide by my word once given, or you would have died that night."

I'm not sure why I did, but I asked him, "You did all of this because Zero's dad made you do it? *All* of it?"

"Do not fancy that my minutest actions were at Lord Sero's

father's will," he said. "Promises have been made and sealed, and I will not be unrewarded for my service. I will receive...everything that I am owed."

"I won't let you hurt Zero," I said, feeling the wobble of my chin again. It wasn't as if I could stop him, of course: I probably couldn't even stop Athelas from killing me if he really was going to try it. "You can't do stuff like this for him when you know he doesn't want it."

He laughed; a soft thing that was more shadow than sound. "It's for Zero's sake: he'll be king of the world Behind."

"Yeah? Reckon he's going to see it that way when he finds out?"

Into Athelas' tired eyes, there came a faint smile. "I am quite certain he will not," he said. "But that doesn't concern you, Pet."

"Yeah it does."

"I don't think you understand."

"I understand, all right," I said. "You killed my parents, and Morgana's and Ralph's, and you and Zero's dad are going to try and force Zero to take a throne he doesn't want to take."

"That was not what I meant," Athelas murmured. "I am very much afraid that I'm going to have to kill you, my dear. I shouldn't bother to call for Zero if I were you: he wouldn't get here in time even if I hadn't dismantled that tracker spell he always seems to have on you."

"That was a pretty flamin' stupid thing to say," I said, my mouth dry.

I didn't need the spell: I'd never needed the spell. I don't know if Zero always knew that, and it was just one more way of keeping distance between us—pretending that he needed it to tell him when I needed him—or if he was really as ignorant as Athelas seemed to be.

"Reckon you'll regret threatening me," I added.

"There are many things I regret, my dear," he said, and started across the room toward me, swift and predatory.

"Zero!" I screamed. "*Zero!*"

I didn't have time for any more than that because then Athelas' long fingers were around my neck, and through the vague, fuzzy lethargy spreading from my neck and outward, I knew he wasn't just strangling me.

I saw the veins in my eyes tracing red across my vision and felt the stifled numbness blocking from nose to upper lip as my final thoughts floated free and disconnected. Zero had to come. He had to get here first because if he didn't, Jin Yeong would get here first. And if Jin Yeong got here first, Athelas would kill him in a savage heartbeat.

One heartbeat, one more flash of red veins.

Thunderous silence. Depthless suffocation.

CHAPTER THIRTEEN

THE FIRST THING I felt was pressure: immense, crushing pressure around my forehead and temples that could have been a band of steel, and a weight on my chest. I heard the breath leave my lungs, thready and final, and there was enough life to me to know that I had to draw in another one before it was too late. But the weight on my chest was too heavy. I didn't even fight to breathe; didn't feel the spasms as my body tried to force itself to do so.

I lay prone and unable to move, until someone snatched me from the carpet and crushed me to their chest, tumbling the world around me and flopping my head to their shoulder.

"Wake up!" said a voice insistently. "I will not bite: wake your-self up."

I must have started to breathe again, because suddenly I was breathing in perfume as the house woke up into tattered, deadly life around me, offering power without limits and safety without question.

"Wake *up*!" said that same voice, disrupting the call of the house—or maybe the call of Between.

Behind that voice, another one commanded, sharp and cold, and I woke with what felt like a terrible surge of electricity, shrieking. I tried to lunge to my feet as I woke, already running, but my arms and legs were tangled with someone else's, and they held me tight until I stopped trying to push forward and leaned back instead.

A pair of black, dangerously liquid eyes danced in front of me, and I stopped struggling. I think I sobbed, then I wrapped my arms around his neck, clinging for dear life. I wasn't dead. *How* was I not dead? No time to wonder; no time for anything except action. I grabbed at all the bits of Between in the house, the network of power and safety—grabbed them without hands, without touching—and heaved it up and over the three of us like a blanket, sealing off the house inside a suffocating bubble of magic so that Athelas could never get back in.

I heard a familiar, icy voice say, "*Stop* her, Jin Yeong!"

Jin Yeong's chest shuddered with the laugh I heard in my ear. "That—how could I stop it? You could not do it."

"That's why I told you to stop her!" Zero said, even more sharply. "Talk to her! Pet! Pet, listen to me! You need to stop it!"

It was a sentence, but it didn't make sense, because if I stopped what I was doing I couldn't keep myself safe. I couldn't keep Jin Yeong safe. I couldn't close the house around the three of us and keep out whatever Athelas was about to bring down on us now that he no longer had anything to hide.

Maybe I really was dead. Maybe I was just a revenant of myself now, fighting on instinct. But Jin Yeong was warm, and his perfume was strong, so I concentrated on that. The confusion of voices commanded, and magic, ice cold and sharp-edged, tried to cut through the denseness of the house magic I had woven around us, but I just made it thicker and more absorptive, and that icy magic sank in without effect.

I heard the softness of a groan in my ear. Jin Yeong caught his breath, then said gently, "You are *squashing* me. It hurts."

I don't know if he or I were more surprised at the suddenness with which the house released us all: the suddenness of a bubble popping, and the freshness of being able to breath properly. I heard another groan, but this one was Zero's, and I couldn't look to see if he was all right, because I was crying in huge, wracking sobs that battered against JinYeong and left me blind and deaf to everything else except the fact that I had come to love Athelas, had found a place for him in my heart, and that he had killed my parents.

JinYeong let me cry into his neck, one hand behind my head and the other pressing against my ribs, hissing something over his shoulder at the voice behind us that demanded, "Where is Athelas? What did you do to the house, and what has Athelas done to you?"

Every breath hurt, but every thought hurt much more; I thought that the ache in my throat might even be the end of me, but Zero's voice, a constant, cold pressure, still pushed to know, "What happened, Pet? There's magic all over you, and it belongs to Athelas. I need to know what happened."

JinYeong moved very slightly; I felt his chin graze my ear as he turned his head to gaze at Zero. "Go away, *Hyeong*," he said.

"Pet, *tell me what you know*."

"I," said JinYeong, in snarling, heavily accented English, "will *tear. Out. Your. Throat.* Go away!"

"Don't," I said, my voice thick with tears. "It was Athelas, I *told* you it was Athelas, and you *didn't believe me*!"

"Athelas did this?"

"Ask your dad," I said. Maybe I screamed it over JinYeong's shoulder, because I was shaking and Zero was pale, and two scented arms tightened around me. "Ask him where Athelas is. Ask him what Athelas did. Bet he'll tell you now. They're probably both together now."

"My father is—" he stopped, and I saw the same awful uncertainty on his face that I had felt twitching across my own when I first realised that it could only be Athelas. "Athelas was with you that night—and my brother—"

"Your nurse was probably the only one he didn't kill," I said, catching a breath that didn't give me enough oxygen. "Reckon someone wanted to make sure he got caught for your brother; they came for the knife and you woke up—led you right to him and gave Athelas an alibi instead. And he got home just before Jin Yeong that night. Left blood all over his chair, too; he says he exploded the body to make sure Jin Yeong had too much blood on him to be able to smell the stuff already in the house. If you don't believe me, just *look*!"

The memory was there, terrible and present: I took it and I shoved it into the cold spikiness of his mind. I heard him hit the wall as if I'd physically struck him, felt the tug as he took in the memory, but I didn't want to look. I sank back into Jin Yeong's neck instead, shivering, wishing that his warmth could make me feel warm again. I did see when Zero dropped to one knee and then the other, as if his huge body was suddenly too much to bear.

That made the tears well over again, hot and too big to stay in my eyes. Everything could be fixed. Everything had been fixable until now. They were psychos but every now and then they were still human, except that Athelas had never been human. He had just pretended to be human. Pretended to like me. Pretended to like Ezri, and—

"Pet!" That was Zero's voice, short and gritted. "Pet, what is it?"

I picked my head up from an almost noiseless wail into Jin Yeong's neck and met eyes that were as sick as my own.

"Abigail," I said to Zero huskily. The words wouldn't come out right; they stuck in my throat in a hot, choking lump. If Athelas had come to the conclusion that it was time to cut his losses and loose ends both, there was no way he wouldn't go after Abigail and the humans. Tuatu had the dryad and North, Morgana had Daniel and the pack: Abigail and the others only had themselves, and I knew how little that would mean against Athelas or anyone he and Zero's father might send after them.

I pulled away from JinYeong and pulled my boots on, then staggered to my feet, heavy with dread. I wasn't dead and I needed to think about that, but right now Abigail needed those thoughts more.

"Abigail," I said again, panting. "We gotta get to Abigail before he does!"

I heard a stifled sound from Zero that could have been a guttural "*No!*", but he was already turning, already on the run; he surged through Between without regarding walls or doors, or furniture. JinYeong grabbed my hand and we dove through the shifting world after him, JinYeong lean and fast, me stumbling and heavy. It felt as though my legs couldn't—or wouldn't—work, and I'd never felt Between drag at me so much as it did right then. So I let JinYeong cut the surface ahead of me and just followed him, one foot after the other and the constant pull of his hand around mine.

With my free hand, I felt for my phone and pulled it out as we ran. Someone would answer. Someone had to answer.

I nearly dropped it, and when my hand gripped convulsively around it to stop that happening, I felt the buzz of a message coming through. I looked down at it briefly, hoping for a bright, relieved moment that it might be Abigail herself, or even Ezri.

It wasn't. Detective Tuatu's number flashed up at me, along with a message.

Pet. What do you know about vampiric pumpkins?

I stared at it, but couldn't comprehend it. Later. I'd ask Zero about that later. Right now, I had to get to Abigail, whether in person or by phone.

I tried to call while we were on the way. Tried and failed more times than I remembered, my phone buzzing with sporadic texts from the detective that would have to be dealt with later but that I didn't have the energy for right now.

I was still trying to get Abigail on the phone when we arrived, Zero just barely in the lead and JinYeong once more beside me instead of towing me. I must have gotten quicker as we went, though I could only remember the dragging of time and space.

I shoved my phone back in my pocket and started for the gates, my heart in my throat.

"Careful," said Zero sharply, holding me back with one huge hand that covered nearly my entire upper arm. "The wards aren't up."

I stared at him. "The what?"

"There were wards here: the same sort of thing that I put up at home but set to be triggered by fae in particular instead of behindkind in general. They've been smashed to pieces."

"Ah heck," I said, starting forward again. I didn't move too quickly, just so that Zero knew I wasn't about to do anything rash, but I needed to keep moving. I needed to see that Abigail and the others were all right.

Jin Yeong, a silent shadow of perfume, flanked me as I stepped through the grass and toward the house. There wasn't anything different about the place. Nothing to see, I mean. Nothing was different about the awning or the plants, and there was no difference to be seen in the stone gargoyle out the front either.

So why was it that I already knew what I would see? Why was it that when I walked through the concrete doorway, I could feel the dead emptiness of the place: a lack of life rather than a lack of physical bodies?

Shivers ran across my skin as I stepped down into the hallway, a constant tremor that ran beneath the skin although I wasn't remotely cold, and suddenly I knew exactly what it was that I could feel.

It was Between—no, Behind. And not even the essence of behindkind themselves, but the kind of greasy residue they leave behind when they've been in a place. Little bits of Between sloughing off like scales from a fish or skin from a snake.

I didn't consciously decide to run, but when I started trotting, and then outright running, my footsteps echoed through the whole of the place, lacking warmth and softness to quiet them. Zero didn't try to stop me this time; he ran, too, just ahead of me as if he knew exactly where I was going, and we headed straight for Abigail's office, sprinting around corners that had never seemed so sharp or so cold before.

I caught myself up at the door, my gaze darting wildly around the room.

Was she here?

If she was, was she alive?

It wasn't until the dazzle from the sunlight outside faded from my eyes that I saw exactly why the room was so dark. It wasn't just shadow creeping from the edges of the room to the far-too-textured middle of the room: it was blood.

So, so much blood.

There were bodies, too, but they didn't look much like bodies. With a ringing in my ears and the sound of my own breath far too loud, I saw a foot. A foot, a few fingers that bled into the carpet and merged with a sticky pool of blood that spread out in a glistening trail of what might have been muscles, shredded and useless. There was more, but JinYeong's shoulder edged in front of me and gave me something else to concentrate on instead.

There was lantana on his shoulder, a few tiny flowers with the pollen still clinging to the inside of the flower. I looked at that, and JinYeong stuffed his hands into his pockets, surveying the scene as if he had stood there to get a better view. I tried to catch a breath that just wouldn't come, and beside me, Zero said through a groan, "Too late."

I already knew. I knew the style—could you call it *style?*—of the killings. I had seen it before in my dreams, in real life. I had seen the mess and the welter of blood; I'd smelt the heaviness of blood in the air. I'd *stepped* on—

Zero dropped to his haunches, still just slightly in view behind JinYeong, his head bowed as if he had no more energy to hold it up.

A rumble that was his voice said to himself, "I knew it would end badly. Why did I do it?"

"It's not your fault," I said thickly, wishing that the smell of it all didn't coat the back of my mouth so completely. "You didn't do this."

"I called them in."

"I called 'em in," I said harshly. "Stop trying to take responsibility for everyone! They knew the risks, and they chose to do this. They would have been doing it even if you didn't ask them to help out with a case: it's what they do with their lives."

"They didn't," he said, and I saw the faintest movement to his huge form. A very slight rocking, back and forth. "They didn't choose to be in this fight; not this one."

I stepped out from behind JinYeong and stared at him, trying to push away the awful feeling that I knew what was coming. "What are you talking about? What do you mean *this fight?*"

"They were *safe* until they got involved with Heirlings," he said, burying his face in his hands. "No one would have been interested in them if they weren't trying to help protect Heirlings."

"You knew where to come," I said numbly, dropping down on my haunches in a smaller, mirror version of him. "You knew how to get here. I didn't tell you that. And you knew what the wards used to be."

"*Hyeong,*" said JinYeong, his eyes dark and warning. "You have been playing games again."

"I asked them," Zero said, as though it hurt to speak. "I told them that if they helped keep you safe, if they joined in this fight, they could have you after I leave. They were meant to keep you safe after...everything comes to an end."

When Zero was dead—or the King Behind—and the world Behind settled back beneath the human world like silt in a puddle and stopped muddying the waters.

"You can't just *give* me to—" I stopped and took in a deep

breath between my teeth, fighting off the nightmare that was reality. It seemed awful to fight where Abigail and the others had come to such a horrible end. I said quietly, "Thanks for trying to keep me safe. I appreciate it. We'll talk about this later."

I'm not sure he understood. I'm not sure he was in any state to understand anything just then. I wanted to be able to go over and hug him: comfort him, tell him it was all right. But it wasn't all right. Nothing I could say would make it all right, and I didn't know how much I wanted to say when a least half of what he was going through was directly related to the dreadful not-rightness of the entire situation. I didn't have the *energy* to do it.

Zero stood, and I thought for a moment that he was going to switch back into his usual, icy demeanour to move around the room and investigate as he always did. Instead, he turned, or flickered, and then he was gone.

"Ah," said Jin Yeong, clicking his tongue. "*Hyeong* should not be alone right now."

"He'll be all right," I said. My voice sounded distant and emotionless, and I didn't seem to be able to make it say more, or mean more. I didn't know for sure, but I was pretty sure that Zero had at least a few more resources these days to cope with the emotions he was currently dealing with than he'd had in the past. At the moment, maybe more than I did. "He'll come back."

"*Ung,*" Jin Yeong hummed, but he didn't seem entirely satisfied. He didn't leave me, though, and that was enough.

Zero came back, of course—maybe half an hour later. I don't know exactly what he did, or where he went, but when he got back, there was a hard, fragile sort of capsule around him. I couldn't bring myself to hug him, but I did wrap my hands around his wrist for a bit, and he stood still to let me, so maybe it did some good after all. It made me snuffly and teary again, which was maybe a nice change from the cold *feelinglessness* that had settled over me, but at least Zero didn't seem as though he was going to sink through the floor any longer.

JinYeong, who had begun to prowl his way carefully around the room, sniffed a bit but returned to our side of the room without being too obstreperous. There was a narrowness to the look that he shot around the room again, but that could have been because of how dark it had become around the edges.

"It would seem that we're too late," said a female voice behind us, as I was trying to figure out why it was suddenly so dark around the edges of the room.

Zero turned, sweeping up with the sword that was suddenly and impossibly in his hand while the voice was still speaking, and a silver blade met his, parrying and then disengaging in a single, ringing beat.

"Don't kill Palomena," I said to him, on a sob.

Zero's sword dropped. He said, "*Please* stop crying."

"I'm not crying," I said, wiping away the tears with my cuffs. "Don't tell me what to do."

That made him release a breath that was almost a laugh, which loosened my chest enough to make me able to realise that there was a warmth around my shoulders, front and back. I only recognised it as JinYeong's arm wrapping around me from behind when Zero shot a hard, not-quite-cool look at it. I could have shrugged off the arm, but I left it there instead. Today, I was prepared to accept all the comfort I desperately needed, from JinYeong at least.

"I would have something to say about that, I promise you," Palomena said reassuringly to me. She took a lingering, regretful look around the room, and her eyes came to rest on me for a moment before flicking back to Zero. She said, "This is a bit of a shame."

"Yes," Zero said baldly.

"Maybe it's not what it looks like," I said, my tears dry but my voice a bit too wobbly for the professional human I was supposed to be. "Maybe it's like when A—when we found the dead bloke who wasn't who we thought he was?"

"We'll investigate properly, Pet," said Zero. "We won't just assume that everything is as it seems."

"Ah," Palomena said. "Then before you investigate too thoroughly, do you think it would be a good idea to send me away?"

I think I would have been hopeful if Zero had agreed. He didn't: he shook his head and said, "There's no need. Athelas has been...very thorough. We'll call in the detective to verify the remains by human methods, but I can see the remnants of the work."

Remnants, he said.

The shadows were actually shades.

I'd thought I was just tired of the mess and death, that there were black spots dancing around the edges of my vision because I was sick and dizzy. That the edges of the room had collected shadows due to the time of day, not because they were peopled with shades of people who had once been alive.

One of them separated from the wall closest to me, heading for the door, and I briefly saw Ezri's young face as the shade wafted toward me. She grinned at me, sharp and mocking, just like she'd done when she was alive. As if she knew something that I didn't know and enjoyed the fact. Or as if she was making that expression at someone else—someone I couldn't see.

She was just a kid. Just a kid who'd carried a cricket bat and tried to be tough enough not to die in a strange world that could kill her in a heartbeat.

I don't know who she was grinning at, but it seemed as though she looked right into my eyes for those few seconds. Then there was just darkness that seemed to howl and scream: a darkness that joined itself to the rest of the shadow in the room, a darkness that silently howled and writhed and finally bubbled away into the floor.

"Can you make 'em stop doing that?" I asked Zero, looking away from that roiling mess in the middle of the room that would soon resolve into the remaining mess that was physically there.

Shadows—no, shades—were already gathering again around the room to do it all over again.

"No," he said, and I thought for a moment that he might actually throw up. His eyes fluttered shut and then open again, and he drew in a breath through his nose, making it pinch in. When he spoke again, his voice was as cold as it had been when I first met him. "Leave the room. It's no good staying here, and they won't stop spawning for a few years yet, I'd think."

"He could have left them to live," I said, my chin crinkling again. "He knew they would have died in a few years anyway. Why do it now?"

"The king must have found out about Blackpoint and his human associates," Zero said, still in that awful, calm, cool voice. "He might not have thought it worthwhile to seek out a small group of humans if it were only a matter of them helping a human or two, but he wouldn't put up with one of his own joining them to expose the world Behind."

I felt so tired. "Reckon he's dead too?"

"We haven't found him yet," Zero said.

"Yeah, but that could mean the king's got him, couldn't it?"

"If the king has him and he is not dead now, he will be dead soon," Jin Yeong said. "Perhaps they will keep him alive to get some information, but I think there is not much to tell."

Palomena said, warningly, "I've heard no news that Blackpoint is anything other than dead, as we reported a little while ago."

"Yeah," I said remembering in the dim recesses of my mind that weren't occupied with the nightmare around me that we still needed to be careful what we said around her. "He's dead all right. We already knew that."

"I would like to suggest once again that I be retired," Palomena said.

When I looked at her, she wasn't looking at me—or the room, in fact. She was very carefully not looking at the room, as if trying to make sure she saw as little as possible.

I don't know if Zero saw it too. At any rate, his gaze rested on her for a few moments before he said, "Jin Yeong, take Pet out. I need to do a last sweep here with the lieutenant."

"I can stay—" I began, but Jin Yeong tugged at me.

"There is too much blood here," he said. "I am hungry. I should not be hungry when my allies die."

I stiffened. "What about Vesper?"

"The little lady is safe," he said, still gently tugging me away from the smell and the sight of the dead humans. "I gave her a...thing."

I resisted the pull for a moment, right on the cusp of the doorway. "You didn't—you didn't turn her—?"

"Pft," he said, the dismissiveness of it a balm to my soul. Jin Yeong had done many things, but he hadn't ever actually lied to me. "She is just like you: she would never let me do that."

So I let him pull me out of the room, out of the house, and into the sunshine. And then I sat down with him under a tree and hugged his arm around me with my back to him, shivering away the tears until there remained only an ache in my throat.

Zero emerged alone before much longer, still edged in ice and barely-contained fury, but he moved as though he had a purpose again, which I suppose meant that he was dealing with stuff. I wondered if I would look like that soon.

"Home," he said to us; a single word with a complex meaning.

I couldn't bring myself to stir and get up, so maybe it was a good thing that Jin Yeong got up and pulled me along with him. I'd spent so long anchored to my house and desperate to keep it that I hadn't ever considered how tight-knit that bond was. Athelas... Athelas had pointed it out more than once, and I'd seen a vague reflection of it in Ralph's bond with his house—and Morgana's, if I'd ever had enough nous to realise it—but it was only now that I came to consider exactly what that bond was.

The bond had been Athelas, too—or had, at least, come from him. He hadn't been able to kill me, thanks to my parents, but he had done the next best thing: he had made as sure as he could that I would never leave the house. And if I did leave the house, he knew that I wouldn't go far. Even in his games, Athelas had made sure that he had a winning hand, no matter which way things went.

And now my home didn't feel as though it could be home anymore. Not because of what it had been without my realising it, but because of the home it had become while I *was* aware. At first, while I was alone, it had been a refuge: a place of safety from the outside world where no one knew I was. Security and a promise for the future, a hope to keep me going when it felt like there was no warmth or hope in the world. When my psychos had first come it had been a more perilous place, but it had been a place where I could learn and grow and try not to die in the vast new world that had opened up to me.

And after they had been there for a while, the house had become a home again. A place I could leave in the security that it was there, and would still be *there*, and *mine*, when I got back. A place where I could care for the people I loved and be cared for in return, as slow and often problematic as that care had been as it grew.

It was a place where I had grown to love Athelas—a place where he had made his mark as indelibly as Zero and Jin Yeong had made theirs—and I didn't think I could bear to see the shades that had almost certainly been left by his complete and final absence. I didn't even know if it was still home, and this time I didn't have the ability to forget it all and live there anyway.

I mean, it wasn't like I could go anywhere else. I just followed Zero as though I was the brainless pet behindkind usually thought me to be, Jin Yeong's hand around mine and his presence beside me. He didn't try to talk, and that was nice because I didn't think I could make much sense right now.

Maybe none of us really thought of it as home anymore. Maybe I was the only one who ever had, because as soon as we got back, Zero vanished out into the backyard, and I felt the pull all through the house as he started whatever exercises he did while he was out there alone. I'd seen him doing those exercises, but I was always pretty sure he was doing more than it looked like he was doing. At any rate, he was honing that concentration, that purpose of life, pushing away the emotions that had brought him to his knees earlier, and I wished I could do the same.

JinYeong didn't seem to be able to settle, either; he prowled from one end of the lower half of the house to the other, pattering around me like a cat as I put the kettle on and started meal prep.

What are meals when the sneaky old fae you've started to think of as family turns out to be a murderer—especially the murderer of your parents?

What are meals?—but also people have to eat. Even fae have to eat. And it was something to do that didn't leave me able to think too much: not if I didn't want to burn the pancakes.

I fell asleep with JinYeong on the couch, shivering and heavy but not troubled by nightmares. I must have slept for longer than I remembered, because the day and night passed over while I shivered, and Zero came and went. I felt a brief hand on my forehead as he passed every now and then, and shivered a bit more, then slept again.

Maybe you can't die of grief, but it took all the energy out of me, and by the time I seemed to have enough energy to sit up again, it was early evening. The faint pinkening of the sky touched the edges of the windows, and I felt the coolness of an evening breeze sneak beneath the front door and up the hallway toward us.

I sat up with a heavy head, and JinYeong curled up into a sitting position easily. I wondered if he'd been there the whole time or if I was misremembering the steady, constant warmth that had finally stopped my shivering.

I sat where I was for a few minutes, trying to decide if I had the ability—or maybe just the motivation—to get up. Was there any use in getting up? Was there any reason to not just lie down again?

I didn't so much sigh as a breath forced itself into my lungs and then left again. Maybe I could get up and decide what to make for dinner. Zero must be pretty hungry by now.

I found myself looking at JinYeong instead, with my head tilted back against the couch, until he turned his head and met my eyes. One of his eyebrows lifted enquiringly.

"Nothing," I said. I grabbed his shoulder and used it to pull myself to my feet, and he allowed it with a soft sniff of laughter. I stood where I was for a brief moment, but my hand was already on his shoulder, so I turned a bit and leaned over to kiss his cheek. "Just thanks," I said.

I left him there and wandered away to the kitchen, wondering if I was going to feel like a ghost in my own house forever or if it was just a result of too much sleep. My brain tried to make me think about Athelas when I went to make myself a cup of coffee, so I left the kettle alone and just drank a cup of water instead. I was alive and I didn't know how, because Athelas had definitely tried to—

I pushed that thought away, too, hurling my cup into the sink with the remaining water still in it, and went back into the living room. JinYeong was still on the couch when I stepped back down onto carpet, and I felt the vague suggestion of Zero in the back-yard. I left them both where they were, left Athelas' empty chair cutting into the living room, and went out to the front patio instead to try to wake up a bit.

The next-door neighbour was watering her front yard, and that was kinda nice and normal to see, so I stayed where I was for a lot longer than I'd expected. It was too hard to go inside and see

Athelas' chair so empty and dreadful. Here, outside the house, it was possible to believe for just half an hour or so that things like watering the lawn in your pyjamas while yawning and picking up a weed or two and throwing them into the garden bed instead of getting rid of them properly were the real world. Real, and sleepy, and safe.

I propped my feet against the veranda railing and wondered if the cool breeze sweeping in would do something about the hot, miserable feeling that was currently sitting right in the centre of me and pushing upward every so often, making my face feel hot and tight.

I didn't know some of that heat had pushed up even further to make tears well in my eyes until JinYeong came out with an ice-cream in either hand.

He shoved one at me and said, "Eat," and sat down beside me to eat his.

I blinked away the tears, surprised to find them there, and asked him, "What did you do?"

"I did nothing," he said, looking faintly guilty. "If you do not want the ice-cream—"

I surprised myself with a soft choke of laughter, and since it seemed to make me feel better for a little bit, I went a bit further and licked my ice-cream. "Not that. I mean when everything got—you know, *messy*. When your friend walked your team into that place to be drained by vampires. What did you do?"

"I made other things...very messy," he said. "What I did...you should not do."

"I'm not gunna go on a rampage and kill people, if that's what you're worried about."

JinYeong's grin was very sharp and not at all amused. "I did not kill people," he said. "Not human people. *Hyeong* made sure of that."

"Yeah, he's good at looking after people," I said, and there I was at the point of tears again. I said accusingly, "Heck, you're supposed to be cheering me up."

"You should not be cheerful just now," he said. "Now, it is enough to be sad."

I shifted a bit, and maybe it was by accident, but I didn't think it was: I found myself pushing into the warmth of his arm. I could have moved when I realised what I'd done, but I stayed there instead. It was all right to let myself be comforted a bit, wasn't it?

"Know what the worst of it is?" I asked, leaning back a bit more to kick at the railings. I hit them savagely enough to loosen the slats in front of me, and that was satisfying, so I kept doing it. "I feel like I can't even hate him properly."

"The old man?"

"Yeah. I got to know him—got to love him. How am I supposed to hate someone I understood and loved? Problem is, I don't reckon I can forgive him, either. He told me—he told me not to forgive him, too, a long time ago. S'pose he knew this was coming one day."

"That one had plans inside plans," agreed Jin Yeong. He slid me a sideways look and said, "*Hyeong* did not say you have to forgive him. I did not say so. Why would you say so?"

"Dunno," I said, giving the slat one last kick to dislodge it completely. I let that foot drop back to the patio floor, heavy and useless. "Just...I dunno."

"Maybe," said Jin Yeong, licking his ice-cream with great precision and seriousness, "Maybe it is because you are not satisfied."

"No, I reckon it's because I want to be able to do *one* of those things: hate him or forgive him."

"I think you are not satisfied. Something is there in your head, turning and turning, and you can't get rid of it."

I turned a bit to look across at him and folded the arm that wasn't holding my ice-cream underneath the other, warming my ribs on that side too.

"You trying to pick a fight?" I demanded. "If you think I'm

gunna be distracted by a fight—heck, you're probably right. What do you mean about something turning over and over in my head? There isn't anything *left* to turn over: Athelas explained everything and it all makes sense. All the little things that were bothering me, all the little bits that didn't fit in anywhere suddenly make sense and fit. He killed my parents, and he's gotta pay for that."

"If you want to kill him, I will do it," JinYeong said, delicately licking melted ice-cream off his fingers with a fastidious wrinkle of his nose. "But I think you don't want to kill him. I think it would be bad for you."

"No; I want him to vanish," I said. "I want him to not exist so I don't have to think about him or worry about walking into him one day. I want to know I'll never have to hate him, or forgive him, or remember that he's out there somewhere."

"I am not satisfied," said JinYeong, surprising me. "I am very not satisfied."

"Yeah? About what?"

"I do not know. It is *bothersome*."

"Just like me, then," I said.

I caught the twitch of Between somewhere outside the front gate just before JinYeong stiffened and scowled in that direction. My eyes followed his, and with a fizz of shock that made my feet thump into the wooden floor, I saw that there was a man out on the street, his head turning curiously to observe the other side of the road and then this side. Like he was looking for a yard in particular. Like he was looking for *someone* in particular.

Well, not a man, but someone who looked like a man.

And then he stopped right outside our gate, turned, and just... stood there looking over the gate.

"It's the Librarian," I said, blinking. "Heck. How did he find me?"

Had he found me? Or was he here on business with Zero? If so, how had he found Zero?

Jin Yeong, his eyes narrow and calculative, ran his tongue over one of his canines and put his ice-cream down. "I am not sure," he said, "that I should call *Hyeong*."

"Me either," I said, setting my own cone down carefully on the top of the railing in front of me. "I'll go down and talk to the bloke. You stay here to get Zero if we need him, yeah?"

"This person—you know him?"

"Sorta."

"Very well. I will wait here."

I got up and headed for the stairs, and Jin Yeong added, "I shall not wait long."

"Sounds good," I said, and hopped down the couple of stairs to the path. Whatever the Librarian wanted, it was probably best that he didn't get too comfortable around the house.

I'm not entirely sure, but I don't think he could see me before I spoke to him. When I said, "Oi. What do you want?" his left eye twitched just a bit, as if he'd stopped himself from flinching, and he looked straight at me for the first time.

"You really are indomitable," he said. "Hello."

"Thought librarians were meant to stay in libraries," I said. I could feel the tight ball of energy that was Jin Yeong behind me on the patio, and I was feeling pretty antsy myself. Whoever he was after, me or Zero, I didn't like the fact that he knew where to find us. "What are you doing out on the streets?"

"Are you asking me how I found you?"

"No, but you can answer that one if you want to," I told him. "You give me something for free, and I'll take it. I won't give you anything for it, though."

He grinned at me, straw-stubbly cheeks deepening with laugh lines. He reminded me of Athelas for a moment, all soft lines and real feelings, and I didn't want to be reminded of Athelas right then.

Maybe he saw something in my face, because the grin faded away pretty quickly.

"I'd tell you that it's not safe to be as honest as you are," he said. "But I suppose you wouldn't take the advice. Are your owners home?"

"Why would they be here?" I asked. Strictly no lies. I was pretty sure he'd know straight away that I was telling them, and even if I didn't know how dangerous he was, Zero's dad *did* know, and he had backed off. "Unless you know something I don't know, you should know that the fae don't much like living in human houses."

"True," he said, his gaze floating past me and roaming over the house behind me. "But I think this house might be a bit better connected with our level of reality than might normally be thought."

"Yeah, probably," I said. "Maybe it's 'cos of the murders."

It was a risk to say that. If he knew anything about me at all—if he knew anything about Athelas, or Zero's dad—he would have a pretty good guess that I was not just a pet. How much more than that he knew, I didn't know. Enough to know how and why my parents had been murdered? And what that meant?

Like I said, it was a risk, but I wanted to know what he knew.

"If they were the right kind of murders, I suppose so," he said, bringing his gaze back from the house to my face. "I have something for you."

I frowned. "You're going to give me something? What's it cost?"

"No charge," he said, and held up a book. "I've been meaning to give it to you for a little while now, but I couldn't seem to find the appropriate time—or maybe it was the place I couldn't find. Now seems appropriate."

That was flamin' ominous, I thought gloomily, then tried to chivvy myself into a more reasonable frame of mind. It wasn't like it was the Librarian's fault that I was having such a bad day; and who knew, maybe it was a good present? It was a book, after all.

He didn't pass it over the fence, he just held it there until I reached out and took it, almost as if he didn't really want to give it to me. He let it go straight away once I had it, though.

"Good day," he said, smiling at me. "I'll see you next time, I suppose. Good luck."

"Thanks," I said, because I needed all the good luck I could get, even if I didn't know why he was wishing me luck.

I would have reiterated to him that I wasn't planning on paying him anything for the book, and that he shouldn't expect to be able to try and chisel something out of me later, but he didn't give me time. With barely a whisper of Between, the Librarian turned away down the road, and for a moment it wasn't a road but a hall, made of stone but somehow living, curving around him in shadow and light to follow him wherever he wanted to go.

I caught the briefest sight of it and then it was gone, but I couldn't help straining my eyes for another sight of that smooth, peaceful corridor. I saw nothing, not even another flutter of Between: it was gone utterly and completely.

I breathed in a sigh, held it, and let it go. Then I looked down at the book he'd given me and caught my breath again—this time so suddenly that I nearly choked on it. I heard Jin Yeong strolling down the path toward me, but now all I could see was the book: a hefty, clothbound copy of *Dad and Dave* that was warped from a bit too long in the sun and had a big, discoloured patch on the bottom at the spine where it had been half dunked into the bath-water one day.

"What is it?" asked Jin Yeong, looking over my shoulder. "This, why did he give it to you?"

"Dunno why he gave it to me," I said, a prickle of what might have been either fear or excitement in my heart. It should have been fear, but I couldn't help being excited, too, because here was another piece of my past that I'd forgotten about. "It's mine, though: my book. I had it when I was a kid."

I flipped open the clothbound coverboard and flipped two

pages in quick succession, the paper thick and familiar beneath my fingers, looking for the thing I knew would be there.

Never write your name: it can be used as evidence against you.

Not even your initials.

But there it was, on the title page of the book: my single, tiny act of rebellion against my parents. Only really half a rebellion, but still.

Jin Yeong, leaning over my shoulder, touched a finger to the sunken letters in blue ballpoint pen and asked, "*Nuguya?*"

"It's me," I said, surprised as my voice came out sounding light and cool. "That's my name."

He flipped the book shut with a suddenness that made me jump and took it from me, his fingers pinching the coverboards together as though my name might suddenly try to jump from the pages and escape.

"How did he get this thing?"

"Dunno," I said, the chill of uncertainty spreading across me again. "Heck, how *did* he get it? He said he's a librarian, but I could have sworn this book was still in the house: it's been here for *years.*"

Jin Yeong's eyes were distant, though his head was cocked to listen. "Did you read it recently? When did you read it?"

"Heck," I said, staring at the book. "That's another one of those things I forgot, I reckon."

There was a vague fluttering of remembrance that wasn't so hard to dig out now that I knew how to do it. I allowed it to come out and felt again the dismay I'd felt one day when I was much younger and coming home from the park, when the way home had become suddenly...*not* the way home. The first thing I had noticed was the way that the road became sticky beneath my shoes and tried to slow me down. I wasn't too worried at first, because it wasn't enough of a tug to make me think that it was actively trying to swallow me up while under the conviction that it was actually quicksand. I hadn't reckoned on the mailboxes starting to come to life, maws snapping and elongated poles stretching to coil toward me.

The nearest one got to me first, green lid snapping against maroon base, with a tongue that looked a lot like a letter, but furrier.

"You're a mailbox," I told it sternly. "You can't eat me."

I had known about Between then—known enough to remember how to use it, at least. And I had remembered more quickly back then. Despite making myself forget every time, once I was Between, I seemed to be able to remember what things were and how to use the place.

When I was a kid, that was. Turns out that if you do a big enough number on yourself to make yourself forget the death of your parents, you can make yourself forget a heck of a lot of other stuff, too. It made sense of the way I had been able to use Between so instinctively when I first found it again: I'd had the experience and mental mechanisms for it. I'd just been lacking the actual memories to go with it.

And now that I remembered that, I remembered exactly what had happened with this book. It hadn't dropped into the bathwater, it had dipped into the creek as I forded it to escape the behindkind that chased me home that day. I'd left it out on the patio to dry off, and it had probably never made it back into the house, though I couldn't be sure when it had vanished from the property entirely.

"Never mind," I said to JinYeong. "It's another one of those wriggly memories I had to dig out. We'd better go in and show this to Zero."

It wasn't until we got inside again that I saw it: the Heirling Sword, halfway in and halfway out of the umbrella stand, far too sharp and bright to be an umbrella but not blue enough to be a sword.

JinYeong snarled and shut the door with a force that shook the house, setting a great big *something* sweeping around the whole place from the front gate all the way around to the last fencepost behind.

"Yow!" I said indignantly. "Let me know before you do stuff like that!"

"It was not me," said Jin Yeong, his teeth bared and his expression almost feral in its intensity. His eyes were still on the sword, as though he could force understanding from it by the potency of his gaze.

"Who was that bloke?" I demanded. "He said I could call him the Librarian, but you can't tell me he's just a librarian. Not when he did that to the sword."

I saw the raw horror sweep across Jin Yeong's face as he came to a conclusion just a bit quicker than I had.

"*Hyeong!*" he shouted, as pale as I'd ever seen him. He broke free from his trance and started through the hallway with a long, hasty stride. "*Hyeong!* We are discovered! *Hyeong!*"

"Flamin' heck," I said, left alone in the hall to rock on my heels in shock. "That was the king, right? It was the King Behind."